NOT
WITHOUT
MY
SISTER

MARION KUMMEROW

NOT
WITHOUT
MY
SISTER

Bookouture

Published by Bookouture in 2021

An imprint of Storyfire Ltd.
Carmelite House
50 Victoria Embankment
London EC4Y 0DZ

www.bookouture.com

ISBN: 978-1-80019-231-7
eBook ISBN: 978-1-80019-230-0

TWO SISTERS

Bergen-Belsen, Germany, April 1944

Mindel walked as fast as her little legs would carry her to keep up with her big sister. The unfriendly men in black uniforms used their usual "*Schnell! Schnell!*" shouts to propel the mass of women and children forward. From experience Mindel knew that they never hesitated to use their batons or whips on the people who were too slow.

But she had an entirely different problem: her shoelace had come undone during the long walk from the train ramp and she had to tread carefully so as not to fall over it.

"Hurry up, we need to stay together," Rachel hissed and pulled at her arm.

"Ouch!" Mindel protested, since it felt as if her sister was tearing her limb from limb. Clenching her teeth, she carried on because the thought of being all alone, without her big sister to protect her, was so horrible she felt the panic creeping up inside of her.

More and more people were herded together. Mindel barely reached up to the hip of those surrounding her and suddenly felt as if a wall was closing in on her. She quickly looked up into the sky, but all she could see was a mass of bodies.

"You, get over there," a guard barked and Mindel felt a sharp tug on her hand. She scrambled to follow in the direction where

Rachel pulled her, but there were too many people blocking her way. Slowly, her hand slipped from her sister's and she screamed at the top of her lungs, "Rachel! Wait!"

"Please, I can't go! Not without my sister!" Rachel pleaded with the guard, although Mindel couldn't hear a response.

In her desperation Mindel dropped to the ground and tried to crawl between the forest of legs in the direction where she heard Rachel calling her name. But there was no getting through. "Rachel! I'm here!" she screamed once more.

"I'll find you," Rachel yelled back, and then, much further away already, "Mindel, I love you. I promise, I'll find you."

Somehow Mindel managed to get back on her feet and was moved by the mass of bodies in one direction, when all she wanted to do was to turn around and rush after her sister, who'd been shoved in the opposite direction.

She pressed her doll, Paula—whom Mindel always carried beneath her dress—against her heart, tears flowing down her cheeks. "Don't you worry, Paula, we'll find her."

CHAPTER 1

Six months earlier in a tiny village in Bavaria

Rachel Epstein sat with her mother in their cozy kitchen, peeling potatoes. The wooden tabletop, like the entire farmhouse, had seen better days and was in urgent need of repair, but to Rachel it was home. Sitting here, working side by side with her mother, always gave her a sense of belonging and safety, something the world outside didn't provide anymore.

While Rachel peeled the potatoes, her mother hurried about with flour, butter and precious sugar to bake an apple cake for Rachel's baby sister's fourth birthday.

"Could you please run into the garden and get me another apple? It looks like I'm short a few slices and I want this cake to be perfect." Her mother had always been petite, but she'd grown thin these past years, making her look older. Her dark brown hair showed ever more grey streaks and the brightness in her eyes had dimmed with all the hardships the family had had to endure.

"Of course, Mother, I'll go right away." Rachel stopped peeling potatoes for dinner and tucked a wisp of hair behind her ear. She left the kitchen through the back door that opened directly into their vegetable and herb garden.

Being farmers they had always grown their own fruits, herbs and vegetables, but in the past few years when the restrictions for

Jewish people had increased on a weekly—if not daily—basis, they had become dependent on their own produce to be able to eat at all. Rachel simply couldn't fathom how Jews in the bigger cities, without the produce nature provided them with, could survive.

The farmhouse had definitely seen better days, despite their mother's incessant cleaning and father's repairs. There just wasn't enough money, time, or materials to stay on top of all the repairs needed. But what could be expected from a nation at war?

Their farmhands had left many years ago, either because they'd joined the Wehrmacht or because they didn't want to work for Jews anymore. Rachel sighed. Things had become so complicated. Walking into the orchard with the old apple trees, Rex, their Alsatian watchdog, greeted her with a wagging tail, and she patted him on the head, which he took as an invitation to follow her. She heard laughter and loud voices even before she saw her three younger siblings: Israel and Aron, ten and seven years old and inseparable as twins, and the birthday girl, Mindel.

A smile crossed Rachel's lips. Thirteen years older than her, she treated Mindel more like a daughter than a sister, especially now that Father was working the fields day and night, and Mother had her hands full with running a household that used to have several maids, before the Nazis had come to power and changed everything.

Her smile faltered when she spotted Mindel hanging precariously from one of the apple tree's branches, while her brothers were sitting comfortably a few yards up and looking down at her.

"What do you think you are doing?" Rachel yelled at them.

"Nothing," her three siblings replied in unison.

"It doesn't look like nothing to me. Israel, you should know better than to get Mindel to climb up there. She could fall down and break her neck!"

"We didn't tell her to, she wanted to follow us all by herself," Aron defended his older brother.

"Why do we even have to drag her around? She always spoils our games." It was Israel who complained and Rachel had to suppress a smile. She doted on Mindel as much as she could, and had done so since her birth, but the two boys wanted to have time alone. A part of her could understand that: while they loved Mindel as much as Rachel did—although they would never admit to such a female emotion—they were boys and wanted to play wild games where a little girl would only bother them. Unfortunately both she and Mother were too occupied with the household and garden chores to constantly keep an eye on her, and thus this task had fallen on the two boys.

"You should be cleaning the cowshed, not gallivanting through the orchard and eating the apples we need to preserve for winter."

"I already finished my chores," Israel protested and looking at the dirt-smeared faces of all three children it was clear that he'd enlisted the younger ones' help with his chores, most probably promising apples from the tree in exchange or some other gift he wasn't actually allowed to dole out.

She sighed. Times were hard enough, maybe they should have some fun. "Can you at least hand me another apple for Mindel's birthday cake?"

Mindel's eyes shone with pride. "I'm gonna be four tomorrow. Then you can't say I'm little anymore."

"Little, little!"

"Baby!"

"Little baby!" came the yells from further up the tree.

"Stop teasing her!" Rachel scolded them. "And now hand me an apple, but one that's nice and ripe."

Mindel tossed one down to Rachel, but Israel said, "Not from down there, the ones up here taste much better." Giggling, he tossed another one down to Rachel. She shook her head disapprovingly; at seventeen years old she was much too mature to participate in these kinds of shenanigans.

Returning to the kitchen, she felt a wave of nostalgia wash over her. Back when she had been their age, life had been good. But that was before the Nazis came to power, when Jewish people had possessed the same rights as all other ordinary German citizens, and when the farm had still truly belonged to her parents.

Over the years, things had gradually worsened for them. Almost imperceptibly at first and then faster and faster, until it was like a snowball crashing downhill. As of now, they, like so many of their fellow Jews, had lost all civilian rights and privileges. Rachel had been forced to leave school, and—as her parents liked to remind her when she complained about their life—it was only thanks to living in this godforsaken place in the middle of nowhere, that their family had not been deported to some ugly place like most of the Jews who lived in bigger cities.

Israel and Aron had an inkling about the general situation in Germany, but never seemed to give it more than a passing thought. They were too occupied roaming the fields and forest, while Mindel at her young age was completely oblivious to what was going on outside the farm.

Rachel wasn't entirely sure it was good to shield Mindel from the happenings in the world, but she had no say in this. It was entirely her parents' decision. She entered the kitchen through the back door, exchanging her sturdy boots for house slippers before doing so.

At the sight of her father in the kitchen—a place he rarely frequented outside mealtimes—she stopped in her tracks, staring at him. His lips were pressed into a thin line, a deep furrow creasing his forehead.

Holding up the two apples in her hands like a shield, she asked with a barely audible whisper, "What has happened?"

"Old Hans has died."

Mother didn't even look up from the cutting board, but Rachel clearly observed her shaking shoulders. The news must be worse than she'd thought. Old Hans was the kindly elderly man who'd bought their farm years ago after it had been declared that Jews could possess no land. Then he had immediately employed them as his farmhands, effectively giving their family the opportunity to live on the property as if it was still theirs.

Rachel looked at her father. "What will become of us?"

"Hans doesn't have children and in his will he left the property to me, although I had hoped he wouldn't die until after the war," Father said.

Mother's eyes got a dreamy look. "Then the farm will belong to us again."

"But Jews can't own property," Rachel said.

"The authorities might not notice."

Rachel thought that was wishful thinking, especially because the ghastly mayor, Herr Keller, had had his eyes on the farm for years, and had pestered Old Hans many times already to sell it to him—or at least to get rid of the Epstein family. As far as she knew the only person who'd been standing between them and deportation had been Old Hans, who'd been in his nineties already and cared little about Keller's strong-arm tactics, knowing that he'd lived most of his time on earth. Hans' fierce protection, along with the fact that farmworkers were scarce and Herr Keller as the mayor of the nearby town had to fulfill quotas of produce, had allowed them the tiniest window of freedom.

But now that the kind old man was dead, what would the horrible Nazi do?

No, Rachel certainly didn't share her mother's opinion that he'd not notice when Father retook possession of his own farm. And being the mayor of the nearby town, he was going to find out soon enough, because everything that was important in the entire region went across his desk.

"There's nothing we can do but wait," Father said.

"Maybe nothing will happen," Mother replied.

Rachel wanted to scream at them. How could they be so oblivious to the dangers? Hadn't they impressed on her and Israel never to venture out into town, not to attract unwanted attention? Hadn't they had the idea to sell the farm to Old Hans in the first place? And now they suddenly believed everything would be just fine?

In their village there'd only been two other Jewish families and both of them had left many years ago. One of them emigrated when it was still possible; the other one had disappeared in the night, never to be seen again. Since then she'd heard about others taken away and not coming back, but her parents preferred to stick their heads into the sand and pretend they were safe on the farm, since it was too far away even from the tiny village of Kleindorf to be of the Nazis' interest. Despite her parents' warnings to keep away from any and all other people, she'd kept a very loose contact with her former classmate, Irmhild, who now worked in the town hall with Herr Keller. Nothing that Irmhild had told her over the past years had indicated there was a reason to feel safe. If the decision had been hers to make, she and her family would have left a long time ago.

"We should leave the country," she blurted out.

Her mother raised her head and cast Rachel a scolding gaze. "And where do you think we should go?"

"I don't know. Anywhere other than here… Maybe England?" Rachel's shoulders sagged. She shouldn't have spoken out against her parents.

"We don't speak English!" Mother said, as if this was reason enough to stay in the precarious situation they were in, only able to hang onto their old life because of the kindness of a man who'd died recently.

"We could learn."

Mother glared daggers at Rachel as if the mere mention of learning another language was insult enough. "I'm not going to leave this place. This is my home, where I grew up, where my grandparents and parents lived for years, where I married your father. Upstairs is the bedroom where I gave birth to you four children. I won't go just because some Nazis decided they don't want us here."

"Your mother is right. Besides, that ship sailed years ago. As you know it's forbidden to emigrate for the likes of us. Even if it were still allowed, we wouldn't have the money to pay all the fees and bribes." Her father rarely talked that much and now he looked outright exhausted. "No, staying here is the safest course of action. Much better than taking the gamble of leaving for who knows where and being exposed to all kinds of danger while trying to escape Germany. I never want to hear another word about this."

CHAPTER 2

Two weeks later

Mindel was excitedly running from tree to tree, the doll Rachel had given her for her fourth birthday strapped to her back. She happily thought back to her big day with the sweetest apple cake she'd eaten in her life and all the wonderful gifts. Her parents had given her a new dress with a beautiful flower pattern, and even her brothers had been on their best behavior the entire day and had let Mindel decide which games to play. But Rachel had taken the biscuit with the gift of the wonderful rag doll she'd made with her own hands.

"Now you have a special friend who'll always be there for you," Rachel had said as she'd given her the doll.

For once, Mindel had been rendered speechless. Such a wonderful gift, a friend only for her. She'd wrapped her arms around her big sister and told her, "I love you so much, you're simply the best big sister in the world."

Rachel in turn had smiled in the happy way she used to but nowadays rarely did, though Mindel couldn't understand why, and had said, "I love you too, sweetie. What shall we call your friend?"

Mindel hadn't hesitated for a single second as she blurted out, "Paula."

"She does look like a Paula to me," her mother had said, and Rex had barked his approval as well.

Since then, Mindel never went anywhere without Paula, who had become a trusted friend, someone to play with, besides her often-annoying brothers. She loved her even more than Rex who wasn't allowed inside the house because, like everyone on the farm, he had chores to do.

She didn't understand why she wasn't allowed to play with the children they sometimes saw at the neighboring farms when out on one of Aron's discovery expeditions. But none of her whining and complaining had softened Father's determination to keep her away from the other children in the village.

Even Aron—who'd become her only real playmate since Israel nowadays barely had time, due to his increasing share of chores on the farm—was adamant about staying away from other people.

He never told her the reason why, but always said in an important voice, "It's not good to meet others."

"But why?"

"You're too young to understand."

She hated when he did this, but reluctantly gritted her teeth and obeyed, fully aware of the good smacking both of them would receive if Father found out they'd ventured into the village.

Since Aron loved to be the boss and order her around, she usually stuck out her tongue at him. "I'm only doing it, because Father said so, not because of you."

Paula, in contrast, understood her and liked to play girls' games. She never wanted to be the boss and rarely disagreed with Mindel. Paula truly was a special friend and the best companion Mindel could have wished for.

Today, though, Rachel had taken them out into the woods all day to search for mushrooms and blueberries. Mindel loved being out and about and picking berries, but she loved it even more when she got to stuff the sweet delights directly into her mouth, so her little basket was still half empty, while Rachel had already filled a second one.

"Stop dawdling, and come here," Rachel called out.

Mindel stopped talking to Paula, picked up her basket and rushed toward her big sister, who talked and behaved like an adult most of the time. When she was grown up Mindel wanted to be just like her. Knowing the answer to everything, while still being kind, unlike her brothers. She adored her big sister, who always made her smile. When she scratched her knee, Rachel would blow on the scratch and say a few healing words or sing a silly song to make Mindel laugh. And just like that, the pain was forgotten and she could rush away to play some more.

On her birthday she'd secretly wished for it to only be Rachel and herself, because she could very well do without the constant nagging, badgering and fighting from her brothers.

"We need to return home, it's late already and we have lots of work to do."

"Work, always work," Mindel complained, looking around for her brothers who came walking toward them, their baskets filled to the brim with chanterelles.

"Look what we found, there's a great spot over there," Israel said.

"Well done. Mother will be so pleased."

"Can we go back and collect more?" Aron asked.

Rachel shook her head. "No, it's a long walk home and we are supposed to be back before dinner."

As soon as Rachel had spoken the words, Mindel remembered just how long the walk out here this morning had been and her legs suddenly felt tired. "I can't walk that long. I'm tired," she complained.

Rachel only laughed. "You're young and have healthy legs. You'll manage."

Pouting, Mindel whispered to Paula, "You have it good, being carried around all day."

Rachel must have overheard her, because she said, "Do you want me to carry Paula for you?"

"No. She wants to stay with me," Mindel said and then looked down at the basket in her hand. "But maybe you could carry my basket? It's really heavy."

"I can certainly do that for you." Rachel took the basket and hung it across her arm next to the other two. Her sister was so strong, Mindel really wanted to be like her when she was grown up.

After about an hour's march, they passed the hut of an old woman who lived at the forest edge. From there it wasn't that far to her farm and squinting her eyes she believed she could see a plume of smoke from their farmhouse. Their mother must be heating the range. Mindel sidled up to Rachel holding onto her sister's skirt.

"She's not a real witch you know?" Rachel said with a laugh, as if there was no reason to be afraid of the ancient woman her brothers called *the old witch* and insisted could do magic. One of the witch's favorite tricks was to turn people she didn't like into a toad.

Aron turned around to stare at Mindel and said, "Ribbet."

"Why do you always have to scare her?" Rachel scolded him.

Mindel shivered. She surely didn't want to be turned into a toad and normally gave the witch's hut a wide berth. "Can't we take another way?" she whispered for Rachel's ears only.

"It'll take us at least half an hour more and I thought you were tired?"

Mindel sighed. What a difficult choice! Sidling up nearer to her big sister, she decided that if Rachel wasn't afraid, she wouldn't be either. But, just in case, she kept hidden behind Rachel's back as they approached the hut.

Much to her chagrin the haggard old woman must have seen them because she came outside, leaning on her stick, her white hair standing in all directions. She wore a green-brown skirt that went all the way down to her ankles and a red blouse that had been patched up in several places.

"*Halt*! Aren't you the Epstein brats?" the witch yelled, showing a few yellow-brown teeth in her otherwise empty mouth.

Frightened to death by the sight of the crazy woman, Mindel jumped behind Rachel's back, clinging to her legs. Memories of Hänsel and Gretel rushed into her mind, and she feared the witch would want to eat them in her soup, instead of turning them into toads as Aron had said she would do.

"Yes, we are," Rachel answered, seemingly unfazed.

Mindel couldn't help but admire her sister for her poise.

"Come here," the old witch said and shook her finger at them. Given the choice whether to follow Rachel toward the witch or stay a safe distance away, Mindel let go and instead grabbed Aron's hand. Together they slid behind Israel's back to hide and observe as Rachel moved toward the woman.

"She's so brave," Mindel whispered.

"I would do the same," Aron replied, but Mindel had her doubts because she could see the fear in his eyes. Surely he didn't want to be turned into a toad either.

"Shhh... I want to listen to what she's saying," Israel scolded them.

"You can't go home," the haggard woman said. "Herr Keller is at the farm, taking your parents away. You need to hide."

Mindel didn't understand what Herr Keller was doing at their farm and why they couldn't go home and say hello, but looking at Rachel's face, she saw fear. It was both a frightening and reassuring experience to realize that even her big sister was afraid of something.

"But where should we go?" Rachel asked in a shaky voice.

The witch looked at the children with surprisingly kind eyes. "I can't keep you here, my hut is much too small and too close by. Go deep into the woods where nobody can find you."

Now, that sounded like an adventure, but moments later fear took over again and Mindel shivered despite the warm autumn afternoon. In all the fairy tales the people walking into the woods rarely fared well. Hänsel and Gretel almost got eaten by the witch, Little Brother was turned into a deer and Snow White was only saved because she came upon the kind dwarfs.

Another thought crossed her mind and she involuntarily grabbed Aron's hand tighter. It was dark in the forest at night. It wouldn't have been so bad if they at least had Rex with them, but he'd stayed at the farm barking at strangers trying to steal from them.

No, she wouldn't sleep out there with wild animals, monsters, ghosts and who knew what else. How bad could this Herr Keller be anyway? And wouldn't Rex bark at him too if he tried to steal their farm?

CHAPTER 3

Rachel sat in the cold and damp cell and, try as she might to appear strong in front of Mindel, she could barely hold back her tears.

Two weeks had passed since that fateful day when the old woman had warned them to hide. Since it had been too cold at night to sleep outside, they'd been hiding in a neighbor's rarely used barn until the owner's niece had found them. About Rachel's age, she'd taken pity on them and promised not to tell anyone. After three days without being discovered Rachel had nourished the hope that everything would end well, especially when her former school friend Irmhild came up with a bold plan to produce fake Aryan papers for all four siblings. It had been a crazy and terribly dangerous undertaking, but miraculously it had worked. A friend of Irmhild's chipped in as well and contacted a Catholic convent in Kaufbeuren that was running an orphanage. The nuns had kindly agreed to admit the four children to their orphanage, no questions asked, as long as their papers would withhold a perfunctory inspection.

And then, the awful moment when things had gone wrong. Goosebumps rose on her arms as she remembered the scene that had happened the day before.

Walking down the road after dark to reach the convent at first light in the morning, her two brothers had skipped on ahead, while she and Mindel lagged behind. It was difficult walking in the darkness and poor Mindel had been afraid.

"Look, can you see the bright star up there?" Rachel said to distract her sister.

"Yes. It's beautiful, but where's the moon?"

"The moon is hiding, because it doesn't want to give us away. Remember, we're playing hide-and-seek?"

Mindel nodded with a very serious face. Rachel had impressed on her that this was a game and they had to steer clear of any other people if they wanted to win.

"What is our prize if nobody sees us?"

Survival. "A cup of warm milk with honey." Rachel had no idea whether the nuns in the convent had milk or honey, but one lie was as good as the next one, since all she cared about right now was keeping Mindel's spirits up throughout the night. The convent was about twenty miles away and she dreaded the moment when her little sister wouldn't be able to walk anymore.

"Why do Aron and Israel always have to go ahead of us?" Mindel complained after a while.

"Because we are in two different teams," Rachel said, although that wasn't the real reason. She had realized that with four children wandering about at night the risk of being seen was too great. Israel had protested at first, because despite all his bravado he was still a child and afraid to be out on his own at night. But, after appealing to his masculinity, he'd relented and agreed to walk ahead with his brother, although he'd insisted on always being in hearing distance.

Caught up in her thoughts, Rachel hadn't been vigilant enough and by the time she heard the approaching vehicle it was too late. A police car stopped beside them and Herr Keller and his henchmen jumped out.

For the agonizing duration of a breath Rachel stared at them, until she regained her wits, grabbed Mindel's hand and shouted, "Run." Adrenaline pumping through her, she mobilized all her energy, running as fast as she could while dragging the poor mite behind her. They made good progress and Rachel noticed the thick undergrowth to the side of the street. Too thick for the men chasing them, but not for two very thin girls.

Just as they jumped across the ditch, Mindel stumbled and fell. Rachel desperately tried to drag her along by sheer willpower, tearing at her arm, but after a few moments had to accept that it didn't work. She jumped into the ditch to pick up her little sister and kept running with her in her arms. But after only a few steps she realized there was no point and she came to a standstill, trembling with fear at the realization that all they'd done had been for nothing and they'd been caught.

It was over.

Herr Keller's eyes showed a mean glint. That man had been nasty even before the Nazis had come into power, always scolding children for any perceived infringement to *his* rules in *his* town. As well as being mayor, he had embraced his new position as chief of the regional Nazi Party—and all the powers that entailed—with open arms.

"If it isn't the Epstein *Judenpack*. You didn't think you could escape me, did you?" He laughed cruelly. "Not in my district. The Führer is right. Germany must be free of all of your kind. Heil Hitler!"

He did not actually expect her to return the salute, but even if he did, carrying Mindel in her arms made it impossible. She was tempted again to try her luck running away, but the extra weight in her arms painfully reminded her that that idea was an impossibility.

Defying her fear, she took a step toward him, hoping all the rumors had been exaggerated. Just as she glared at Herr Keller, she noticed movement in the shadows of the trees alongside the road and her heart felt like it had stopped beating.

Despite her orders not to get involved should they be discovered, her brothers had returned, looking for them. Afraid they might show themselves in the misguided attempt to help her and Mindel, she deliberately looked away from where she'd seen the movement, locking eyes with the despised Herr Keller instead and driving her brothers away with a gesture she disguised as waving a fly away from her ear.

There was nothing more she could do, except to trust in Israel's cleverness and hope he was old enough to know how dire their situation was. She said a short prayer to God in her mind that Israel would do the rational thing and keep himself and Aron away from them, continuing their journey to the convent once it was safe to leave their cover.

"Where are your brothers, Jew?" Herr Keller asked.

"I… I don't…" She suddenly had an idea. "They were caught about an hour ago by the police."

Keller looked first puzzled and then pleased. By the time he returned to his office and figured out that nobody had caught the boys, her brothers would be long gone and would have hopefully arrived safely at the convent.

Keller's henchmen manhandled her and Mindel into the waiting vehicle. Before she was pushed inside Rachel glanced back down the street, but her brothers weren't anywhere in sight.

Dear God, please get them to safety.

CHAPTER 4

April 1944

Once again, she and Mindel were being moved to some other place. As was customary, the Nazi guards never explained where they were taking them or how long the journey would be, nor gave any information at all. In fact, they didn't even announce the prisoners were being moved.

But Rachel had learned to read the signs, as she had learned never to ask a question if she didn't want to feel the end of a whip lashing into her skin. During the past six months, the sisters had been to at least ten different places; transit camps, collection camps, temporary camps. Despite the different names, they all looked and felt the same: appalling.

Hectic orders were given, prisoners counted, and then a squad of black-clad SS men marched into the assembly yard, where the women and children wearily stood, awaiting new orders.

"Hurry up, lazybones, I don't have all day," the leader barked at them.

Rachel's impulse to get riled up over injustices or insults had long ago dissipated and she merely grabbed Mindel's hand tighter, putting her feet into motion as she followed the group of women heading toward the camp's exit gate.

Forcing herself to look down at her toes, she took step after step toward an uncertain future, her only hope being that the journey wouldn't take them east. Rumors of so-called death camps in the Generalgouvernement—the Nazi-occupied land formerly known as Poland—had reached her many times over.

These Polish camps were said to have conditions a million times worse than the camps she had been in this past half year, mythically-awful places that could only be compared to one of Dante's circles of hell.

Although Rachel didn't believe all of the whispered rumors, especially not the claim that new arrivals were being killed even as they walked down from the train ramps. But she wasn't naïve enough to believe anything good ever came out of the Nazi machine.

"Are we going back to our farm?" Mindel asked, holding onto Rachel with one hand, while carrying her doll Paula in the other one.

"I'm not sure." Rachel had never had the heart to tell Mindel that the farm hadn't been theirs even before Mindel was born, and that by now the appalling Herr Keller had surely stolen it.

"Paula misses her home very much," Mindel said in a feeble voice.

"I know." Even while walking in step with the rest of the group, Rachel brushed a hand across her sister's filthy hair. "Tell Paula we'll soon return home again and then I'll make an apple cake for all of us."

"She would like that very much." Mindel's face brightened at Rachel's answer and she pressed the filthy doll against her face to give her a kiss. Paula looked a lot worse for wear and barely resembled the pretty rag doll Rachel had sewn six months ago for her sister's birthday.

Her mouth watered at the memory of the apple cake her mother had made for the occasion. It had been the only sweet they'd eaten for months, since sugar rations in general were minuscule and those for Jews basically nonexistent.

Only thanks to their orchard, vegetable garden, and the food-stuffs the children found in the forest, had the family been able to feed themselves sufficiently. But even their meager rations had been a feast compared to what the Nazis fed them in the camps.

Rachel had been hungry since the day Herr Keller had captured them and her heart broke a little bit more every day when she saw how her sister's chubby cheeks had hollowed out. During the first weeks, the poor mite had whined and complained, and cried herself hungrily to sleep every night, but that had stopped months ago.

Alongside the grief over their separation and possible deaths, Rachel felt an increasing rage at her parents for taking things too lightly. If only they'd fled Germany years ago instead of trusting that the kindness of Old Hans would keep them safe forever.

At the train station a cattle train was waiting for the prisoners.

"Not another one of those!" a young woman complained.

To Rachel's eyes the wagons already looked full, but the SS men mercilessly pushed more women into the cattle carts, making vicious use of their batons if a prisoner didn't jump up fast enough into the dark open mouths that marked the entrance to another hell.

Picking Mindel up, Rachel told her, "Hold me tight!," before she scrambled up onto the cart, screaming when a truncheon went down on her back. She all but threw Mindel inside and crawled behind her, frantically pushing up to her feet, so she wouldn't be trampled to death by the women pushing and shoving to get away from the hitting, punching and lashing SS men.

The jostling mass of bodies soon blocked the light coming through the open door, thrusting Rachel further into the back of the cart.

"Push your daughter against the corner and shield her with your body or she'll be squashed to death," a woman with a baby strapped to her chest said, and angled her body sideways, so Mindel could duck beneath the baby and get into the corner, where another girl her size was already standing.

"Thank you," Rachel said, as she positioned herself next to the other woman, their backs turned to the onslaught of bodies and their hands pressed against the wall to keep a little breathing space for the two little girls in the corner.

Another woman about Rachel's age was thrown against her. She had the loveliest brown eyes and wore her pitch-black hair in a hilarious haircut that resembled a boy's style that had grown out. Rachel angled her body and stretched out a hand to help her up.

"I'm Linda," the woman said.

Rachel stared at her in disbelief. People usually didn't mention their names, especially not at the first encounter. All prisoners had grown weary of forming friendships or even connections, because they never knew how long the other person would still be alive.

"I'm Rachel."

"Nice to meet you," Linda said. She might easily be the most peculiar person Rachel had ever met, because who on earth said *nice to meet you* when thrust against another person in an overcrowded cattle cart on a journey to hell? "How old is your daughter?" Linda pointed at Mindel.

"She's four. And she's not my daughter. She's my sister."

"Oh. She must be glad to have you."

"I really am. Rachel is the best sister in the world," Mindel said from her corner.

That was true, because on her own Mindel would never have survived this long. Rachel's heart squeezed at the thought of that and then again as she remembered her brothers. As she did every time they crossed her mind, she sent a prayer to heaven for their safe arrival at the convent. Although it felt highly unlikely that two young boys on their own would have managed to walk the twenty miles to a destination they'd never been before, she clung to the idea. The alternative was… No, she wouldn't go there. Would not allow herself to entertain the idea of what might have happened otherwise.

Every morning she woke, dreading to find the boys among the new arrivals, and every evening she sighed with relief when they hadn't appeared. Though, of course, that didn't mean they weren't in some other horrible camp.

"I have to pee," Mindel suddenly said.

When they'd been shoved into the cart, Rachel had seen two buckets: an empty one and another one filled with stale drinking water. From the experience during prior transports she knew that by now the drinking water was gone, while the waste bucket overflowed.

"I'm sorry, sweetie, you'll have to hold on a little longer," she said.

"I can't," Mindel whined.

Linda came to her aid. "Can you pee on the ground?"

"How can you even suggest that?" Rachel snapped.

"We don't know how much longer we'll be in here. For all we know it could be days. So just let her pee now and save her the pain of holding it in."

Rachel made a disgusted sound.

"What do you think you're standing in? The crap and urine of dozens of women who've been in here for many hours."

"Dear God." As soon as the words had left Linda's mouth, Rachel became aware of the awful stench and the feeling of feces seeping into her shoes. The urge to bolt from the locked cattle cart became overwhelming.

"See?" Linda smiled. "There's nothing we can do." Then she turned to Mindel. "I'll hold up your skirt and you try not to pee on your underwear, will you?"

The unsavory business was finished rather quickly and Mindel seemed to feel better until she started to complain. "My legs are hurting."

"I know, sweetie, but the journey won't take much longer."

"You always say that, and it's never true!"

The fury in her sister's voice hurt Rachel and she gave an exasperated sigh. Why on earth had God decided that she should be the sole caregiver for a child in the worst circumstances imaginable?

"Can I at least sit down?"

With the women in the cart packed like sardines in a tin, Rachel knew there wasn't a single spare inch of space. "You can see there's no room to sit."

"I'm so tired!"

"I can hold her for a while," Linda offered and took Mindel in her arms, who instantly fell asleep.

"Thank you. Why are you so nice?" Rachel asked.

Linda laughed. "If we're not nice to each other, who will be?"

"I guess you're right." Rachel was still pondering the truth of Linda's assertion when one of the women started singing a modern Jewish folk song in Hebrew. Despite not speaking a single word of Hebrew—her parents and grandparents had been so-called assimilated Jews who talked and behaved like Gentiles—Rachel knew the lyrics to 'Hava Nagila', and sang along. One by one the women joined in and the happy melody filled the cart, dispersing the sad reality for as long as the song lasted.

An eternity later, the train stopped and they were hurried outside and onto a train ramp. Cold fear grabbed Rachel's heart and she held tighter to Mindel's hand, who seemed to almost be sleepwalking.

"Are we going home?" Mindel asked with closed eyes.

"I'm afraid not yet, my darling."

Mindel's eyes shot open, and the fear she saw in them broke Rachel's heart. "Where are we then?" Her small hand in Rachel's trembled.

"I don't know. But you just keep by my side and we'll be fine."

"Do you think Aron and Israel are fine?"

"I'm sure they are. They will stick together just like the two of us."

"I'm afraid."

"There's no reason to be afraid. As long as we are together, we'll be fine."

CHAPTER 5

Mindel pressed her doll Paula against her heart, tears flowing down her cheeks. Ever since those awful men in black uniforms had captured her and Rachel, they'd been sent from camp to camp—each one worse than the one before.

After the last horrible train ride, Rachel had grabbed her hand and pulled her behind her for an interminable walk until they arrived at yet another camp. Mindel knew all too well the sight of a wrought-iron gate and barbed wire around the place.

Every place those awful men in black uniforms—SS as the adults called them—had brought them looked the same. And Mindel still didn't understand why they were even there.

Nobody, not even Rachel, had answered her questions about the why. *Why am I here? What have I done? Wasn't I good?* Shame crept up her body as she remembered how she'd fought with her two older brothers, Aron and Israel, that morning they were taken. She'd pinched Aron and broken Israel's precious catapult. But the SS men couldn't possibly know about that.

More tears flowed as she thought of her brothers, whom she hadn't seen in such a long time. At seven and ten years of age, she adored and admired them immensely—at least most of the time. Would they find her, knock down the SS men and rescue her and Rachel? She hoped so.

But then desperation tore at her again. Her sister was gone.

Upon arrival at the camp, one of the guards had separated them and put her into another line, ignoring Rachel's protests and Mindel's frantic cries.

And now she'd been searching this desolate place for hours, but there was no trace of Rachel anywhere.

"Now it's only you and me, Paula," she said to her doll between sobs. "But I will take care of you, don't you worry."

Mindel made Paula nod and pressed her tighter against her body. Desperate to protect her doll, the girl squeezed her beneath the long-sleeved white-and-blue striped dress she'd been given in the last camp, when her old one had fallen apart. More women arrived, the crowd pushing and shoving. Mindel stumbled against a young woman and in her effort not to get trampled by the mass of bodies she clasped her hands around the woman's skirt.

Either the stranger didn't notice or didn't mind, because she kept on walking, dragging Mindel behind.

"Nationality?" the guard asked the woman.

"Dutch."

"Star camp, over there." He pointed to another line and then looked down at Mindel and up at the woman. "The child, too."

The crowd organized itself, everyone falling into different lines of five people wide each. Mindel kept clinging to the stranger, because she had no idea what else to do.

Hours later, when her grumbling stomach was giving her vicious stabs and she could barely feel her legs anymore, the line came to a stop and the woman turned around. "Now, get away from me, you filthy urchin!"

Mindel had become used to being called names, and "filthy urchin" was one of the nicest things people had thrown at her during the past months. Nevertheless, she let go of the woman's skirt and moments later found herself standing all alone.

"I'm hungry," Mindel imagined Paula saying from beneath her dress.

"I'll go and look for something to eat. Usually they have soup somewhere." Mindel trotted off to where she saw another line forming, and just like she had hoped there was a pot at the end that was even bigger than her.

With renewed energy she took her place at the end of the line, forewarning her doll, "Paula. I know you don't like the soup, but you have to eat every drop of it because it will keep you strong. Promise?"

Valiantly she kept her eyes dry as she repeated the words that Rachel had told her so many times. If only she could find her sister again.

When she finally arrived at the soup pot, the food bearer, an old and emaciated woman with hollow eyes, filled the ladle and was about to pour the soup for Mindel when her arm stopped midway. "Where's your bowl?"

"I... don't have one."

"No bowl, no soup," the woman said and beckoned with her arm to the person behind Mindel. "Next one."

Mindel was shoved out of the way, stumbling along the dusty ground. She watched with envy as others filed past, each and every person holding up a cup or bowl of some sort. Up until now she'd never given it a thought, but it became all too clear that Rachel had both of their cups, and without one Mindel wouldn't eat.

She felt like screaming out loud. But if she had learned one thing in these past months, it was that nothing good ever came of screaming. Most of the time it resulted in nothing but kicks, lashes or punches. So instead she ran off, her only goal to find her sister.

Gathering up all of her courage she asked one of the friendlier-looking guards, "Do you know where my sister is?"

"What do I care, you filthy Jew?"

He made a movement as if to hit her and she ran as quickly as her feet would carry her, bumping into a small group of women with shaved heads. "Please, I need to find my sister!"

"You won't find her here."

"But…" Mindel was about to sit down right there and wait until she died, because at least then she'd be able to fly to the clouds and spot Rachel from up there.

An older woman who spoke with a peculiar accent said, "Go back to your barracks, I'm sure your sister is waiting for you there."

Barracks? "But… I don't…" Mindel's mind raced. Usually she and Rachel had been assigned to a barracks together and her sister had handled everything, from choosing a bunk for them, to getting blankets, to lining up for soup when it was time to do so. "Nobody told me where my barracks are."

The woman looked slightly incredulous, but patiently asked, "You just arrived here?"

"Yes. Today."

"Alone?"

"No, but my sister was put in some other line and I was left here."

"How old is your sister?"

Mindel furrowed her brows, thinking. "Really old. She's been taking care of me."

"That would explain it," the woman murmured before she said in a louder voice, "They probably took her to a sub-camp to work in one of their factories."

Big tears rolled down Mindel's cheeks, but she didn't utter a single sound.

"Oh, hell," the woman cursed. "You can sleep in our barracks, but don't think I'll take care of you! I have enough on my hands just keeping myself alive."

Mindel nodded. At least she'd have a place to sleep tonight. Feeling for Paula nestled beneath her dress, she followed the woman to one of the ugly barrack buildings. It wasn't much different from those she'd slept in before—a one-story white building with tiny windows, and one door at each end.

As soon as the woman opened the door, an atrocious smell wafted into Mindel's nostrils and she involuntarily gagged. Once her eyes had adapted to the dim light inside, she noticed the three-story bunk beds lining the walls.

"Take the last bunk in the back," the woman said and turned on her heel to leave. If it weren't for Paula, Mindel would be all alone and miserable.

She did as she was told. Most of the people were outside, but some had stayed in their beds, filling the hut with groans, sniffs, coughs and broken wind.

Dear God, I will never be mean to my brothers again if you help me find Rachel, she promised before she reached the last bunk. It was right next to the buckets used at night when the inmates weren't allowed outside to the latrine. The stench of urine and feces was horrific. She gagged several times, but since she hadn't eaten for so long, nothing came up.

Rachel had always preferred the uppermost bunk, so she climbed up there, and stretched out on the bare wood, pressing Paula against her face. Tears fell into the doll's dirty dress and she barely noticed when two other people climbed into her bunk and shoved her into a corner, grumbling. Exhaustion took over and she fell into a deep sleep, murmuring, "Rachel, where are you? Please, come and find me."

CHAPTER 6

Rachel came awake at the shrill sound of a siren. Out of habit she fumbled about the bunk, searching for her little sister, when the events of the day before rushed to her mind. The image of Mindel's panicked face when the guard separated them and dragged Rachel into another fenced-off compound of this damned camp, was vividly imprinted in her memory.

Linda lay in the bunk next to her and a little ray of hope entered her heart. Linda was positively crazy, but somehow managed to maintain a positive attitude in all of this. She touched the other woman's shoulder. "Wake up, Linda."

Linda slowly opened her eyes. "Why? Nobody came to wake us."

Rachel all but laughed. "You slept through a siren that could wake the dead."

"Well, I am not dead yet." Even as she said the words, Linda rubbed her eyes and climbed down from the upper bunk. After extensive experimentation in different camps, Rachel had come to the conclusion that the upper story of the three-story bunk beds was definitely the best choice, as long as one had the energy to climb up and down each day.

The lower bunk seemed more convenient at first glance, and mostly the old and very weak coveted a spot on the ground floor. But those people were always the first ones to endure an extra inspection or feel the wrath of a guard, since most guards never bothered to climb up to the upper beds.

The middle bunk was a compromise between convenience and exertion, but Rachel found it combined the disadvantages of the other stories. The guard's sharp eye and truncheons could easily reach up there and you still had to fear the people above peeing and shitting on you.

"No dawdling," yelled the *kapo*—a prisoner who was given privileges in return for supervising other prisoners—and Rachel hurried to climb down from the bunk bed. On the way out of the hut she passed a sick old woman called Denise, who was too weak to get up from her bunk.

Last night, after her arrival, Rachel had talked to Denise, a woman who'd claimed to be thirty, but looked like she was sixty. From her Rachel had learned that this concentration camp they were in was called Bergen-Belsen and that it was divided into several compounds, separated from each other by barbed wire fences.

Rachel and Linda had ended up in the biggest part, the women's camp, and she could only guess where Mindel was. Maybe in the star camp, which was close to the main entrance and had gotten its name because instead of prison garb, the inmates wore civilian clothes with a yellow star sewn onto them. Though most inmates were Jews in all of the compounds, the star camp was apparently mostly for the Dutch. Either way, even if Mindel was there, it would be difficult to get to her because traffic and communication between the compounds was strictly *verboten*.

Guilt crept up her spine. She should have fought harder to stay together with Mindel when the SS guard had torn them apart and shoved her in the opposite direction away from her sister. At four years of age, Mindel was little more than a baby, and without

Rachel to look after her the way she'd done since their parents had been captured, how could she survive?

Rachel could only hope that a kind woman would take little Mindel under her wing, to care for her and keep her safe. Desperate, she rubbed a hand over her head, cringing at the feel of the stubble there instead of the long dark hair she'd once loved to brush and braid.

They'd shorn her hair in the camp before this one, and while she still reeled from the humiliation, she acknowledged that with the disgusting living conditions it might well be a good thing. At least the omnipresent lice couldn't hide in her hair. Not that it helped much—she was infested with these little buggers from head to toe, and the constant itching and biting was one more nuisance to bear. Mindel, though, had not been shorn, and Rachel had spent time each night picking lice and other critters from her head.

As much as she had hated the task of plucking the lice from her sister's scalp with her fingernails, now she would have given her right hand to do so again. Before all of this happened, Mindel's dark brown hair had been soft like silk, much like their mother's.

She rubbed her arms, hoping the motion would force some warmth back into her skin. April was still chilly at night and she'd not been able to scrounge a blanket the night before. Every time they were moved from one camp to the next, they'd had to start from scratch, fighting for a bunk, a blanket, and apparently now for the privilege of staying together.

Her hand touched her most precious possession: her soup bowl that she always carried tied to her waist. No bowl—no soup. With a shock she registered the second bowl. *Good heavens, I hope someone gave Mindel a cup to eat from.*

"Hurry up or do you want us all to be punished for your dawdling?" someone yelled and Rachel quickly followed the rest of the women outside to stand in line for the godawful roll call.

"I still have Mindel's cup," she whispered to Linda who was standing beside her.

"Not good," Linda murmured without moving her lips.

"Do you think someone gave her a cup?"

"Surely. At least I would have."

Rachel wasn't so sure, because kindness was a rare sight in the camps and from what she had gleaned so far, Bergen-Belsen was far worse than all the other places Mindel and she had been to so far.

"How long does this roll call last?" Rachel asked after what seemed like hours, when her legs were hurting and her tongue stuck to the roof of her mouth with unbearable thirst.

"It can take hours until the SS has counted all of us, making sure the numbers of living and dead prisoners match up," the woman to her left said.

Her eyes glued to the ground, Rachel whispered back, "Have you been here long?"

"Too long."

"I'm looking for my baby sister. She's in one of the other compounds."

"You'll never find her, there's no way across."

Rachel felt as if she was shrinking in size with the utter hopelessness of her quest. "There must be some way."

"The infirmary is the only possible way to get to the other side, but you must have a verifiable emergency to be allowed in there," another woman whispered.

"Like a severed arm," the first one said.

"Shush, or you'll get us all killed," someone behind them hissed and moments later the guards came up to their row, inspecting each of the women closely.

Desperate to find her sister, Rachel formed a plan. If the infirmary was the one place where people from different sub-camps could meet, she had to go there and ask questions about Mindel. It was a long shot, but someone might have seen her.

With this plan conceived her most important move was to stay in the camp and appear sick enough to be taken to the infirmary in the star camp. When roll call was finally over and the women were allowed to receive their morning soup, Rachel told Linda her plan. "I have an idea how to find Mindel."

Slurping the disgusting and murky liquid that served as soup, Linda glanced up. "Tell me."

"I'll pretend to be sick."

"How? Haven't you listened to the women who have been here for quite a while? Short of a severed arm, you won't be considered sick enough to be taken to the infirmary."

"There must be something. I'm not willing to give up that soon. I must find her. She won't be able to cope without me. She's just four." Rachel finished her soup and sank back on her haunches, the guilt about not having clung to her sister more fiercely threatening to overwhelm her.

"It's not your fault, you know that, right?" Linda said.

Rachel nodded. On a rational level she knew this, but emotionally she still felt responsible. She missed her sister so much. Mindel's small hand in hers, her skinny arms wrapped around her waist. Yes, she even missed Mindel's incessant chatting with Paula about their lives back home. "But how will she cope without me?" Then she had an idea. "What if I asked the Lagerkommandant? Surely he'll let us be together."

Suddenly the ever-positive Linda seemed to shrink two sizes and hissed, "Don't do that. Don't! You can't!"

"But why not?"

Linda's brown eyes seemed to fill with an ocean of grief. "Nothing good will come of it."

Rachel decided not to ask for details because Linda's face spoke of so much pain and guilt she didn't want to add to it.

"The thing is…" Linda murmured. "My sister wanted to save my mother. See… my father is a Gentile, so we're *Mischlinge*, half-Jews. The Nazis forced my father to divorce my mother, and about a year ago, the Gestapo came for us. My sister and I were given the choice to work in an ammunitions factory as civil workers, while Mother was to be deported. But Roberta begged the men to let Mother come with us. The officer in charge only laughed and said if she loved her mother so much, she'd be deported alongside her. Then he stared at me. 'What's your choice, Fräulein? Would you rather join your family or support the Führer and *Vaterland*?'"

Rachel's eyes all but popped out and she whispered, "What did you do?"

"It was the hardest decision of my life and I had only a few seconds to make it. By that time we knew that the tale of relocation to better lands in the east was only that—a tale. We knew about the camps where people are worked to death or give in to hunger and disease. If I joined them I would surely die, but on the other hand… how could I work for those who'd made my life a living hell? Had taken my father away? Forced him to cut all contact with us? And were now sending my mother and sister to their sure deaths?"

"Oh my goodness."

"I stared back at him—I will never forget his steely eyes, mocking me to do the wrong thing. Because, make no mistake, both alternatives were so wrong in different ways."

"What did you do?"

"I told him I'd rather work for the Führer and *Vaterland*."

Rachel hissed in a breath at Linda's statement.

"You should have seen the disappointment, yes, even hate, in my mother and sister's eyes. They were devastated. And I never got the opportunity to explain my reasoning to them. They were taken away immediately, probably hating me forever." Linda's voice was laced with emotion. "But after a week working in the factory I ran away and went into the underground. Six months later, someone betrayed me and I was caught again. This time they didn't give me a choice."

"I'm so sorry." Rachel wrapped an arm around Linda's shoulders.

"Don't be sorry. I learned two things from that exchange: first, you'll only worsen your situation if you plead with the Nazis for something. And second, I will do everything to help others, because I don't know what their story is."

"You're exceptional and I'm so glad I met you," Rachel said.

Linda blushed slightly. "I'm really nothing special. Let's think about ways you can get into the star camp."

CHAPTER 7

The horrible sound of a horn woke Mindel from her sleep and she rolled over to snuggle against Rachel's warm body.

"Hey, get off me, brat!" the person lying next to her yelled.

Mindel swallowed down her fear and opened her eyes. Then she remembered. Rachel was gone. Tears fell down her cheeks as she wallowed in misery. *It's so unfair! Why did they take Rachel away? What have I done to deserve this?*

She clutched her doll to her chest as she blindly climbed down from her bunk. She urgently had to pee, but didn't want to be late for roll call, since she'd been beaten several times before for not arriving on time. Torn between going to the latrines and being late, she finally opted to scramble for the stinking buckets next to her bunk. Holding her nose tight with one hand, she scrambled to push her underwear down with the other.

In her hurry she missed the bucket and urinated on her leg, but there was no time—or water—to clean herself. She ran after the others and reached the door just as the last person walked through. Unsure what to do next, she followed a girl who looked slightly younger than Rachel and didn't leave her side as everyone lined up for roll call.

While walking past rows and rows of inmates, she glanced into each and every face, hoping to find Rachel somewhere.

"You new here?" the older girl asked.

"Yes. I lost my sister when we arrived."

"I'm Heidi, what's your name?"

Finally, a friendly soul who didn't scold her or send her away. Mindel gave her a grateful smile. "I'm Mindel."

"I saw you last night at the food line and then in our barracks, but you were asleep already. Take this." Heidi held out a tin cup for her. "I stole it from a stiff last night."

Mindel nodded and reached out to take the cup, weak from hunger. "What's a stiff?"

"A dead person." Heidi looked straight ahead and told Mindel to do the same, before she added, "Guard the cup with your life. Tie it to your body. Put it beneath your dress at night. Don't ever leave it unattended. Do you understand?"

"Yes." Mindel understood well enough. "No cup, no food."

While standing more or less motionless for the eternity of the roll call, she clandestinely removed Paula's hair ribbon, slung it through the cup's handle and tried at least a dozen times to make a bow. With every failed attempt, her desperation grew.

When the guards had passed their row, Heidi turned around and said, "Let me." Then she made a sling with a knot and pushed it over Mindel's wrist. "There you are. Don't lose the mug."

"Thank you."

Mindel hated the roll call with a passion; it was the most awful thing she'd ever experienced, even more than the constant hunger and abuse. In the beginning of her captivity, she'd wanted to jump, run and play, but Rachel had forced her to stand still.

Then, as time passed, she'd become hungrier and weaker and all she wanted was to sit down, but again Rachel had forced her to stand up. Didn't those SS men have anything better to do than to keep everyone out in the cold, rain or sunshine? Didn't they see how exhausting it was having to stand still for all that time? Mindel didn't understand why they had to keep counting everyone. It wasn't as if there was a way out of this horrid place.

When the roll call finally ended, she trotted off to take her place in the queue, waiting for soup. She carefully removed the sling from her wrist and grabbed the cup with both hands and for good measure gave a fierce grimace so nobody would dare to steal it from her, because she was really, really hungry. When it was her turn, the food bearer filled the mug up to the brim and gave her a small piece of bread.

Mindel bit on her lip, trying to balance the mug with one hand and the bread with the other one. When the soup spilled, she almost started to cry.

"Hold it in both hands," Heidi, who'd come up behind her, said. "Like this." She showed Mindel how to put the bread between her teeth to have both hands free for the mug. Mindel nodded, focusing on stepping lightly as she looked for a place to sit down and eat. Even with both hands it wasn't easy to keep the liquid from spilling over, and she stopped several times to steady the wild movement of the precious soup.

It tasted atrocious and even a month ago she would not have eaten this horrible gruel, but with her aching tummy she'd eat just about anything. Even the dirt on the ground. She had learned never to ask for more, even though she didn't understand why. The SS people were eating all the time, so why didn't they give her something when her tummy hurt?

The mug was empty all too soon and she scraped out every last drop with her fingers, licking them clean. If her mother could see her now, she'd be struck with an open hand. Back home the rule was "*no fingers in food.*" Mindel had hated that stupid rule, because eating with a knife and fork was so hard, but she didn't like having to lick the rest of this disgusting gruel, either.

Thoughts of her mother filled her with sadness. Rachel had told her their parents had been sent away to work for the government and would soon return.

"But why can't they work on our farm? Mother always says there's more than enough work to do," she had asked and Rachel had answered with a typical adult turn of phrase. "You're too young to understand."

As if! Mindel understood quite well that adults had some very strange opinions and didn't seem to know how things really worked. Or why would they stay in this awful place? Why didn't they tell the SS to let them go?

Since Heidi had been so nice, Mindel gathered all her courage and asked, "I lost my sister. Can you help me find her?"

Heidi's eyes took on a sad expression. "What's her name?"

"Rachel."

"And her last name?"

Mindel furrowed her brow, thinking hard. She knew that the adults sometimes had called her mother Frau... something. She just couldn't remember it. As hard as she tried, nothing came to mind. "I don't know."

"Well, that makes it difficult. There must be hundreds of girls with the name Rachel in the camp. Do you know how old she is?"

Mindel did not. She put up four fingers. "I'm four. Aron is seven." Then she put up all ten fingers. "This is how old Israel is. And Rachel, she's much older."

Heidi gave a deep sigh. "Aron and Israel are your brothers?"

"Yes."

"Are they here too?"

"No. When the SS caught us, they were walking way in front of us. They started running so fast, the men couldn't catch them!" Mindel was immensely proud of her brothers. They were true heroes. If her own legs weren't so short, she would have run with them, and then… She began to sob. "It's all my fault that we're here!"

"How can you say that? It's the Nazis' fault."

Mindel trembled with guilt and rage. "I fell when we were running. Rachel picked me up and carried me, but then she was so much slower. That's why the men caught her. It's all my fault!"

Heidi wrapped her arm around Mindel's shoulders. "It's not your fault. You're still so little."

"I don't want to be little!" Mindel burst out. "I want to be grown up and strong and then I will hit all the SS men with their stupid batons and tell them to let us go."

This time Heidi smiled before she said, "Unfortunately it doesn't work like that. We can search for your sister in the evening if you want."

Another horn sounded and Heidi stood up, pulling Mindel with her. "The adults have to go on their work details. You'd better return to your bunk and stay out of the way."

"Work?" Mindel asked, perplexed.

"Yes, almost everyone above fifteen has to work, except for those in the special camp. The Nazis use us prisoners to keep the war machine at speed."

Mindel didn't really understand, but nodded and walked back to her barracks, proud that she'd memorized which one it was. Once she arrived in the mostly empty barracks, save for a few sick people groaning, she climbed into her bunk. The stench was repellant, but she held her nose and pulled out Paula from under her dress. The poor mite hadn't had anything to eat yet.

Lying on her bed, talking to Paula, her belly was aching and growling again. She tried to ignore it, but being all alone was awful and boring. She wished there were other children to play with… Sitting here with nothing to do only made the hunger worse. She started to get off the bunk a few times, but then she realized she didn't know where to go.

Rachel had always impressed on her the need to stay out of the way of the guards. Now that she was on her own, she really didn't want to come across one of them, because they could be so mean. She lay back and tried to daydream about their life on the farm back home, and how she had played with her brothers, but it was getting harder and harder to remember those days. She barely remembered what her mother looked like, let alone her father.

Loneliness sucked her into a deep hole and she barely noticed when the back door of the barracks opened and three children rushed in. They stopped dead in their tracks, glaring at her, whispering to one another, before they turned around and rushed back out the way they had come.

Fear fought with curiosity and in the end Mindel climbed down from her bunk, cautiously leaving the barracks. She spotted the children between two outbuildings and walked toward them.

A tall and incredibly thin boy with a shock of pitch-black hair noticed her and hurriedly waved her over. Mindel looked around and when she saw two guards coming down the path, she took off running for the shelter of the outbuilding.

Completely out of breath she crashed to her knees and skidded toward the thin boy. She wanted to scream with pain, but remembering the scathing remarks of her brothers for behaving like a baby, she didn't want to show any weakness to this boy and gritted her teeth. If he was anything like them he wouldn't want to hang out with a crybaby.

"Well done," he said. "Never let them spot you. I'm Laszlo, and you?"

"Mindel."

"I haven't seen you before, are you new?" he asked, flashing a double-toothed gap, just like her brother Aron, who'd been so proud of his first missing tooth. Mindel wished she had a wobbly tooth, too, because that would make her a big girl.

She nodded and when she noticed Laszlo looking at her doll, she tucked Paula behind her back. He didn't have to know that she still played with dolls.

Laszlo pretended not to notice and asked, "How old are you?"

"Four. And you?"

"I'm already seven. You can play with us if you want."

Suddenly she didn't feel quite as lonely as she had just a little while ago.

CHAPTER 8

After eating her meager breakfast, Rachel found herself following the others as they lined up, shoulder to shoulder in long rows. All around her were exhausted-looking women, and it was easy to pick out the ones who had been there for a while. They were emaciated, their hair—if they still had any—tangled and falling out, their clothing just barely hanging on their bodies.

"What are we doing?" she whispered to an old woman standing next to her.

"Work details," the woman said in an expressionless voice.

"They make us work?" So far, Rachel had been to several transit camps and detention centers, but nowhere had she been forced to work.

The other woman gave a dry cough. "Bergen-Belsen itself is for the sick and dying. Everyone else gets sent somewhere else."

Rachel watched as the guards walked up and down the lines of women, choosing the healthier ones and ordering them off to one side. A sense of panic began to well up inside her. She couldn't be sent off to someplace else. She had to stay here and find Mindel.

"I can't be sent to work," she hissed in Linda's direction.

As the guards drew closer to her place in line, Rachel desperately thought about how she could evade being sent elsewhere. Compared to the other women she definitely looked healthy and able-bodied. Just as the guards reached the row before her, she broke out into a fit of coughs, bent over, clutching her stomach with one hand while she forced her fingers down her throat with the other.

All of the ugly gruel she'd had for breakfast rose in her throat and she spewed it onto the ground. It wasn't difficult to look faint and aggravated, because if the soup had tasted horrid on its way down, it certainly hadn't improved coming back up.

"Disgusting filthy whore," a female guard with the most scathing, vile, blue eyes yelled. "You clean that up!"

Rachel bent down, swiping at the ground with the hem of her skirt and keeping her eyes down until the shiny black boots in front of her walked by. When she was sure the vile guard had moved on to the next row, she slowly got up.

"Whatever did you do that for?" her neighbor on the other side to Linda whispered.

"I need to find my sister."

"Stupid girl! In here, you have to take care of yourself first. The women who work have a chance to live. In the sub-camps everything's better—less crowded, more food, and a shower once in a while."

Coming from this older woman it sounded like the Promised Land. Rachel caught a glimpse of her wistful expression and shook her head with disbelief. But just as quickly the cold hand of fright closed around her heart. She saw herself reflected in the eyes of that cynical older woman. In a year's time, would she look and think the same way too? Panic welled up in her, making her stagger. A year from now Mindel would surely be dead if she didn't find her first.

Roll call ended and another setback hit Rachel squarely in the chest. Naturally upbeat and always-positive Linda had looked much too healthy and had been selected for a work detail. Despite knowing the other woman for just a few days, she felt like her best friend was being ripped from her and tears pricked at her eyes as the two were separated into different groups.

"Don't lose hope, I'm sure you'll find your sister and then the two of us will meet again. Never give up, because if you do they will win."

Rachel had no words to respond. All of a sudden she felt inadequate. If Linda could keep a positive attitude, she should be able to do the same. But somehow she couldn't. The separation from Mindel weighed heavily on her conscience and dragged down her spirits and her will to resist.

After the different work details had left the camp, the non-working women were basically left to their own devices for the rest of the day. Most flopped down on the ground, leaning against the walls of the barracks, soaking up the April sunshine. It was such a beautiful day, the sun shining brightly from a cloudless sky, completely oblivious to the suffering that was going on beneath it.

Rachel gave in to the overwhelming tiredness in her bones after the endless journey in that godforsaken train and joined the group of skeletal women on the ground. *Just for five minutes*, she said to herself.

She must have dozed off, because she found herself back home on her parents' farm, the first seedlings peeking through the warming earth, braving the frosty nights. She walked across the field, carefully weeding and watering the plants. A wave of nostalgia washed over her. Life wasn't easy under the Nazis' rule, but their secluded farm on the outskirts of the tiny village of Kleindorf was still a safe haven—thanks to Old Hans.

Once he'd taken possession of their property, and had installed her parents as working tenants on what had once been their own land, nobody had bothered them. Rachel had been apprehensive, and even as the months went by and nothing happened, she'd never fully believed her parents, that they'd sit out the war and then everything would go back to normal again.

"Kleindorf is too small and remote to attract a Nazi raid," her father had said.

"We're the last Jews around here, so why would anyone bother?" her mother responded.

"As long as we achieve our quota and Hans can sell the required amount of produce to the farmers' association, they'll leave us in peace."

"Even if there is a raid, the Kleindorf farmers will stand by us."

Rachel wanted to believe their words with all her heart. In her mind, she walked back to the orchard with the apple trees in full blossom, when a howling sound disturbed her. She opened her eyes, finding herself in a grey and dreary place instead of the lush green field. After blinking a few times, her disorientation faded and she recognized her surroundings. The concentration camp of Bergen-Belsen.

Her parents had been wrong. Sadness filled her heart. She made an effort to get up and walked around the compound asking every woman about her sister. Most of the haggard figures simply shook their heads, others advised her to "forget about the brat," but finally she found a kind soul.

"Sit down for a while, will you?" the woman in a drab gray dress with the yellow star sewn onto it said. "I'm Doris, by the way."

"Rachel."

"When did you last see your sister?"

She recounted the story of how they'd been separated on arrival.

Doris frowned and then used her forefinger to etch a map of the camp into the dirt. The form looked a bit like a tank with a sharp end on the right and a broader one on the left.

"We are here in the women's camp, over there behind the fence is the SS clothing store and the workshops, and right next to it, with only a small connection to our compound, is the star camp, where they keep Jews of different nationalities as hostages to exchange for German prisoners of war."

"Really?" Rachel had never heard of these sorts of dealings.

"Yes, but don't get your hopes up. Since I came here a year ago, nobody has left this place alive—other than for work details. Here," she pointed to the right of the star camp on her map, "we have the Hungarian camp and the special camp. These special camp inmates are privileged. They don't have to work and get extra rations, because they have paid for their escape already and are waiting to resume their journey to Palestine."

Rachel was perplexed. There were actual people, German Jews, allowed to emigrate to Palestine? Her parents had only ever spoken with disdain about the ones they called Zionists, claiming they were the root of discord among the Jews.

"Next the neutrals camp, filled with Jews from nations that are not at war with Germany, like Spain or Argentina. And a small men's camp, like this is the women's camp. Behind that row there's another camp that's not guarded by the SS, but by the Wehrmacht. They keep wounded Soviet soldiers there, and from what I've heard, conditions are a lot worse than here."

"Worse?" Rachel involuntarily gasped and held a hand in front of her mouth.

Doris cackled a laugh at her. "Much worse. But back to your sister. My best guess is she'll be in the star camp."

That much Rachel had already gathered from the woman yesterday. "How can I go there?"

"You can't." Doris leaned back, suddenly reaching under her dress and then pulling out her hand with a victorious expression. "Got you!"

Rachel didn't even have to look to know that Doris had just plucked another of those nasty critters from an intimate body part, because she'd become so used to doing this herself since everyone in the camps was lice-infested. Once again, she remembered combing her fingers though Mindel's long hair every night. Once, in her first camp, they'd all been sprayed with some stinking chemical that stung in her eyes for hours. But the critters had returned the very next day, adding one more misery to their already miserable existence.

Desperation washed over Rachel. Despite Doris' declaration that it was impossible, she clung to the idea that somehow she could find a way to get into the infirmary in the other compound and search for Mindel there. "I must find her!"

Doris turned her head with a stunned expression at Rachel's outburst, but then her face softened and she put her bony hand on Rachel's. "I wish I could still be like you, but look what the camp has made of an old hag like me."

CHAPTER 9

"Watch me and learn," Laszlo whispered to Mindel as they hid outside the back door of the kitchen barracks.

"What are you going to do?" Mindel whispered back, goosebumps rising on her skin. She was scared someone might see them, especially as Laszlo looked like he was up to no good, but she wasn't going to let him see her fear. The other children in the group had argued that she was too little to hang out with them, but he'd stuck up for her.

She looked up at him with pure adulation. He seemed so grown-up and was so courageous, he was her hero and she'd do whatever he wanted. For the past days she'd followed him around, always eager to please him and make him proud of her. She'd prove the other children wrong and show them she wasn't "too little."

Laszlo peeked around the corner of the building and then pulled her over until she could see as well. "That bucket is my goal."

Mindel looked at the woman in the kitchen who was pulling potatoes from a large gunnysack and peeling them into a bucket—the same bucket Laszlo had pointed to.

"Those are potato peels," she whispered back.

"And they taste really good. I'm going to get us some."

"But that's stealing," Mindel said, appalled at his heinous plan.

"So what?"

She stared at him, her mind wandering back to her parents' farm. One time, her mother had made a birthday cake for Israel, but everyone had only been allowed a small slice before she'd covered it and put it away for the next day. Mindel and Aron had waited until her mother walked out to milk the cows, snuck into the kitchen pantry and each grabbed a huge slice into their hands.

Out of fear of being caught red-handed, they'd crouched in the pantry and stuffed the cake into their mouths as fast as they could. Once the deed was accomplished, they snuck out and into the garden, pretending nothing had happened.

But the moment her mother saw them, her lovely face turned red and she called them out for stealing the cake. Even today, Mindel had no idea how her mother had found out, since they'd been so careful.

It had been a horrible moment when her mother had taken Mindel's sticky hands, turned them with the palm upward and hit her with a wooden spoon. Aron hadn't fared much better either, and both had been sent to their bedroom without dinner that day.

Mindel had never again stolen even a morsel of food from the pantry.

"Please don't. You'll get in trouble. They'll beat you," she pleaded with Laszlo.

"Only if I get caught. And I'd rather take a beating than starve to death."

Mindel heard his words and the truth behind them, but she wasn't sure she agreed. In the camp people got beaten all the time for tiny misdeeds and it wasn't with a wooden spoon, but with truncheons and whips. She'd even seen people fall down and never get up again after a beating. She didn't want that to happen to Laszlo. He was her friend.

"See that little cubbyhole by the shelves?" Laszlo asked.

She craned her head until she saw it, and nodded.

"You're fast and small, so you sneak inside and hide there. I'll stand guard out here. Once the woman turns her back to you, grab as much from the bucket as you can and run back here to me. I'll create a distraction if I need to."

All the blood drained from her head and she suddenly felt dizzy. "You want me to steal the potato skins?"

"It's called 'organizing' food, not stealing. If you pass this test, I'll make you a member of our gang."

Mindel swallowed. She so badly wanted to be part of the gang. To belong somewhere. And she was hungry. Very hungry. But stealing was wrong. Her mother would be so disappointed.

Laszlo saw her wavering and insisted, "I dare you. You can't be with us if you're a chickenshit."

She hated this word. Aron had often name-called her this, mostly when she hadn't obeyed his stupid rules. She squared her shoulders and said, "I'll do it, because I'm brave."

Quivering with fear, she bit her lip, thinking of a way to get out of this dare. She repeated Laszlo's words, telling herself it wasn't really stealing—because the SS men were so mean and didn't give them enough. But not even that helped to calm her nerves.

Laszlo nudged her forward. "Ready? Then go."

Mindel nodded. Gathering up all her courage she crept forward, intent on pretending this was simply a game of hide-and-seek. Back on the farm she'd been a master, hiding in the smallest crevices without making a sound. Most of the time, her brothers would walk right by her, never knowing that she was mere inches away from them.

Suddenly, excitement pushed her fear away. The kitchen worker and those stupid SS guards would never know she was even there, and Laszlo would praise her master skills at playing hide-and-seek. As an added benefit she'd return with a handful of potato skins for their group to eat. She gave a slow smile, encouraging herself, before she squinted her eyes, focusing on the task at hand. Silence was the most important factor, because adults seemed to go more by ear than by sight where children were concerned.

She crept toward the door and waited until the woman wielding the potato peeler turned her back, then Mindel quickly slipped into the kitchen and pressed herself into the small hiding place. Barely breathing, she watched and waited until the woman picked up the tray of peeled potatoes and walked over to the stove.

Mindel wasted no time. She rushed forward, plunged her hands into the bucket, grabbed two handfuls of potato peels and ran for the doorway where Laszlo was waiting for her. She ducked out of the kitchen just as the sounds of the woman's feet returned. Clutching her bounty to her chest, she ran with Laszlo toward another building where they'd left the other kids.

"Good job," Laszlo said once they were sitting behind the hut, breathing hard.

Mindel smiled broadly at him and presented her spoils. "I did it."

"Yes, you did it." Laszlo was eyeing the potato peels and Mindel held out her hands toward him.

"Eat some."

"You stole them, you get first dibs."

Mindel put the food on a not-so-dirty patch of ground and ate two peels. They were slightly bitter and smelled like dirt, but tasted much better than the horrible gruel they were given for soup. Then she divided the bulk into five equal parts for each of the children in the group: Laszlo, Ruth, Fabian, Clara and herself.

"Here," she invited them.

Almost reverently the children each took their share and chewed the unexpected treat. Once they finished eating, Laszlo grinned. "See, I told you she's not too small."

Fabian pouted, but Clara said, "You were right. Now let's make her a member of the gang."

After Laszlo nodded his approval, Ruth produced a strip of washed-out gray-brown yarn from her pocket, tied it around Mindel's left wrist and said rather ceremoniously, "Welcome to our gang!"

Everyone shook her hand and Mindel felt herself grow a few inches with pride. The other children had accepted her as part of their group. She wasn't alone anymore.

But all this changed when it was time to climb onto her bunk after dinner. The barracks were still mostly empty, as the adults milled about doing one thing or the other before curfew. She found her bunk empty, too. Not even the disgusting smelly blankets lay there anymore. Mindel waited for the two adults who'd shared her bunk last night to return. But nothing happened. The barracks filled and once the *kapo* announced night's rest, she was still alone—and scared.

Her bunkmates hadn't been exactly welcoming, although they mostly hadn't been unfriendly either and had allowed her to share the blankets with them. Now she'd be all alone, and without the warmth of a blanket and two more bodies by her side.

She shivered at the thought of the upcoming night, because even though the days could be quite warm, the nights were still cold—although not as horrid as they'd been during the harsh winter.

The memory of cuddling with Rachel to keep warm under the threadbare blanket brought tears to her eyes and she took out Paula, kissed her dirty face, and cried as silently as she could because she didn't want to hear the adults curse her for waking them up. But apparently she hadn't been silent enough, because a short time later she heard a hissed curse, creaking wood and then steps on the floor. Panicked about the punishment she might receive, she breathed as shallowly as possible, pretending to be fast asleep. But she couldn't suppress the odd sob erupting in her throat and wished so much for Rachel to be by her side to soothe her. Or any other human being stroking her head and whispering words of comfort.

A small hand reached for her and she started. It was too dark to see who it was, but when she heard a familiar voice whisper, "Don't cry. I'll stay with you," she relaxed.

"Thanks." She smiled through her tears and eagerly nodded despite the fact that he could not see her and moved back to allow Laszlo to climb onto her bunk.

He brought a blanket with him, covered them both with it and they huddled together. She instantly felt warmer, clutching onto his arm with one hand.

"I will protect you," he said.

"Won't you get in trouble with your parents?" Mindel knew that the star camp was separated into men's huts and women's huts, but families could see each other during the day. Usually girls stayed with their mothers and boys with their fathers, but if they didn't have one, they were allowed to stay with their mother or another female relative in the women's barracks.

His arm around her shoulder tensed and she was scared she'd said something wrong and made him angry at her. The prospect of alienating her best friend made her shudder.

"My parents died a while ago," he whispered in a restrained voice before he gave a deep sigh. "No one pays any attention to me. If anything, the other people in my bunk will be happy to have more space."

"This is such a horrible place," Mindel murmured.

"It is. I hate it here, too."

"I'm so scared." Mindel pressed herself tighter into his arms.

"You don't have to be scared, I'm here to protect you."

She gave a barely audible giggle. "That's what Rachel always said. Without her…" she forced herself to continue speaking "… she did everything. Chose us a bunk, got us blankets, always knew when it was time to queue for food, everything."

"Hm." Laszlo seemed to struggle to find words. Mindel didn't actually believe he was scared, too, but it almost seemed as if he were about to cry.

"I'm so glad you're here."

Laszlo had found his voice again and whispered, "I always wanted to have a brother or sister and now you're mine. Don't you worry anymore, everything will be just fine. We can fight better than Nazis do. We just have to stay alive a little while longer. You know, it won't be long before the Allies come and rescue us."

Mindel had never heard talk about the Allies before, but if they were friends of Laszlo and planned to rescue them from this awful place, then she would consider them her friends too.

After a while, his breathing evened out and she snuggled even tighter against his warm body, soaking up the protection he offered. Rachel used to hold her just like this while they slept, and even though she missed her sister like crazy, she felt reassuringly safe in Laszlo's arms. Plus, he'd told her, his allies were coming to rescue them.

She lay there trying to figure out why the SS guards, both men and women, were so cruel to everyone. Searching her conscience, she couldn't find any misdeed to draw their ire, and yet they constantly snarled at her and even threatened to hit her with their horrible whips.

There were no answers and she finally fell asleep full of worries. When the nightmares and tears came, as they inevitably did each night, Laszlo was there to soothe her fears with promises to watch over her and keep her safe.

Mindel believed him. Laszlo seemed so grown-up; he'd brought a blanket with him, had made her part of his gang, and had shown her how to organize food. A proud smile appeared on her lips as she remembered how she'd outwitted the kitchen woman. Just a tiny nagging voice insisted it was stealing and stealing wasn't right.

She ignored the voice, because having an aching, growling tummy was even worse. Drifting back to sleep, she dreamt about Rachel and how she'd find her with Laszlo's help.

CHAPTER 10

During the day few people seemed to be in the camp as most of the women had been sent away on work details and those too sick or weak to work were lying either inside or outside soaking up the sunshine, which is what Rachel had been doing while figuring out her next move.

Invigorated by the need to find her sister she wracked her brain to find the best way forward. Finally, she came up with something akin to a plan and got up. Carefully, she made her way to the other side of the women's camp, where the gate to the star camp and the infirmary was. She had no idea how to actually get in there but suspected it would rely on chance.

In front of the building next to the camp offices and workshops, Rachel hesitated. A female SS guard came out of the office looking at her. Since she didn't immediately begin to yell, Rachel gathered her courage to walk up to her and to ask, "*Verzeihung, Frau Aufseherin*, I am looking for my little sister. I believe she was assigned to another compound by mistake when we arrived yesterday."

The young woman had straight brown hair and a well-fitted uniform showing off her rounded hips, and she stopped to glare at Rachel. "What do I care about your sister? She'll soon be dead anyway. Just like you. And now get out of my way, you ugly scarecrow!" The guard put her hand against the truncheon tied to her hips to emphasize her words and Rachel hurried to follow her orders and make herself invisible.

What she had seen so far didn't encourage her to ask more questions. None of the guards in all the detention centers or transit camps she'd been in in the past six months had been particularly friendly, but the SS men and women in Bergen-Belsen were in a class of their own.

When she finally arrived at the fence that separated the two compounds, she lingered out of sight until a woman in nurses' attire crossed through the gate, barely acknowledged by the guard who opened and closed the gate for her.

As soon as she entered the women's camp, the nurse lit a cigarette for herself. Rachel hesitantly approached her and asked, "Excuse me, I'm looking for my sister. She's just four years old, about so high." Rachel demonstrated Mindel's height against her hip.

"Haven't looked after anyone that age today." The nurse was very obviously a prisoner herself, despite looking better nourished and clothed than the rest of the women. She squinted her eyes, scrutinizing Rachel while taking another pull on her cigarette.

Rachel didn't smoke, but since she'd heard that the nicotine decreased the feeling of hunger, she felt a sudden longing to take a drag. "She's not… a patient."

"If she's not a patient, why are you asking me?" The nurse was obviously puzzled.

"It's…" Rachel didn't know how to explain, but looking at the impatient face and the dwindling cigarette, she quickly continued, "My sister, she's only four, we were separated yesterday upon arrival and I believe she's in the star camp."

"So, now you want to go look for her on the other side of the fence?" The nurse's eyes lit up with an emotion Rachel couldn't quite place.

Rachel nodded eagerly.

"Well, it can be done…" The nurse looked squarely at Rachel, measuring her up, while taking another drag. "But it will cost you."

"Cost me?" Rachel almost toppled over. She had nothing to give.

"Yes. I have to bribe the guards… And it's a big risk for me, too."

"But… I have…" She wanted to say she had nothing, but thought better of it and decided to let the nurse state her conditions first. Perhaps there was a way to get what the woman wanted. "How much would it cost?"

"Ten cigarettes."

Rachel felt the blood draining from her face. Ten cigarettes were worth a fortune. Some prisoners always seemed to have them, but since she'd been too occupied caring for Mindel all this time to become versatile in the finer arts of black marketeering, she had no idea where and how to get hold of them.

Despite her hopelessness, she forced a confident expression on her face. "I'll get you the cigarettes as soon as I can." If she had hoped that the nurse worked on a promise, she was disappointed.

"When you have them come back here just before dinner time. Don't tell anyone. Don't ask the guards for me if I'm not here. And don't ask another nurse, because they will turn you in. Understood?"

"Yes." As she walked away, a shiver ran down her spine, realizing how incredibly risky this conversation had been. The nurse's warning about her colleagues maybe turning Rachel in might have been said out of spite… or it could be the truth. In hindsight she recognized the glint in the woman's eyes as greed. It didn't bear contemplating what would have happened if she had talked to another nurse who wasn't as open to bribery as this one apparently was.

Rachel had seen with her own eyes how insolent prisoners were punished. On the other hand, the guards oftentimes doled out favors to those who snitched on their fellow inmates, converting them all into appalling henchmen, doing the Nazis' dirty work. Perhaps she could… Disgust boiled in her stomach at the mere thought of getting the cigarettes needed to sneak into the star camp by turning on a fellow prisoner.

But how else could she get them? If only Linda was still with her. She would surely know of a way. Since Linda was always so kind and generous to everyone, it seemed people went out of their way to help, even if only with advice. Instead of waiting for the feeble possibility that Linda's work detail might return for the night, Rachel went to find Doris again and ask her how one got hold of cigarettes in this camp.

"Hey, Doris," she called out as she spotted the old woman leaning against the wall with her eyes closed.

Doris opened them to slits, and then asked, "Who are you?"

"I'm Rachel, remember? We talked about my little sister this morning and you explained to me the outline of the camp."

It took a few seconds until the light of recognition lit up Doris' eyes. "Oh yes. You're looking for your little sister. My brain isn't the way it used to be. The camp changes a person. Soon we'll all be like the *Muselmänner* over there." She cackled and sunk deeper against the wall.

Rachel followed Doris' gaze to a group of men. They were the only males, apart from the guards, in the women's camp, and came inside during the day to take care of the worst chores: they belonged to the work detail that had to collect the corpses and shove them into the ever-burning crematorium. Rachel had never in her life seen such raw agony as in those men walking past her.

"*Muselmänner?*" she asked.

"*Kretiner* if you prefer. Cretins. Poor sods. Too far gone already. They'll all die soon. As will the rest of us."

Rachel couldn't tear her eyes away from the men, who barely resembled humans anymore, and Doris' words echoed in her head. *Too far gone.* The absence of a human spirit in these creatures struck her. There was no light in their eyes, no recognition, no trace of intelligence. Their souls had left this world long ago and left an empty shell behind. A zombie that breathed, walked and carried out orders, without an actual human being to fill the shell with life.

She shrugged off the listlessness taking hold of her, determined not to become one of them. Deliberately looking away from the sorry sight, she returned her gaze to Doris, who had closed her eyes again, and remembered why she'd come here in the first place.

"How can I get cigarettes?"

Doris' eyes popped open. "You have a cigarette for me?"

"No, I asked you how I can get some." Rachel wanted to scream. It had been a mistake to ask Doris for advice, since the woman obviously was soft in the head or… too far gone and about to become a *Muselmann* herself.

"You have to work for them," the old woman answered with sudden clarity. "There are ways, especially for a pretty young girl like you. If you want, I can direct you to one of the SS men who are half-decent and happy to pay."

"To do what?"

"Satisfy their lust."

Rachel's face contorted into a disgusted grimace. She was willing to do a lot of things to find her sister, but becoming a whore was not one of them. Her parents had always instilled upon her that she should save herself for marriage, like any good girl would do.

Doris must have noticed Rachel's disgust, because she added, "Or, if you're a sapphist, I can point out the female guards to you who like to play both sides."

Rachel shrunk backwards. She hadn't known these kind of people existed until she'd been to her second camp and seen it with her own eyes. It had been a shocking sight to witness a female guard doing all these things with a prisoner, almost on par with many of the other atrocities the Nazis committed. How could she even entertain the idea to… Vomit rose in her throat.

"Isn't there anything else I can do?"

Doris cackled again. "Maybe, but it pays much less. Ask one of the *kapos*—the camp royalty—and offer your services to her. You can wash their laundry, do chores for them, or…" Doris cast a long glance at Rachel's comparatively healthy figure "… you could sell your food rations."

"Thank you." It was a lot to take in and Rachel quickly disappeared to a quiet place to ponder her next steps. She could certainly offer to do laundry and other work, especially since she wasn't on a work detail and had nothing to do all day. But would it be enough? She had no idea how much these chores were worth and how many days she would have to toil for the elusive contraband. Even if she managed to earn the ten cigarettes, she was afraid she might not earn them in time to rescue her sister.

CHAPTER 11

With the help of Heidi and Laszlo, Mindel combed through the entire star camp asking each and every person if they had seen her sister. But nobody had.

One of Heidi's friends even sat down with Mindel for hours to sketch Rachel's face onto a torn piece of a paper bag she'd found somewhere. The result looked amazingly similar to her sister and Mindel said with excitement, "You know, you can paint pretty well. That is super!"

The girl blushed at the praise and handed the crumpled paper to Mindel. "Keep it and show it to everyone, maybe you'll be lucky and someone will know your sister."

But even with the sketch, nobody recognized Rachel. As the days went by, Mindel stopped looking for her sister and instead focused her energy on hunting for food.

The Gang, which was what they called themselves, met every morning after roll call and started searching the camp for whatever might be useful. It was amazing how many things they found every day that could be traded for other useful stuff. Laszlo became her teacher and she was a fast learner, always eager to please him.

On one occasion a guard dropped the butt of a cigarette and as soon as he was out of sight, Laszlo raced toward the spot to pick up the remains.

"Yuck! What are you doing with that?" Mindel asked. Her father had smoked, but he'd always said it wasn't for children, especially not for girls, and, to be honest, she disliked the musty, burnt smell of it.

Laszlo looked at her with that indulgent expression he sometimes used indicating how utterly stupid she was. Now, he would give her a lengthy explanation not only about the cigarette, but about the inner workings of the camp in general.

As much as she loved him, on occasions like this one she hated his know-it-all attitude, that was so eerily similar to the way her brothers had treated her, always claiming they were better than her, just because they were older. She quickly pushed the thought away. Thinking of them always made her sad and she didn't want to be sad.

"A cigarette is worth more than gold," Laszlo said with an important face. "There are adults who will do almost anything for a cigarette."

"But it's not even a real cigarette, it's just a butt," Mindel protested.

"You have no idea," Laszlo boasted. "An entire cigarette can buy you almost anything you want, but the butt alone is worth a lot, too. I'll teach you to fiddle the tobacco rests out of the paper and once we have gathered a good amount, I know someone who'll exchange it for food."

"People really do this?" Mindel couldn't hide her astonishment. Exchange cigarettes for food! She thought that was very strange, but adults did all kinds of peculiar things, so why not use cigarettes for money?

"I'm telling you. But if you don't want to believe me…" Laszlo grimaced. He could be so sensitive at times.

Mindel hurried to appease him. "I believe you. Adults are strange like that."

Immediately he smiled again. "They are. Butts are a rare find. Because they are so valuable, everyone wants them. So, if you see a guard dropping one, don't hesitate even for a second and grab it as fast as you can."

"I will." She determined that she would scour the camp for butts and bring them to Laszlo to show him how much she deserved his trust in her.

CHAPTER 12

Rachel looked at her raw and calloused hands. Working for cigarettes had been a lot harder than she'd anticipated. Following Doris' advice she had approached the *kapo* in her barracks to ask for work. Unfortunately, the *kapo* already had her own personal servant, but agreed to hire Rachel out to others for a small percentage of her income.

It was a rotten deal, but Rachel was too afraid to contradict her. And so she had been scrubbing dirty clothes, sweeping floors, and sewing dresses for eight days straight, until she finally received her tenth cigarette.

"Thank you," she told the woman with the beaked nose who'd hired Rachel to clean the latrines in her stead. It had been the most disgusting work she'd done during the past week—far worse than she had been able to imagine, since most of the inmates suffered from chronic diarrhea and oftentimes couldn't hold it in long enough.

"Tomorrow again?" the other woman asked.

"No, for tomorrow I have other chores lined up." Rachel never wanted to sign up for this particular task again. But then she thought better of it. Once she had found Mindel she had to take care of her and any additional income would alleviate their situation a tiny bit. For Mindel she would even scrub latrines again. "But maybe the day after? I'll come looking for you."

"Don't wait too long, or I'll just find me someone else."

Rachel knew it was an empty threat, because only the most desperate women were willing to do this chore that was usually doled out as penalty to truculent inmates. She held out her hand to receive the cigarette and carefully stashed it in the pocket of her dress together with the others.

Back in her barracks she fell onto her bunk completely exhausted, but strangely happy. Tomorrow after the roll call she would walk to the fence between the compounds again and wait for the nurse. With some luck, she'd buy her way into the star camp that very day. If Mindel was there, she would surely find her and somehow come up with a way for the two of them to stay together. She had no idea how this was supposed to work, but she'd take things one step at a time. First she had to find her sister, everything else would follow.

In the morning she jumped from her bunk eager to start the new day. Another trainload of newcomers had arrived the night before and the already full camp was bursting at the seams. Rachel stood in line for roll call, musing about her efforts to find Mindel. She'd asked what felt like every inmate in the women's camp and her little sister definitely wasn't in this compound. The limited communication across the barbed wire fence into the other compounds hadn't produced any results either, but as soon as roll call was over, she'd go to the infirmary in the star camp.

Her legs aching from standing still for hours, she quietly shifted her weight from one leg to the other and moved her toes in her dilapidated shoes to get the blood flowing again.

In fact, she wondered whether her body even had blood left to circulate, since the rations were so minuscule, her stomach was painfully rebelling against its emptiness at all times—even keeping her from sleeping at night.

One hour went by, and then another, and everyone still stood outside, waiting. There seemed to be a problem with the lists counting the newcomers and the horrible blonde guard began her count again, generously cracking her whip at anyone not showing the perfect "Aryan posture": legs straight, shoulders squared, eyes ahead. If it weren't so awful, it would be funny to watch the women sagging as soon as the vicious guard had passed.

Lost in her musings, she didn't notice how one of the guards entered her row, came to a standstill in front of her and yelled, "You, over there!"

Rachel flinched, taking two seconds to realize he'd meant her. Before he could crack his whip at her, she hurried to nod and scurry over to a group of waiting women. As soon as the roll call ended, her group was herded toward the exit gates, where a truck was waiting for them.

She inwardly cursed, frantically searching for a way out, but there was none. She had to climb onto that damn truck whether she wanted to or not, and minutes later the vehicle sped out of the gates, loaded with miserable women.

As the despised Bergen-Belsen camp disappeared in the distance behind their truck, her heart sank. After everything she'd done, scrubbing, begging… now she'd never see her little sister again. Since she was too dehydrated to cry, she leaned against the railing and squeezed her eyes shut, conjuring up the image of her baby sister. Mindel would be as good as dead now and it was all her fault. Rachel should have grabbed her hand tighter, shouldn't have allowed the guards to separate them, should have… Her shoulders trembled as she hung on to her morose thoughts.

As with every previous transport, the Nazis hadn't given a single word of explanation. Not where they were headed or why, nor how long it would take. And certainly not whether they'd be returned one day. One woman lamented that she'd left a slice of bread hidden under her bunk and another one said, "I'm sure your bunk neighbor will find it and feast on it." The heartless comment caused the first woman to spring at her, attempting to scratch out her eyes.

A ruckus ensued and Rachel was shoved, pushed and knocked against the railing, until everyone's energy was exhausted and the agitation petered out like the ripples from a stone cast into a puddle. Rachel reached into her pocket, feeling for her treasured cigarettes.

As always, rumors and speculation about their destination abounded, and the women who prided themselves on being in the know tossed names of sub-camps and work details around the truck, arguing about which one was preferable.

Rachel didn't care either way. All she wanted was to go back and find her sister. She knocked her head against the canvas of the truck in desperation, but there was nothing she could do.

Almost an hour later, the vehicle stopped and the SS screamed, "*Los! Raus! Schneller!*"

She had no idea why they were always urging them to move fast, when on the other hand they dawdled for so many hours during roll call. But since the SS had the whips, she quickly jumped off the back of the truck and lined up behind the other women. The wrought-iron gate was similar to the one in Bergen and read, "*Arbeit macht frei.*" Work brings freedom.

She sneered at the words. Did working hard on the farm all her life not count? Maybe she should ask those bigoted Nazis to let her go?

"Prisoner number?"

Rachel rattled off her number. In the transit camps where she'd been before the Nazis had at least appeared to consider the inmates human, but in Bergen-Belsen everyone had been given a number and they'd been told it was *verboten* to use their names.

"Nationality?"

"German."

The guard spat at her. "You're not German, you're a filthy Jew. Do you hear me? Next time someone asks for your nationality you say 'filthy Jew'. Do you understand?"

Rachel nodded.

The guard gave a vile grin. "Nationality?"

"Filthy Jew," she answered without flinching. It didn't matter. Nothing mattered anymore. For a moment she considered attacking him in the hopes he'd shoot her dead, but of course she couldn't. She had a baby sister to find.

"You're a quick study," the guard said with a satisfied grin. "I'll reward you with a nice job. Get over there."

She hurried to follow his commands and walked in the direction of his pointed finger to a small group of women forming another line. The line turned out to be for handing out new prisoner dresses and each woman received one. Rachel held the coarse, blue-and-white striped dress, which was made of rough half-linen, with the same deference as if it were a royal robe. She inhaled the smell that was so different from her own stinking dress that she'd worn day and night for the past months.

She was so elated at this unexpected luxury, she didn't even mind having to stand naked in front of the male guards while changing into the new dress. The cloth felt scratchy on her skin, especially without a camisole beneath, but it still gave her a sense of protection that her old, threadbare and see-through dress hadn't been able to.

Apparently, her neighbor during roll call had been right and a work detail in one of the ammunition factories was as close to heaven as life could get under the Nazi yoke, because as soon as she'd slipped on the dress, she was ordered into another queue, where she received a plate and a spoon. Within less than a minute Rachel had multiplied the possessions she owned.

The barracks' *kapo* seemed to be a bearable woman, not one of the vile creatures who were usually awarded the lowest positions of power in the Nazi hierarchy. Maria, a thickset and sturdy woman, wore the red triangle on her prison uniform to identify her as a political prisoner. Rachel, of course, had been given the yellow triangle, branding her as a Jew—the lowest of the low, beneath the cockroaches and lice that infested the beds. A Jew had to take orders, and derision, from everyone else including common criminals, asocials, and homosexuals.

"Ladies, I'll show you your bunks," Maria said with a tone that brooked no argument, but wasn't laced with the usual disdain or curses. Together with the other new arrivals, Rachel followed her to a spick and span barracks, with two-tier bunks on either side of the small passageway. After assigning every woman a bunk all to herself, Maria launched into a short speech, detailing the chores every woman was expected to do, mostly sweeping, cleaning, washing, and keeping the barracks tidy. She closed with the following words, "Do as I say and I can guarantee you'll be treated fairly. But if you laze about or start a fight, you're out of here and into a penal unit faster than you can blink. Understood?"

"Understood," Rachel murmured together with the other newcomers. Despite Maria's tough speech, she liked her a lot better than many of the other barracks elders she'd known so far. In Bergen-Belsen most *kapos* were common criminals who craved the little power given to them and relished tormenting other prisoners.

After being processed they were ordered to line up in front of the kitchen where each woman was given two ladles of broth and a dry piece of bread. Rachel wasn't even sure the bread was made with actual flour and the stinking liquid smelled and tasted the same as in Bergen-Belsen, but at least it was twice as much and Rachel found a few potato peels, a one-inch-piece of carrot and some other indefinable rubber-like chunks in her bowl.

Information as always was hard to come by, but when the resident inmates returned from their work details in the evening Rachel found out that she was now in the village of Tannenberg, about twenty-five miles east of Bergen-Belsen, and the group she'd been assigned to was designated to work in the Rheinmetall-Borsig ammunition factory, located half an hour's walk from the camp.

As it turned out, the guard had indeed rewarded her for her obedience, because the residents all agreed that the Rheinmetall work detail was preferable over the alternatives of lumberjack work or road construction.

Rachel involuntarily shuddered at the thought of wielding a heavy axe to cut a tree in her weakened and emaciated condition. She pushed the thoughts away and—alone—climbed into her bunk, which was fitted with a scratchy straw mattress and a blanket, a huge improvement over her sleeping arrangements at the main camp.

She sent a prayer to heaven for her three younger siblings, hoping against hope her brothers had made it to safety and that Mindel had found a kind soul to take care of her. Her belief in God had all but vanished during these past months, experiencing atrocities she never could have imagined, but even if a prayer didn't help, it wouldn't hurt either.

Rachel sighed and closed her eyes. She dreamed of happier times with plenty of food, sunshine to enjoy, and the smell of flowers and grass. She saw her mother smiling as she watched her children play and slowly drifted off to sleep, hoping that one day those happier times would return.

CHAPTER 13

Summer 1944

Spring had come and gone, and the sun scorched the dry ground in the camp, making it dusty and difficult to breathe.

Mindel still thought of Rachel once in a while, but had accepted the truth that her sister wasn't going to come back. She was gone, probably dead. Mindel tried not to dwell on it. These things happened. Here at the camp they happened with surprising frequency. One day a person was there, the next day he or she was gone.

Struggling from day to day, she hung out with The Gang, not answering to anyone except to Laszlo and the SS. Naturally the gang members steered clear of the guards as much as they could, though, avoiding confrontation at all cost.

But the other adults? They were weak and couldn't make the kids do anything. In a way it was better than at home, where her mother had always bossed her around and forbidden everything that was fun. Here she could do what she wanted, as long as the SS didn't catch them.

Her only gripes were the roll calls and the lack of food. But even that could be helped up to a certain point, since Mindel and Laszlo made such a great team organizing food from the kitchen. He would stand guard while she squeezed through the tiniest holes and grabbed whatever was available.

One morning during roll call she made an astounding discovery. One of the kitchen workers stood across the parade space from her. Mindel opened her eyes wide, not believing what she saw, but there was no doubt. The woman standing there was the same one who peeled the potatoes day after day.

"Did you know that the kitchen workers are prisoners like us?" she asked Clara at the next opportunity.

The slightly older girl laughed. "Of course they are, or did you expect the SS to do the work themselves?"

Mindel furrowed her brow in concentration. This idea had never occurred to her. "But if the kitchen workers are only prisoners, they can't punish us. So why are we afraid of them?"

"Because they will report us to the SS."

Mindel wasn't convinced. By the time that woman told the SS, she would have run away. From that day onward, Mindel became bolder in her stealing.

One afternoon, she was waiting outside the kitchen building, biding her time until the worker inside turned her back and Mindel could sneak inside. She'd seen that particular woman before. The woman was old, at least thirty, and had dark hair, a pale skin and high cheekbones. Sometimes she talked to herself in a language Mindel couldn't understand. It sounded funny, like gibberish, but Ruth had told the other children it was Russian.

Nobody had been able to explain what Russian was and why these people talked so differently, but it didn't really matter, since Mindel had no intention of ever speaking with the woman.

It was hot outside and the stabbing pain in her stomach made her impatient to go for the peels. Usually Mindel waited until the kitchen worker finished the bag of potatoes and carried them over to the stove. But when the Russian woman turned for a moment to massage her back, Mindel seized the opportunity. On her hands and knees, she crept inside, hiding behind a shelf.

The stupid woman, though, made no attempt to walk over to the other side of the kitchen. When she finally did, Mindel was so desperate to sweep down on the waste basket that she didn't even wait until the woman had disappeared around the counter.

She reached into the bin with the potato peels, and stuffed a handful into her mouth, before she grabbed more, stuffing them into the pockets of her dress.

"*Ty chevo tvorish?*" came a harsh voice behind her and Mindel felt her stomach drop.

She spun around to find the Russian woman standing between her and the doorway. Mindel swallowed the peels in her mouth and edged her way to the left. The woman moved with her, looking her over from head to toe. This time she spoke in heavily accented German: "Hey, what are you doing?"

"I… I'm hungry."

"We all are. That's no reason to steal."

Mindel felt the shame burning her ears and nodded. She'd been so proud of her organizing activities, and now this woman was calling her out on it. Defiantly pressing her lips together, she edged backward, trying to reach the door and run, but the woman anticipated her movement and cut her off.

"You'll get into real trouble when the wrong person catches you," she said and looked around to make sure no one was watching. "Here." She reached up to a high shelf and pulled down a tin from which she took a handful of breadcrumbs. "Take this and go. But don't ever come back stealing here again."

Mindel looked at the crumbs being offered, not sure if she was being tricked. In the gang it was the common belief that adults couldn't be trusted. Not the SS, and not the prisoners. Everyone who wasn't your mother or father was more than willing to exploit the children and take their possessions for their own benefit.

But hunger won over caution and she reached out to grab the treat. The woman stepped aside and Mindel dashed for the back door. She darted out of the kitchen, running full tilt until she reached the place where Laszlo waited for her.

"Whoa! What happened?" he asked when she reached him, out of breath and shaking like a leaf.

"I got caught."

"Holy shit! How did you get out?" Laszlo's eyes darted around, waiting for the guards to appear.

Mindel pulled on his arm. "She didn't tell anyone. She even gave me breadcrumbs." Mindel opened her hand to show him the bounty.

"Let's go and tell the others."

Behind the row of barracks was an empty space that at one time might have been a meadow, but now consisted merely of dirt. For Mindel and her gang it was heaven on earth, because it was a place mostly away from the prying eyes of the SS guards and other adults. Only the posts in the tall watchtowers could see them, and they were too far away to eavesdrop.

When they arrived at the dirt spot they'd made their headquarters, the other children were already waiting for them.

"What took you so long?" Ruth asked.

"I—" Mindel started to say, but Laszlo elbowed her side and said, "The woman wasn't peeling potatoes, so we couldn't get peels, but Mindel managed to scrounge breadcrumbs."

The children eagerly formed a circle and each of them put what little things they'd been able to scrounge into the middle. Laszlo then divided it into five equal parts and they ate together. It was almost like being back home, sitting at the dinner table with her family—just now these four children had become Mindel's family.

Except for Laszlo and herself, the other three still had a parent or older sibling in the camp, but since the adults had to work during the day, they were on their own most of the time.

When they'd eaten Fabian suggested, "Let's play something."

"Jews and SS," came the immediate reply. It was the children's favorite game.

"I'm SS," Laszlo, Fabian and Ruth said with one voice, leaving Clara and Mindel to be the Jews.

"I hate being the Jew," Mindel complained.

"Just to start with," Laszlo said. "Later, we'll switch roles. Everyone gets to be SS."

Clara and Mindel were given a head start, while the others turned their backs and counted to ten. Mindel ran off right away, looking for a place to hide. There really weren't many, apart from the huts. She pressed herself against the wall, hoping the others wouldn't notice her.

She heard Laszlo call out, "Coming," and soon after the footsteps of one of the children approaching her hiding place. She waited until the last moment before she darted away, hoping to have the element of surprise on her side, but Fabian was too quick for her. He grabbed her arm and dragged her behind him to the *punishment place*. Clara was caught soon thereafter and the two of them stood in the middle of the circle, while the others pretended to tie them to a stake, singing, "The Jews will burn! The Jews will burn!"

Mindel and Clara had to pretend to beg for their lives and offered the "SS" food, clothing, money and whatever else they could think of. Once they were officially "burnt alive," the game ended and they started again with roles reversed.

That part Mindel liked a lot better, because the SS always won and the Jews never had a chance. They played several more rounds of the game, until they were all exhausted and collapsed to the ground.

It was quite strange to feel so tired, because her brothers had always told her she'd become faster and stronger when she grew older, but in reality the opposite seemed to be true. Every day she could run less and had to sit down to catch her breath more often.

But sitting around doing nothing soon became boring and Ruth, who was thinner than a stick, said, "Let's see who's thinnest." She straightened her dress and pushed her fingers up beneath her lower ribs. Her hand disappeared up to her knuckles.

"Ha, that's nothing, I can beat that," Fabian boasted and pushed up his shirt to show how he could make his entire hand disappear beneath his ribs. "What do you say now?"

The other children murmured with admiration and Mindel nodded very seriously as she said, "You are really thin."

"What about you, Mindel? Show us how thin you are!" Fabian urged her, but she answered, "I don't like this game." She could only squeeze the first two digits of her fingers behind her ribs, another disadvantage of being the youngest and smallest in the group. She always lost at these games.

Much too soon dinner time came around and, despite being so hungry, she loathed the moment when she had to put the disgusting gruel into her mouth. Why couldn't the SS feed them something nice? A flashback hit her and suddenly Mindel was sitting at the kitchen table, watching her mother knead bread dough.

"Can I have some dough?" Mindel asked.

"No, you have to wait until the bread is baked." Mother continued to knead and then to form the dough into two nicely shaped loaves of bread. The moment her mother turned around, Mindel couldn't wait any longer and leaned across the table to pinch off a piece of dough, but Mother was faster and swatted her hand away.

"Off I said. You can't eat the raw dough or you'll get worms in your stomach."

Mindel didn't want to have worms, so she looked longingly at the yummy-looking loaves that disappeared one after the other in the oven.

"How long until they come out again?"

Mother laughed and rubbed the back of her hand across Mindel's head. "You'll have to wait until dinner."

"That long?" To tell the truth she hadn't known what time dinner was, but she knew for sure that anything later than right now was much too long. Especially because soon after the delicious smell of freshly baked bread coming from the oven filled the kitchen. Sure enough, one after another, her brothers, Rachel and even Father arrived in the kitchen, sniffing, and asking when they could have a piece of fresh bread.

"Hey, you dreaming or what?" a loud voice said and Mindel looked up into the face of Laszlo. As much as she loved him, in that moment she hated his presence, because it had brought her back into this ugly camp.

"Do you ever miss fresh bread?" she asked him.

His face took on a dreamy expression, before it hardened again and he said, "Every single day."

CHAPTER 14

Rachel was torn from her slumber by loud yelling and it took her a moment to remember where she was. She jumped out of her bunk, put on her shoes and ran outside for the inevitable roll call. But much to her surprise, there was no roll call, only a queue in front of the field kitchen.

She'd gotten so used to the awful gruel, she didn't even smell the stale and musty odor anymore and hastily spooned every last drop into her mouth—just in time to line up with hundreds of other women. Even before the line had fully formed, they were marched from the camp in rows of four.

It was already light outside, and the entire population of the rural town seemed to be on their feet already, heading out to work. As soon as the group of prisoners came nearer, though, the townsfolk diverted their steps into side alleys, or looked away—apart from some intrepid ones who hurled terms of abuse at the prisoners.

Rachel walked on the outside of her row of four and faltered in her step as a glob of spit landed on her arm. But even as she wiped it away, the guard behind her lashed out with her truncheon, shouting, "Keep walking, filthy Jew!"

She stumbled onward, furtively glancing around. Never had she felt more humiliated in her life; she didn't understand why these people hated them so much. She was a German just like the townsfolk, the only difference between her and them being that her ancestors had practiced Judaism. But her parents had long since assimilated and she and her siblings were raised like anyone else, except that they didn't attend church on Sundays.

In the distance, she could see a large building, presumably the factory they were assigned to. Despite the early morning, the air was warm and she feared the walk back in the evening, when the asphalted street would be scorching hot. Grateful for her dilapidated shoes, she glanced around and noticed some other women had nothing but rags wrapped around their feet.

After a tiresome march they finally arrived at the Rheinmetall-Borsig ammunition factory that stood like a giant, gray sentry at the far side of the town. The resident inmates hurried to their workstations, but Rachel had to line up alongside the other newcomers to be assigned their line of work.

She just hoped it would be something where she could sit down because, in her weakened condition, she was completely exhausted from the half-hour walk that back on the farm she'd have been able to do several times a day without a single complaint.

"You, come with me!" a male factory worker said, pointing at Rachel and five other women. He led them to a workstation, where, with a jubilant heart, Rachel noticed several high stools. The foreman told them to sit and showed them how to fill bullet shells with explosives, then he left them alone, assembling the next work group.

She didn't dare to talk or even look around, but focused exclusively on the task at hand. It was not physically challenging like street construction work would be, but she had to concentrate hard not to spill the explosives when stuffing them by hand into the shells.

As the morning passed, the air inside the factory grew unbearably hot and stifling. In addition, the smell of the various chemicals stung her nose and eyes, and after a while she could barely see through the veil of tears that ran more freely than they would have done cutting a dozen onions. Once she used her fingers to swipe at her eyes, only to yelp with excruciating pain as she smeared the chemical residues on her fingertips into her eyes. After that it was certainly preferable to have the tears dilute her vision than to endure that unbearable pain again.

But the acid stench did not stop at just irritating her eyes. After hours of inhaling it, her lungs burned and she began coughing continually.

"It will get better," the woman working next to her offered.

"How do you know?" Rachel asked before another violent coughing spell shook her body.

"Because I've been here for a long time."

Though Rachel had been positively surprised last night about the sleeping conditions, she realized she hated the work so much it certainly wasn't worth it. And it wasn't because she was a spoiled city brat either, since she'd worked hard for so much of her life on the farm. Despite the better bed and slightly better food here, she found she couldn't help but wish herself back in Bergen-Belsen, where she hadn't had to march an hour each way to her workplace in addition to working a twelve-hour shift. But what stung most was that she was helping the war effort of the very people who'd vowed to exterminate her kind—and who'd torn her sister from her.

Though, as she found out during dinner time, working in the ammunition factory did come with one perk: every woman received a glass of milk together with her thin soup. It was the first time since her capture that she'd seen or tasted milk. Real milk. Fond memories of home flooded her brain and made her smile.

"Why do they give us milk when they haven't done so in any of the other camps before?" she asked one of the women who'd been there for quite a while.

"Not out of the goodness of their hearts, obviously," the thin, bald woman said. "It makes the acid taste in our mouths less bad, and supposedly stops the poisoning effects of the vapors we inhale all day."

***

Several weeks passed, the days blurring into one another, and while the work didn't get any easier, it was mindless. Performing the same exercise over and over, for twelve hours each day, was boring and tedious, but Rachel became more or less accustomed to the grind and, as the other woman had promised, the coughing diminished.

One evening after dinner—the same gruel as every day, with slightly varying tastes of disgustingness—the women returned to their barracks and, feeling as hopeless as ever, Rachel lay down on her bunk. These days she rarely did more than lie around in her free time, because she was always so exhausted. A noisy group of newcomers entered their barracks to fill in for those that had died over the past week. It wouldn't make a change in her own workload, but Rachel still liked to see different faces and maybe get some outside news. Every woman in here craved news about the war and the general situation in Germany, some even hoped for news about their family members. Despite the complete lack of outside information, the women in Tannenberg had learned about the Allied invasion in France by carelessly dropped remarks of the civilian foremen at the factory.

Usually the guards would gloat about successful battles, and when they didn't say a word for days, their behavior gave way to wild speculation about the state of the war. Every worried face or abruptly ended conversation was reason for the inmates to assume the end was near. Rachel wasn't the only one whose hopes for survival thrived on the promise of a speedy downfall of the German Reich and her liberation at the hands of the Allies.

Peeking down from her top bunk, she observed a mass of filthy, dreary and exhausted women scuffling past the bunks and wondered whether she looked like them too, dreading that every day in this hell brought her one step closer to becoming a *Muselmann* herself. The memory of the horrid "too-far-gone" creatures she'd seen at the main camp in Bergen-Belsen followed her in her nightmares and if there was one thing she was more afraid of than death itself, it was becoming one of them.

She made an effort to climb down and greet the newcomers, who were assigned their bunks by the *kapo* Maria. Then she saw her.

"Linda!" She jumped down and rushed toward the woman to hug her. Even though they hadn't spent more than a few days together back in the main camp, it felt like seeing a long lost friend again.

"Rachel! How wonderful is this! Coming here and finding a friend."

Like always, Linda had the ability to brighten her day and it seemed as if the sun was shining inside the dilapidated barracks.

"It's so good to see you." Rachel didn't know what else to say. *You look awful*, would have been true, but wasn't an appropriate way to show how happy she was to see Linda again.

"Maria, can Linda have the bunk next to me?" Rachel asked the *kapo*, the resolute woman who kept a strict, but never cruel, regiment over her barracks.

"Sure." Maria wrote down Linda's name next to the bunk number and then continued with assigning the newcomers.

"Did you ever find your sister?" Linda asked, once they had climbed the upper bunks.

Rachel shook her head with desolation. "I was so close to getting into the star camp before they put me on the work detail here."

"I'm so sorry. But I'm sure she's fine. Someone will have taken her under their wing."

"That's what I keep telling myself." Rachel tried to sound confident.

"Don't beat yourself up about this." Linda put a bony hand on Rachel's arm, a gesture that warmed Rachel's heart, reminding her there was still kindness in the world.

"I know I shouldn't… but I feel like I failed her. I promised to take care of her, and instead I let her be ripped away."

"Nobody can go up against the SS. Not you, not me, not anyone in here." Linda sat on the bunk and put Rachel's head into her lap, stroking her as if she were a baby.

"It feels so awful. Not knowing where or how she is." Rachel had difficulty keeping the overwhelming emotions at bay. She had no tears left to shed, but her emaciated body shook under the forceful waves of guilt and shame rolling over her. "I should have held her tighter… not allowed them to separate the two of us…"

"Shush. Don't worry so much. Your little sister will be fine." Linda kept whispering soothing words and soon enough Rachel drifted away, dreaming of a reunion with Mindel.

CHAPTER 15

It was so hot. Mindel's tongue was glued to the roof of her mouth, but of course nobody cared. She wouldn't get a single drop of water before this horrible never-ending roll call was over, and God only knew how long that would take. Stupid SS!

She did not understand why it took that long to count the prisoners. The SS guards were adults, so why couldn't they count the prisoners without having to start over and over again the way she had to do when counting beyond three? It didn't make sense, and doubts about the SS's intelligence crept into her mind.

Next time she saw Heidi, she would ask the older girl about it. She now knew that Heidi was fifteen. Grown up enough to know about such things, but not yet too old to be untrustworthy.

Mindel couldn't help but admire Heidi, who had lived in Berlin before her family had fled the Nazis in an adventurous move to Amsterdam. Laszlo had told her that Amsterdam was the capital of the Netherlands, a country neighboring Germany, where people spoke a different language.

She still couldn't quite wrap her head around how this was supposed to work, since Heidi and her sister spoke the same language as Mindel did.

"Don't be stupid," Laszlo had said. "When they're alone they speak Dutch, but when they are with us they speak German."

"But wouldn't it be easier to speak only one language all the time?" On her parents' farm she'd only ever talked to her family and the odd person who passed by.

"Silly girl! Dutch people speak Dutch, but most Dutch people have learned to speak German since the occupation. Like how I speak Hungarian because my father was Hungarian but also German because my mother was German."

"You speak two languages, too?" That was news to Mindel and she wondered whether she was the only person in the world who hadn't known that different languages existed, let alone spoke another one.

"Three actually, I learned some English at school."

"Did you go to school?"

Laszlo furrowed his brows. "Everyone goes to school when they're old enough."

"My brothers don't." The thought of her brothers sent a stabbing pain through her heart. When Rachel and she had been captured, they'd reasoned that their brothers—who'd been way ahead of them—had probably run away real fast. But during her time in the camp doubt had crept in and she feared the SS might have found and captured them, too.

She shook her head, preferring not to think about this. In her imagination her brothers had returned to their farm, tending to the rabbits, the hens and working the fields. She'd surely find them waiting for them when she finally found Rachel again and they could return home.

"How old are your brothers?" Laszlo asked.

"Seven and ten."

"Don't you know anything?" Michael, one of the older boys and an annoying smartypants said. "Jews aren't allowed to go to school."

Mindel turned her head away since she didn't want to continue talking about this topic. At home everything had been so peaceful.

She'd not even really known her family *was* Jewish, or different from everyone else—not that she had come into contact with many other people.

But since her capture she'd learned so many things about Jews, and not one of them was good. Jews were filthy, mean, cunning… and now she learned they weren't even allowed to go to school. Who had decided all of this?

She knew the answer already. The SS and Adolf Hitler. He seemed to decide on everything in Germany and none of his decisions made any sense. What she didn't understand was why the other adults didn't tell him how wrong he was?

The sun steadily rose higher into the sky, scorching everyone on the ground. Laszlo had said it was August. She remembered that back home August was when the entire village came out to the fields to harvest their crops. But here in the camp they were only standing around, waiting. And the horrid SS guards wouldn't even let them wait in the shadow of the huts, which would have been so much more comfortable. The SS really had no idea about how life was supposed to be.

An old woman standing nearby collapsed and, despite the guard's outrage, whipping and beating her, she wouldn't get up. Mindel watched the spectacle with wide-open eyes, voicelessly mouthing, "Don't be stupid, get up!"

But nothing happened. The woman lay motionless on the ground and, after a while, the guard stopped beating her and moved on. Mindel shook her head. It wasn't the first time she'd witnessed such an event. According to Heidi, the people who stopped moving were dead.

Mother had always told Mindel that after a person's death the soul lived on and went to God's side. So, she stood there watching closely what would happen next. She really wanted to see the soul and how it flew up into the sky. But just like every time this had happened before, there was nothing and the corpse lay there like a stick. Nothing, not even a shadow, or a feather rose up to the sky.

Mindel was disappointed. Somehow what her mother had taught her didn't seem to happen in real life. Could her mother have been wrong, or had she lied to Mindel? The enormity of her suspicion caused her heart to tense painfully.

That was another topic she would have to ask Heidi about. Once she'd tried to ask Laszlo about the souls flying to heaven, but he'd only groaned and told her that she was a baby if she still believed *that*.

It was a disappointment, indeed. If her soul didn't fly up to the clouds after she died, then she wouldn't be able to frolic with the angels and neither could she look down from above to find her sister.

Her thirst was getting worse and standing in the scorching sun she began to feel light-headed, but since she wasn't certain anymore about the whole flying in the skies thing, she decided it was better not to die and forced herself to stay standing upright.

The despicable roll call continued, another woman stumbled, falling into the person to her right and causing quite a ruckus. Mindel watched as the other woman tried to stand up straight again, but an SS guard was already by her side, hitting her with his truncheon.

She cried out and fell forward, and Mindel watched in horror as the guards released the snarling dogs. The scream was stuck in her throat, but for the life of her she couldn't look away as the horrible spectacle unfolded in front of her.

She loved all animals, and dogs especially. Her parents had had a watchdog at the farm, good old Rex. He dutifully barked at strangers and Rachel had told a story about how he'd once bitten a burglar in the calf and kept him in place until Father came running along.

But the camp dogs were neither friendly nor lovable.

Most of them were German Shepherds and kept on very tight leashes. They barked without reason, lunged at the prisoners, and even bit them from time to time. Today, though, what Mindel watched was something she would never be able to forget, something her father had assured her no dog was capable of doing.

The guards released the dogs, and all three of them descended upon the woman who was on her hands and knees, struggling to get back on her feet. The dogs jumped on her, and Mindel finally closed her eyes, and put her hands on her ears, but she still heard the snapping jaws, the ripping of flesh and, above all, the bone-chilling screams.

Then it was silent again.

Mindel peeked through her lids and gasped. There was blood everywhere. One of the guards shook his head and joked that the dogs were going to need a bath. Since nobody else moved or said a word, she removed her hands from her ears, stood a bit taller and looked straight ahead into the distance. Surely, in the mauled body, there wasn't a soul left that could move into the sky.

When the roll call finally ended, many more prisoners had collapsed to the ground. The SS sent every person on a work detail away, leaving only the old, sick and young waiting to be dismissed.

One of the guards looked at Heidi, who was standing several rows away from Mindel. "You! Come here!"

The girl obeyed and he yelled at her: "Take that filthy group of brats and see to it that they bring the living prisoners back to the barracks. Leave the dead for the *Sonderkommando*."

Heidi nodded and called the children around her to explain. "We have to bring everyone who's still alive back to the barracks."

"But how do we know?" a girl about Mindel's age asked.

"If they move or breathe when you poke them, drag them back to their hut. You'd best work in groups of four, because the people can be rather heavy," Heidi said.

That made sense. Mindel admired the older girl for her grasp of the situation. She hadn't even thought about the weight of an injured person.

"What about if they don't move or breathe?" Mindel asked.

"Then they're dead and later the *Sonderkommando* will take them to the crematorium. And don't forget to count how many people you return to the huts and how many are dead. The SS will want to know." Heidi assigned the children into groups, always two older ones with two younger ones.

Ruth and Fabian were in Mindel's group along with an older girl she'd seen before but didn't actually know.

"I'm Laura," the girl said and then beckoned them forward. "Let's get going."

They approached the first person lying on the ground. This one was obviously dead, her eyes wide open, as was her mouth. She was so gaunt she looked very scary and Mindel took a wide berth around her body.

"Can you count?" Laura asked her.

"To five." Mindel put up the fingers of one hand.

"Good, you count the stiffs and Fabian the living."

Mindel nodded, pressing her lips together at the prospect of her very important task. She moved to the next fallen person, while Laura and Ruth were helping someone up and half-carrying her to the huts. Mindel stooped down and looked at the grayish, emaciated woman, who seemed to be asleep. Not sure how to decide whether the person was alive or not, she remembered Heidi's instructions to poke them.

At first, she did so very softly, and when no reaction came, a bit harder. The woman didn't move. Was that enough to determine whether a person was actually dead? Mindel had some doubts and looked up at Fabian, who waited a few steps behind.

"You have to poke harder," he said.

It didn't feel right, but Mindel shoved the woman—hard. She still didn't move. "I think she's dead."

"We must be sure, because they'll put her in the oven."

Mindel felt all the blood draining from her face. The oven. No, she certainly wouldn't want someone to be burned alive. She kicked the woman with all her strength in the midriff. Still no reaction.

"She really is dead," Fabian said and backed off to check on the next person.

"That's two." Mindel hadn't forgotten her task of counting the corpses. By the time Laura and Ruth returned, she'd run out of fingers for counting. "That's how many we got," she told Laura and showed two hands, "and then one more."

"Eleven?" Laura asked.

Mindel had no idea, but nodded anyway.

"And how many living?" Laura turned to Fabian.

"Only three. Come here, I'll show you where they are." He led the small group to the first of the injured and together they managed to get all the people in their assigned rows back to the huts.

"That was so exhausting," Mindel complained and only now remembered her horrible thirst. With the distraction of having to count corpses she'd completely forgotten about it, but now it returned with a vengeance and she hoped the tap behind one of the huts where they got water for sweeping the floors would offer a few drops.

She was lucky and with much patience managed to fill her mug with almost two inches of water that she drank greedily. It tasted foul and muddy, but who was she to complain? Then she shuffled across the courtyard to her own hut, her legs too tired to take proper steps. All she wanted was to climb into her bunk and sleep until the much-talked-about Allies came and rescued her. Not paying attention, she bumped against someone and the next moment, a voice snarled at her. "Filthy brat!"

She looked up and saw a guard pulling a whip from his belt and swinging it at her. It struck her on the back, and she cried out. Stupefied, she stared at him like a rabbit caught in the headlights, until a loud shout snapped her from her stupor.

"Run, Mindel! Run!" a boy shouted.

She didn't know who'd shouted and didn't care either, she simply obeyed and her little legs moved her away from the vicious SS man as fast as they could. Panting, she reached her hut, dropped on the first available bunk and lay there face down. Too exhausted to move, she stayed curled on her side, drifting in and out of sleep, dreaming of life on the farm with her beloved parents, and her three siblings, the dog Rex, the rabbits, the hens, and even the old witch who'd turned out to be a nice old woman when she'd warned them that Herr Keller was taking their parents away.

She thought of the kind neighbor who had given them food and shelter, and of the plan to go to the convent. But then Herr Keller had discovered them again. Tears flowed as she prayed her brothers were still alive and safe. And for Rachel. Despite not having seen her since she first arrived in Bergen-Belsen, Mindel clung to the idea that her sister was still somewhere near. She missed her so much. She missed her entire family so much.

"Mindel, are you all right?" Laszlo interrupted her waking dreams.

"Yes, but I'm so tired. And my back hurts."

"I saw the guard whipping you. Let me have a look." He pushed up her dress and hissed in a breath. "It's only a stripe, not even blood. You're lucky."

"Why did he hit me? I bumped into him by accident. I didn't mean it!" Mindel asked, trying to keep the whine out of her voice.

"It's just the way they are. Mean." Laszlo lay down and she turned and hugged him tight, when she noticed the dampness in his eyes and almost choked. It was the first time he'd shown her that he, too, was sad. Mindel stroked his back, the way Rachel had always done with her and murmured, "It'll all be fine. We just have to stay together."

Much to her surprise this only seemed to worsen his mood and he gave her quite the fright when he started sobbing and the words broke out of him like water through a burst dam. "Damn Nazis! First they shot my father in front of my own eyes because he dared to oppose them, and then my mother died two days after we arrived here." Laszlo's sobbing intensified, sending shivers of terror down Mindel's spine.

He was her rock, her protector, her savior. How could she cope if he broke down? In a helpless gesture she clung to his shoulders, caressing his back and repeating the same words over and over again. "I'm so sorry, my poor pet. Please stop crying."

After a while he seemed to get a grip on himself and swiped the tears away. "I wasn't crying."

She smiled, relieved that the old Laszlo was back and replied, "I know. And as long as we stay together, we'll be fine."

"I will always protect you, because you and I, we are brother and sister now."

He truly was her best friend.

After a while she whispered, "Do you think my sister's still in one of the other compounds?"

"Hard to say. Adults have it so much harder than we do. They have to work."

"I need to find her."

"You tried that, remember?"

"I asked every single person in the compound. Maybe I can sneak across the fence and ask around there?"

"Don't do that. You'll only get into trouble," Laszlo said, before they both fell asleep until the grown-ups returned from their work detail and the owner of the bunk shooed them away.

CHAPTER 16

The Tannenberg camp had a new commandant, who was proving even more sadistic than the previous one. He loved interminable roll calls and delighted in making the tired women stand still for hours after they returned from their grueling twelve-hour shifts at the Rheinmetall factory or on road construction.

Left and right, depleted women collapsed and the vicious guards then beat them until they either managed to get back up or died trying. Rachel's own life felt like it was hanging by a thread, because she'd swayed and buckled several times already, but every time she had managed by force of sheer willpower to stagger upright again.

This night, she was even more tired than usual. The acid taste in her mouth forced her to gag every so often and the stabbing ache in her stomach made her want to lie down and curl into a ball. Instead, she pushed her shoulders back, somehow finding the strength to stand up without locking her knees. That was a mistake many of the women made, thinking it would keep them upright, only it usually rendered them unconscious.

"Oh no, not *Die Schwarze*," whispered Linda.

Rachel glanced to her left and inwardly cringed, her cracked hands clutching her skirt. Susanne Hille, nicknamed *The Black*, because of her pitch-black hair, was striding down the line of women, an evil sneer on her face. She was the youngest guard, maybe only twenty years old, but cruel beyond anything Rachel had ever witnessed before, in fact worse than all of the male guards put together. Her trademark was to randomly strike the inmates with the wooden baton she always carried in her hand.

The vicious thing about *Die Schwarze* was that she never targeted the women who'd fallen, but instead found those visibly hanging by a thread, trying to keep upright. Like Rachel today. Her heart stopped beating as the despised guard entered her row. With that sadistic smile on her lips, she walked down, inspecting the women, until she lunged with her truncheon at the second one in the row.

The high-pitched shriek pierced through marrow and bone, and Rachel involuntarily winced, only to bite the inside of her lip. All the while, Susanne Hille continued her walk, picking new targets every couple of prisoners.

"Not the selections," Linda once again whispered.

"Keep looking ahead," Rachel hissed back and bit the inside of her cheeks so hard she wanted to scream. It was a trick she'd learned from an older inmate to get the blood flowing and put a rosy gleam on her face to look healthier.

Rachel again glanced to the side and watched as Susanne Hille began selecting women from the line. They were shoved to the side and would later be marched away.

"Where do they take them?" Linda asked, once *Die Schwarze* was out of earshot.

"No idea." The one thing Rachel knew was that nobody ever had seen a selected woman again. Rumors had it they were returned to the main camp at Bergen-Belsen, but others were not convinced. A group of Jewish women who'd been transported from Auschwitz to Bergen-Belsen were sure they'd "go through the chimney."

Rachel did not believe this. Naturally, there was a crematorium at the main camp to burn the corpses, but unlike in Auschwitz—if these women were to be believed—nobody had ever been taken to a fake shower block and gassed in there.

Still, she'd rather not find out what happened with the unfortunate chosen ones and kept herself as motionless as she could, while her thoughts wandered, pondering what could have made a pretty woman like Susanne Hille—so close to Rachel's own age—act so callously toward her fellow human beings. What could make any of the SS guards act the way they did?

Naturally, she didn't find an answer to her philosophical musings and mentally shrugged, pulling up instead a picture of Mindel in her mind's eye. Her sweet little sister. Would she ever see her again? Was she even alive?

Probably not. But despite knowing this, Rachel couldn't help but cling to the idea that one day she'd hold her sister in her arms again. One day, when the Nazis had lost the war and the Jews were free again.

From the information the newcomers brought, it felt like there was no doubt that the Nazis were on the losing end. And, as Allied planes crisscrossed the sky high above them with rarely a Luftwaffe craft seen chasing them, some of the prisoners were experiencing that most dangerous of emotions: hope.

CHAPTER 17

The very next morning during breakfast Mindel decided to ask every new arrival if they'd seen her sister. Generally, the women wouldn't listen or gave a sad smile and said, "There are so many girls named Rachel here. Without knowing her last name it's impossible."

If only Mindel could remember… But as much as she tried, nothing came to her. Laszlo suggested jogging her memory by tossing out all the last names he and The Gang could think of, but nothing. One name sounded as unfamiliar as the next one. There was no way around it, she had to go to the women's camp if she ever wanted to find Rachel.

"I'll go to the women's camp and ask there," Mindel said, but the other children only laughed.

"It's impossible to go there, there's a fence between the two camps," Laszlo said.

"Well, unless you have money or goods to bribe the guards," Ruth added.

Mindel wanted to cry. She possessed no money or anything else save the clothes she wore and her doll Paula. And she sincerely doubted a guard would be interested in her doll.

"I don't know why you're still worrying about this. Your sister is probably dead by now, anyway."

Mindel looked at Ruth and burst into tears.

Laszlo wrapped an arm around her shoulder and snarled at Ruth, "Why did you say that?"

Ruth pouted, murmured something and left, while Laszlo hugged Mindel close, trying to comfort her. "Don't worry. Ruth doesn't know a thing. I'm sure your sister is still alive and we will find her."

"Will you help me?" She looked at him from behind a veil of tears.

"Of course, we're in the same gang, remember?"

Suddenly a warm feeling surged in her chest and she leaned her head against his shoulder. At least she had him and wasn't all alone in this world. He might be obnoxious and annoying at times, but he always stuck to her when it counted—just like her brothers. Thinking about them made her burst into fresh tears.

Fabian came around and noticed her crying. Everyone in the camp knew that bad things happened when one cried, so he tried to cheer her up. "Hey, Mindel, how about we play a game?"

"What game?" She sniffed, hoping it wouldn't be Jews and SS, because she had no energy to run around.

"Who's going to die next?" Fabian suggested. It was another favorite game and the winner received a spoonful of soup from everyone else's bowls when it came true. It was a game that didn't require energy and they could talk for hours about the pros and cons of each death candidate.

Mindel smiled. "Yeah, that's a good game. I go first: the old hag in the lower bunk next to the latrines."

"No, that girl with the loud coughing who shares her bunk with her aunt," Clara said.

They all took turns guessing, and filled the afternoon with speculation. Once they were done, there was nothing left but to wait until someone died and see who'd gotten it right.

***

Toward the end of summer, the strangest event occurred. A long line of shiny black vehicles arrived at the camp, and several SS officers—in uniforms adorned with blinking medals—disembarked. The members of The Gang and some older children crept close enough to watch and eavesdrop, without being seen.

The boss of the new arrivals had so many medals pinned to his chest that Mindel ran out of fingers counting them. After the corpse counting, Laura had taught her to count to twenty without fingers, but in exciting situations like this one, she returned to using her hands.

"Have you seen his medals? He must be someone important," Mindel whispered, barely able to contain her excitement.

"Shush," Laura scolded her. "You don't want them to notice us."

Moments later Lagerkommandant Adolf Haas stepped up, shot his right arm into the air and barked, "Heil Hitler, Obersturmbannführer Krumey."

Mindel had always thought this salutation looked ridiculous, but these adults took it very seriously. They even stood motionless for a few seconds, before the hands came down.

The group of men began walking in the direction of the children, who were hiding behind an empty water tank. Mindel's heart beat so fast, she feared the men would hear it. Thankfully Laszlo's hand sneaked into hers and his presence gave her the confidence to stay completely still, barely breathing.

Krumey handed a list to the Kommandant. "These are the people selected for the blood for goods exchange."

"Three hundred?"

"Yes, three hundred of these deplorables have been paid for and will be sent to Switzerland."

Three hundred sounded like many, many people. Definitely more than she could count and probably Laszlo too, who claimed to be able to count to one hundred, although he'd never actually proved it to the other children.

The grapevine in the camp worked fast and Mindel was perplexed when mere minutes later throngs of grown-ups threw themselves at Krumey's feet, begging him to choose them.

"*Glückspilze*." Laszlo sighed. "These lucky ones are allowed to leave the camp and go to Switzerland."

Mindel nodded, albeit she had no idea what exactly Switzerland was, but if everyone wanted to go there, she reckoned it must be a nice place. "How do you know it's a good place to go?"

"Switzerland is neutral, which means they are not in this war. And, according to what my mom used to say, it's paradise on earth. Enough food, clothes, a roof over your head, and no persecution. It seems Jews there can live just like anyone else."

That indeed sounded like a good thing. Maybe living in Switzerland was like living on her parents' farm, far away from all the horrible things she'd seen since the fateful day Herr Keller had taken her parents.

"Do you think Ruth will leave?" Mindel asked. Ruth's father owned a visa to Palestine, and she had often boasted that it was only a matter of time until her family would be released.

Palestine seemed to be another place of dreams. People called it the Holy Land, the land of milk and honey, an entire country only for Jews where nobody would say to them all the awful things the SS said, and—most important—where they wouldn't have to live in horrible camps, taken away from their homes.

"Probably." Laszlo didn't seem too interested in speculating, instead his eyes were riveted on the tumultuous scenes unfolding. The adults begged, pleaded, shoved, pushed, yelled, and cried in an attempt to be added to the transport. Finally, the guards were called and beat everyone with their truncheons until a big enough corridor opened for the Obersturmbannführer to continue his way toward the Lagerkommandant's office.

"We should go see if he will put us on his list," Laszlo said, taking her arm and trying to pull her forward.

For a moment she considered joining him in the adventure of going to Switzerland, but then she remembered her sister. How would Rachel find her there? No, it was better to stay here. With all these people gone, the camp would be all but empty and it would be easy to find her sister. Then a cold shiver ran down her spine. What if Rachel travelled to Switzerland without Mindel? Tears threatened to flow, but she stubbornly wiped them away, whispering to herself, "Rachel would never do that. She's looking for you the same way you're looking for her."

"What's wrong?" Laszlo asked, apparently noticing her shuddering.

"Nothing." She would not admit to him or anyone else that she was still crying over her sister.

"Then come with me."

Mindel shook him off. "No. I don't want to leave. Not without my sister."

"You're stupid!"

His words hurt and Mindel frowned up at him. "And you are mean!"

Laszlo's eyes showed the shock at her outburst, but then he sighed and shook his head. "Look, staying here on the off-chance of finding your sister, instead of trying your luck getting to Switzerland, is plain stupid."

Maybe he was right, but that didn't change her mind. She would not go anywhere without Rachel.

He looked at her for a long time and then said, "I'm going to do it! I'll find a way to sneak onto the transport when it leaves."

The breath caught in Mindel's lungs and raw fear attacked her. "You can't! What if they catch you?"

"They won't. And once I'm out of this goddamn camp, nobody will care. Please, come with me! Staying here you'll surely die, but if you come with me, we can start a new life. We could even find work."

"Work? Like what?" Back on the farm, Mindel had had a few small chores, mostly feeding the rabbits and watering the vegetables, but she wasn't so sure someone would employ them for that.

Laszlo seemed to deflate. "I don't know. Something. Polish shoes maybe?"

Some of the older girls earned food or cigarettes by polishing shoes for the *kapos* or even for the SS, so this might actually be an option. But Mindel was much too afraid to even consider leaving the camp. "That's crazy. We can't do that. The guards will see us."

"Not if we're careful."

Mindel shook her head. "This isn't like sneaking into the kitchen. What if someone misses us? When we don't show up for roll call?" Violent shivers ran down her spine. Every day the guards counted all of the prisoners dozens of times, until their stupid lists matched up. Like that one time, when Heidi had organized them in groups to count stiffs and living. "They will surely look for us and then…" Her voice faltered. She didn't even want to imagine what might happen then. *Not the dogs, please.*

"If you don't come with me, I'm doing it alone," Laszlo said and turned his back on her to watch the crowd.

Mindel's legs had turned to jelly. She had a very bad feeling about what might happen to her best friend and felt the urge to go with him, just to make sure he was all right. And because without him she'd be completely alone. Who would be her friend then?

But on the other hand, she had to stay and find her sister. Rachel's last words echoed in her head. "Mindel, I love you. I promise, I'll find you."

CHAPTER 18

Rachel lived in such a trance-like state she barely knew what day of the week it was. She wouldn't have known what month it was either, except for the passing of seasons, a reality ingrained on her since she could walk, because a farmer's survival depended on living in close communion with nature. Summer had passed and with it the oppressive heat. For weeks now Rachel had observed the leaves on the trees being turned golden, red and orange by the approaching autumn.

Not that Rachel could enjoy the beautiful colors, because it was dim in the morning when she walked to work, and in the evening too, when she returned to the camp. Except for the glimpses through the frosted factory windows, she never saw the sunlight. The cooler daytime temperatures were a welcome respite from the sweltering heat inside the factory building, but they came accompanied by chilly nights, exchanging one discomfort for another. She stretched out her limbs, stiff from lying huddled on her bunk, shivering in the small hours of the morning before their dark walk to the factory and the sun woke up and rose in the sky again.

This morning on her march to the ammunitions factory, she spotted a peculiar sight: a ripe apple lying at the edge of the street. Nobody dared to try and pick it up, because the punishment was either a fast death on the spot or a long and agonizing death after the most horrendous punishment.

Instead, she looked up and saw for the first time an apple tree standing not far from the street. A smile appeared on her lips as she remembered how she'd found her siblings up in an apple tree on the day before Mindel's birthday. And then it hit her square in the chest: this day might be Mindel's fifth birthday. Tears shot into her eyes as she held on to the thought with all her energy and sent a birthday wish to her little darling, hoping deep in her soul that it would reach Mindel.

She marched on, relapsing into the numb mental state that had befallen her over the past weeks, where every thought felt like viscid purée as it attempted to cross her brain. Her thinking had become so slow and incoherent that it had pretty much stopped altogether and now she merely existed, much like the mindless creature the Nazis believed the likes of her to be.

On the other hand, her body had gotten used to the tedious work, doing the required movements all on its own like an automaton. Every day from morning to night she stuffed explosives into casings, never looking left or right, never talking—not even to Linda—never dreaming, and never thinking.

All the other women who'd been at the factory longer than a week seemed to be the same. Walking dead, not actual people anymore, but simply shells that moved, worked, and slept. Even the never-ending roll calls didn't faze her anymore, since she sincerely did not care whether she was selected to disappear, be beaten to death, or allowed to live another day.

Some days, before the wake-up call in the morning, she simply lay on her bunk, waiting for the merciful salvation of death, but it never came. Somehow her body got up, put on her shoes and walked out of the hut to form a line for the thin breakfast soup, without her mind being involved.

It was simply a matter of habit. Day in and day out she lived side by side with her faithful companions: hunger, exhaustion, and pain. Only because of them did she know that she was alive, because supposedly all of those things stopped once a person died.

In Tannenberg the women's hair wasn't shorn at such regular intervals as it had been in other camps Rachel had been in and one day during their meager lunch at the factory she ran her hands through her one-inch-long hair. It was a strange feeling, because she'd grown so used to being bald.

She gazed in abstraction at her hand, until she noticed the loose hair between her fingers. Back at home, she'd had long, soft, dark brown hair, but now the short strands were wiry and stiff, like straw—and orange.

She gasped in shock and cried out, "Good heavens!"

"What's happened?" Linda asked.

"My hair is orange!"

Linda snorted. "Really? You haven't noticed this before?"

"Of course not. The last time I saw myself in a mirror must have been months ago."

Inexplicably, Linda laughed. Rachel's eyes became round as her undernourished brain tried to make sense of her friend's behavior. But try as she might, she couldn't come up with an explanation as to what was so funny.

"Have you had a look around lately?" Linda asked and pointed at some of the other women.

"I know them all, but what does this have to do with my hair being orange?"

Linda came and hugged her. "It's just… Look at them closely."

"Oh!" For the first time in ages Rachel actually looked closely at the women around her, and much to her chagrin, every single one of them—save for two young women who'd only arrived three days ago—had a shock of orange stubble on her head.

She cocked her head to scrutinize Linda, and what she saw made her hiss in a breath. Gone was the woman she'd met on the train to Bergen-Belsen, in fact the person standing in front of her could be a random stranger she'd never met before. Her face drawn and pale, her cheekbones protruding through the parchment-like pallid skin. Dark circles had taken up residence beneath her hollowed-out eyes, suppressing the positive energy that used to emanate from those captivating brown eyes. But it was the bright, glaring orange hair that stuck out, making her look like some horrific clown.

For lack of a mirror, Rachel assumed she looked the same. "Am I? Do I? I mean, do I look like you?"

Despite the change in her body, Linda had not lost her humor and she answered, "I don't know how I look, but you definitely don't differ from the rest of them."

Rachel stared at her, shocked and indifferent at the same time. Fragments of realization permeated the viscosity of her brain. It wasn't just the orange hair. She hadn't given much notice to it, because she was always too tired to care, but for weeks now she'd been noticing a yellow hue on her fingernails and clothing. A stain that wouldn't go away even when rubbing hard. After the first few days she hadn't tried to remove it anymore. Moreover, she'd not given it any more thought and had just accepted it as a delusion of her exhausted mind.

But now she realized this was no delusion; it was very much reality. Whatever chemicals the women were stuffing into the shells, had taken possession of their bodies and had turned them into creatures of horror. Again she wished all of this would end. Soon. She yearned to fall asleep and never wake up again.

But as always when she was truly desolate and ready to give up, Mindel's smile and the trusting look in her brown eyes spurred her on to stay alive.

"What are we becoming?" she asked, looking at Linda for answers. But even her best friend didn't have solace to offer this time.

"I'm afraid we're turning into one of *them*."

Rachel frantically shook her head. "We won't. It will be the end of us." Even though she often longed to perish, in her few clear moments, she clung to the idea that she wasn't on the way to becoming a *Muselmann*. It was too monstrous, too awful to acknowledge. Once a person was *too far gone* there was no way back to life. She struggled through the viscosity in her brain once again, searching for the one thought that always pulled her back into the realm of the living: "I still have to find my sister."

"And you will." Linda held out her hand for Rachel, helping her up. "But now we have to get back to work."

No more words were exchanged during the seemingly never-ending shift at the factory, because apart from costing precious energy, talking was strictly forbidden. The foremen were known for generously doling out knocks with their truncheons and neither Rachel nor Linda wanted to feel the hard end on their skulls.

Still, Rachel forced herself to gather what little spirit she had left in an effort to stay sane and alive to have a fighting chance of ever seeing Mindel again. *If she's still alive.* She must have decreased her work tempo, because the next moment a guard was by her side and yelled at her, "No dawdling, Jew."

When finally the horn sounded to mark the end of her shift, she was even more forlorn than usual. Even if this nightmare ended, would she ever be the same person again?

She barely noticed the long walk back to the camp in the darkness, only lit by the torches of the guards. By now she knew the way by heart and could have walked it with her eyes closed, which she actually had done many times. Usually she, Linda and another woman held hands, so two of them could walk blind, in a state of sleepwalking, while the one in the middle kept them on track and steered them clear of the vicious guards.

The shock about her skin and hair becoming orange, about her being so close to giving up, but for the thought of Mindel's birthday—it all sat so deep, and had set her mind racing for the first time in weeks. So that evening she offered to be the guide, as they called the one in charge of leading the way. Both Linda and Sandra had accepted without protest, soaking up every minute of rest their bodies and minds could get. Rachel held her companions and walked toward the camp, wishing she could step out of the poisonous shell her body had turned into and find a new home for her soul.

If she still possessed a soul.

Upon their return to the camp, another horrible surprise awaited the women. The Kommandant was in a foul mood, more so than Rachel had ever experienced. He made the women stand still an endless time, apparently for no reason at all. After more than an hour, the first women began to fidget and sway. Rachel saw a cruel smirk appear on his lips as he doled out increasingly harsh punishments for the slightest irregularity.

Sandra hissed, "May the devil throw him into eternal hell."

Rachel wanted to respond, when she sensed a baton in her back and stood straighter. She waited, as immobile as humanly possible, not even daring to breathe or blink, when suddenly Sandra stumbled forward and fell to the ground.

"What did you say, filthy Jew?" a guard yelled at Sandra.

"N-n-nothing." Poor Sandra was a quivering mass of fear.

"Liar." He was about to crack his whip at her, when the Kommandant stepped forward and said, "No!"

Rachel kept her eyes straight forward, willing herself to turn to stone. On her other side, she sensed Linda's shallow breathing and heard her own blood rushing in her ears, while she willed Sandra to stand up.

The Kommandant positioned himself in front of Sandra, looking down at her as if she were a disgusting insect, before he stepped on her hand turning his heel back and forth. A bone-chilling creaking sound cut through the silence.

Then he stepped back and said, "Get up, bitch!"

A collective hiss filled the camp as hundreds of pairs of eyes were glued to the poor woman writhing on the ground scrambling to all fours. Rachel willed her to get up, but even as Sandra did it was clear that her hand had been broken in multiple places and she would not be able to work the next day.

Another woman swayed and stumbled from exhaustion. Since the Kommandant was hitting his stride, he sentenced her to kneel on a wooden log for the rest of the evening. It was an exceptionally cruel punishment. Not many women made it through the torture, because they collapsed from the excruciating pain and were then left to die.

Rachel had reached her capacity of emotions for the day and put Sandra and the miserable woman out of her mind, with barely any compassion. If she still possessed the energy to move, she would have shrugged and said, "Such is life."

After hours standing out there, rain began pelting down on them. Within minutes Rachel felt like a drowned rat and the incoming wind tugged at her clothes, making her shiver.

To add insult to injury, the Lagerkommandant disappeared into his dry, warm office and sent *Die Schwarze* out to be in charge. Clad in a long raincoat and a fashionable cap, and with two prisoners in tow holding an umbrella over her, she strode along the rows of miserable women, searching for her next victim.

At last, Rachel felt an emotion well up in her petrified heart. Unadulterated fear. Susanne Hille's penchant for cruelty was unparalleled. She had a plethora of creative punishments in store, each one more atrocious than the next. The sadistic creature bathed in the misery of others and the more pain she inflicted, the happier she seemed to become.

Despite the raging panic in her body, Rachel managed to take on the posture of a rock: immobile, unfazed, eternal. As much as she sometimes longed to perish, she wouldn't give *Der Schwarzen* the satisfaction of doing so at her hands.

A woman standing near to Rachel started coughing, just as Susanne Hille walked past her. The guard froze in her tracks, turned around, and for a moment Rachel could see deep into her cold eyes. She all but recoiled from the impact of getting a glimpse into that soulless monster. If Susanne Hille wasn't the devil incarnate, then Rachel had no idea what she was.

Not a human, certainly.

A split-second later, the guard lashed out at the coughing prisoner with her truncheon, accidentally scuffing Rachel in the process. Rachel's skin flared with pain, but she somehow managed to keep her lips pressed together, not uttering a syllable.

To her right, the poor woman who received the full impact of the punch screamed with pain, as the vicious guard struck her again and again. Rachel forced herself to stare straight ahead and keep her horror locked inside, willing her ears to become deaf and her heart to return to numbness.

She hated herself for being so apathetic, but she simply didn't have the emotional or physical energy to feel compassion for the other woman. She truly *had* become an animal, exactly like the Nazis said they were.

Nobody spoke about these incidents. Ever. In fact, as the days went on the women spoke less and less. Partly because it took up too much energy, but also because if they didn't talk about it, then they could almost pretend it didn't happen. That the nightmare they perpetually endured wasn't quite so horrible as it was.

CHAPTER 19

Laszlo never managed to get onto the transport. Weeks later, he was still moping around about the lost opportunity, especially because Ruth and her parents had eventually been amongst the lucky ones.

Mindel, though, was quite happy to have her friend by her side still, although she didn't say so, instead pretending to be sad for him.

One day she stood beside a woman queuing for soup. The woman turned around and said, "Hey, little girl!"

"Are you talking to me?"

"Yes. You asked me about your sister a while ago. Do you remember?"

Mindel didn't remember, but nodded anyway, since she had probably asked every person in the star camp about Rachel.

"Yes." Mindel squeezed Paula close against her chest as a wave of loneliness assailed her. "I need to find her."

The woman squinted her eyes, but her voice was soft and soothing. "Who's taking care of you, little one?"

Mindel shrugged. What kind of a question was that?

"Anyone?"

"Laszlo."

"Is he a relative? A cousin maybe, or an uncle?" The woman frowned.

Mindel shook her head. "Laszlo is my friend."

A suspicious expression crossed the woman's face. Mindel knew that look, it was the adult look, meant to let her know that this was all wrong. "Exactly how old is this Laszlo?"

"He's seven and he cares for me very well."

The woman shook her head. "I'm sure he does, but he's a child himself. The two of you should go to the orphans' barracks."

"I'm not an orphan!" Mindel refused to believe the woman might have a point.

"Look, there's a couple at the far end of the camp taking care of children like you—who are on your own. The SS know she's doing it. It's fine. The woman's name is Mother Brinkmann. You should go and ask her if she'll take you in, and your friend, too."

"What did that old hag want?" Laszlo asked as he joined her.

"Did you know there's an orphans' barracks in here?"

Laszlo only shrugged and Mindel frowned at him. "You knew and didn't tell me?"

"There was no reason." His face got that stubborn look that often appeared when an adult told him what he was supposed to be doing.

"But… maybe it's better over there?"

"I don't think it will be. People have said Mother Brinkmann has too many children. She uses them to make up for her guilty conscience because she couldn't save her own daughter."

"How awful!" Mindel instantly felt pity for the poor woman who had lost her daughter, remembering how much she had cried after her parents had been taken away. And even more when she'd been separated from Rachel upon arrival at this horrible place.

"It's not awful, it's just how it is in here!" Laszlo glowered at her. "And it's one more reason not to depend on adults, since they can't help us anyway."

"But that woman said the SS know that Mother Brinkmann cares for children like us, who are on our own. That's a good thing, isn't it?"

"We're not on our own. We have each other. Anyway, the SS leaves her and those kids alone, but they don't have more food or better conditions over there. Believe me, we're better off where we are."

"I want to go and see. Please? Can we at least go and meet her?"

He shook his head, but after Mindel pestered him for another hour, he finally relented. "Just to go check it out."

Mindel couldn't get them to the orphans' barracks fast enough, because she was afraid he might change his mind. The Gang rarely ventured into that part of the camp, since they preferred to roam near the kitchen hut and the big courtyard.

Laszlo, though, was dragging his feet and Mindel grew tired of having to wait for him. She turned around, putting her hands on her hips the way she'd seen her mother do and asked in a stern voice, "Why are you dawdling?"

"I don't need no adult telling me what to do. I'm just fine without them."

Mindel admired Laszlo for his wits, his independence and his ability to give the SS the runaround, but the truth was, she often wished for someone a little older to be there for her too. "Don't you wish we still had mothers to protect us?"

"I protect you."

"You do, but you're not as big as an adult. What if things are better over there?"

"I've taken care of myself for a long time now. I've taken care of you, haven't I?"

"Yes, but…" She had no idea what to say, except for her secret yearning to have someone similar to a mother or big sister again.

Someone watching over her. "Please, Laszlo, can we just go and meet Mother Brinkmann? Just to say hello?"

"I already said I would go with you, but I don't make any promises."

"But..." Mindel looked at him, scared that Laszlo might abandon her. "I don't want to stay there without you."

He finally approached her and put an arm around her shoulders. "I won't ever leave you, promise. Let's go meet Mother Brinkmann, she might not be half-bad."

It was like a huge weight fell from Mindel's shoulders. Everything would turn out just fine. She knew it.

"Do you know where it is?" Mindel asked as they walked toward the far side of the compound.

"It's right there. The last hut," he said, pointing at the barracks farthest away. It stood slightly separated from the other huts, close to the electric fence surrounding the entire camp.

Mindel hated the electric fence since the day she'd seen a woman throw herself against it. The furious sizzle as the body connected with the wires still echoed in her ears. She'd been glued to the horrific scene, unable to tear her eyes away, watching the woman twitch and convulse until at long last her limbs became limp. The charcoaled remains were left hanging as a deterrent for the remaining inmates.

She reached for Laszlo's hand, feeling less frightened when he squeezed it back. It took quite a while to cross the huge compound and her heart warmed when she saw a group of children playing next to the hut. The children ignored them, but as they approached, a tall, dark-haired woman stood up. She was as skinny as everyone else, but her brown eyes had a friendly glow to them.

"Good morning, how can I help you?" she said in a soft, welcoming voice.

Mindel instantly liked her, because she didn't shoo them away like the grown-ups usually did. "Are you Mother Brinkmann?"

"Yes, I am. And you are?"

"Mindel." Despite Mother Brinkmann's friendly attitude, Mindel wasn't brave enough to put forward her request, so she nudged Laszlo toward her.

He said in a defiant voice, "And I'm Laszlo. But we only came here to have a look."

Far from being offended, Mother Brinkmann smiled and waved her hand. "Go, take a look around. We don't have much, but the SS more or less leave us in peace."

There was something about her that reminded Mindel of her own mother. It wasn't actually the way she looked, but more her manner. They way she seemed to have control over the situation, no matter how chaotic it was. Mindel remembered how Mother had been able to stop her from behaving badly with nothing more than a stern look. Sadness engulfed her, but also a strange feeling of comfort.

Laszlo strolled around, clearly indicating that he was less than interested in Mother Brinkmann and her children. He could be so stubborn at times. When Mindel saw the cantankerous expression on his face, she feared he'd mess up everything.

She fought off her shyness and stepped forward. "Mother Brinkmann, I was told to come here to ask if I… if *we* could live with you. Me and Laszlo." There, she'd said it. With bated breath she observed the woman's face, bracing herself for a brush-off.

"Who sent you?"

"Some woman." Mindel furrowed her brows, thinking hard. "She said you take in… children like us." As much as she tried, she couldn't bring herself to pronounce the word *orphan*. Her parents just had to be alive. Rachel had assured her time and again that they'd been sent to work for the Reich and would soon return. Although, after having been pushed around from camp to camp until finally ending up in Bergen-Belsen, she had begun to doubt Rachel's words. What if Mother and Father had been sent to a place that was as awful as it was here? Then they might not be alive anymore. Lots of grown-ups weren't.

"I do. What happened to your parents?"

Laszlo had returned and heard her question. With pouting lips, he said, "My mother died months ago, but I don't need nobody to take care of me."

Mother Brinkmann seemed surprised, but she kept the pleasant expression on her face, as she addressed him. "What about your little sister here? Does she need someone to take care of her?"

He looked confused for a moment, but then pointed toward Mindel. "She's not my sister. But I'm taking care of her."

"Do *you* have family in the camp?" Mother Brinkmann asked Mindel.

"No. My parents... I don't know where they are. My older sister and I came here together... I think she's in the women's camp. But I haven't been able to find her."

"So, it's just the two of you, right? No adults watching over you?"

"We don't need someone to watch over us, we can do very well on our own." Laszlo glared at the woman, but she wasn't fazed in the least. Instead she looked at Mindel, who desperately willed Laszlo to keep his big mouth shut. Didn't he see that it would be so much better to live here with this kind woman to look after them?

"What's your full name?" the woman asked.

"Mindel, and he's Laszlo."

"Just Mindel?"

Mindel shrugged. It was too embarrassing to admit that she didn't remember her last name.

Laszlo said, "I'm Laszlo Reisz. My father was Hungarian, and my mother German. And before you ask, I'm already seven. Old enough to take care of myself."

"I never doubted that." Mother Brinkmann smiled at him. "What about you, Mindel, how old are you?"

"Four." Mindel gathered all her courage, made a curtsy and added, "And I would like very much to stay here with you."

"My husband and I have already taken in twenty children since our own daughter died, but we can certainly make room for two more." Mother Brinkmann's smile was so warm and friendly Mindel almost broke down in tears.

She turned to Laszlo and begged him, "Can we stay? Please?"

He nodded with a dour face. Mindel hugged him before he could change his mind. Then she turned toward Mother Brinkmann, who pulled her in for another hug. Laszlo hung back, making sure to seem uninterested.

"Do you have any belongings? If so, go get them, come back here and we'll get you settled in."

Mindel nodded. She carried her most prized possession— Paula—around with her at all times, but they had a few more things stashed on their bunk. For example, their soup bowls. Laszlo had devised an ingenious way of tying them to the bottom slat of the bunk bed so that they didn't have to carry them around and that they wouldn't get stolen. He'd tried to convince Mindel that she could leave Paula behind as well, but she refused. Whenever it wasn't a good idea for Paula to be out in the open, Mindel simply tucked her inside her dress.

She grabbed Laszlo's hand. He was still pouting, but just before reaching their hut, she couldn't stand it any longer and said, "I like her."

"She's an adult, we don't need her. You sure you don't want to stay here?"

Mindel looked at the cramped barracks, the latrine that constantly made her gag, and nodded. "Their hut seems less crowded and much cleaner. And we would have other children to play with, now that Ruth has gone and Fabian is too sick to play."

"It's only a trial. If I don't like it over there, I'll be coming back here," Laszlo said.

She climbed onto their bunk, and grabbed all their belongings: the blanket, several threads of wool, the sketch Heidi's friend had made of Rachel, a sheet of paper, a shard of glass, a piece of chalk, two round pebbles, and several small sticks. She handed their valuables down to Laszlo, who stored them in the big pockets of his pants.

"Let's go."

Clara and Heidi were waiting for them outside when they exited the hut a few moments later. "Where are you going?"

"We're going to stay in the orphans' barracks on the other side of the camp for a few days. But we can still visit each other any time we want," Laszlo answered.

"Really? That's so far away," Clara squealed. "I'll certainly come and visit you."

They made plans to see each other every day, and promised nothing would change, but Mindel somehow doubted that would work. After walking the long way twice this day, she was at the end of her strength, and only the prospect of a better place to live kept her on her feet. She certainly wouldn't walk all the way up here every day.

Waving goodbye to her friends, she hurried to catch up with Laszlo, who'd already walked ahead.

"Laszlo, wait for me."

He stopped for a moment and waited for her, but wouldn't talk to her the entire time until they reached the orphans' barracks.

There, Mother Brinkmann showed them the only vacant bunk bed. "I'm sorry that I don't have a bunk for each of you."

"You should see how crowded our old barracks are. This is actually great," Laszlo said.

"I'll introduce you to the other children." Mother Brinkman motioned for them to follow her and then every child said her or his name. Mindel lost track after the third or fourth one, but they all seemed friendly enough and curious to meet her and Laszlo.

That evening, Mother Brinkmann gathered all of the children together and pulled out a dilapidated book with torn pages and faded images. "It's the only book we have," Mother Brinkmann said. "My children know the story by heart, but I still read it every night."

A warm feeling swept through Mindel's body and she crept nearer to Laszlo. She'd almost forgotten how it was when her mother or Rachel had read stories to her at nighttime. It felt so raw she had to hold back her tears. Judging by the concentrated look on Laszlo's face, he seemed to struggle with similar memories and she took his hand, whispering, "We'll be fine."

Mother Brinkmann opened the book about a bird called Cin-cin and read. "Cin-cin lived with two other birds in the most beautiful castle, where her job was to entertain and amuse the princess. Their cage was made of golden bars and they never lacked for food or drink.

"The princess let them out once a day to play with them and rewarded them generously for every song. The other birds were happy, but Cin-cin wasn't."

Mindel soaked up every word, and even the other children who'd heard the story countless times before, hung on Mother Brinkmann's words as she read of the time when one day the window stood open and the three birds flew outside. Oh, the adventures they experienced!

But the other birds were afraid on their own and wanted to return to their cage. It was just Cin-cin who did not. In the end, Mindel cheered with the other children as Cin-cin fell in love with a wild bird and stayed with him, after helping her two friends to return to captivity.

Mindel was moved to tears hearing about courageous Cin-cin, but she could also understand the other birds who preferred to live in safety.

When Mother Brinkmann finished the book, the children began to beg her to tell them a story about someone called Fluff.

"Who is Fluff?" Mindel asked, confused. She couldn't remember any of the children being called by such a peculiar name.

Mother Brinkmann smiled and answered, "Fluff is a little dog who we tell stories about. He loves all the children and always goes on adventures. Tonight, since you and Laszlo are new, you get to choose the adventure Fluff will embark upon."

Mindel bit her lip while she thought about something exciting and fun for Fluff to experience. Laszlo leaned forward and whispered in her ear. It was a good idea. She said loudly, "I want Fluff and my doll Paula to climb a really tall tree."

Mother Brinkmann nodded and began to talk. "Fluff and his new friend, Paula, are walking through the forest. They have been walking for quite some time, and it is getting late.

"Fluff looks up, trying to see the sky and the sun, but there are too many trees. He walks in a big circle, but realizes he can't remember which way they have come or should be going. They are lost.

"Paula is very scared, and she sits down and begins to cry. Fluff walks over to her and licks her hand, telling her that he will find a way out for them."

"How does he do it?" one of the boys asked.

Mother Brinkmann smiled. "Fluff is a clever dog and he knows that he will be able to see the way out of the forest if he reaches the top of the trees. But there is a problem: Fluff is scared of heights. He has only ever climbed small trees, and these ones are really, really high."

"It's all right, Fluff. You can do it," a little girl murmured.

"Yes, he can. Paula promises to go with him and she climbs onto his back. Fluff climbs the tree, jumping from one branch to another, while Paula holds her arms tight around his neck. It is very hard work, but soon he and Paula can see the blue sky overhead. When they reach the top of the tree, they can both see which direction will lead them out of the forest and back home.

"Paula is so happy, and Fluff too. They climb down and Paula rides on Fluff's back as he walks them out of the forest. Once they are in the meadow, Paula hugs him and thanks Fluff for keeping her safe."

The children all cheered and Mother Brinkmann said, much too soon, "Time for bed, children."

Then they all lined up one by one to receive a warm hug and a goodnight kiss from the woman who was taking on the role of foster mother for them all. Mindel wrapped her small arms around her, not even remembering when someone had kissed her gently like that and then watched as even Laszlo accepted a hug.

She crawled onto the mattress and for the first time since arriving at the camp, Mindel fell asleep feeling confident that tomorrow would be a better day than today.

CHAPTER 20

Rachel's throat was hurting worse than usual. Her hair had grown some more, and—if the clumps that were falling out were anything to go by—its orange hue was getting stronger. She coughed constantly and her eyes were stinging like hell. There was nothing she could do about it but take a couple of shallow breaths, relieved when the tickle in her throat subsided slightly.

"Are you all right?" Linda, who was working next to her, whispered.

"Is anyone working in here fine?" Rachel asked. The sentence was followed by another coughing fit. She wished for a bit of water to swallow down the irritation, but food and drink was forbidden during work.

Talking was forbidden, too, but Rachel knew that Linda was worried about her insistent coughing because she kept casting side glances at her whenever she could. As soon as the foreman was out of earshot, she hissed, "You should ask to go to the infirmary."

"As if that would help." The infirmary wasn't actually a place for healing, but more of an antechamber of death. The only medicine given at the infirmary was rest: the women who were considered unable to work would be allowed to sleep all day—with reduced rations, of course. Rachel had no wish to go anywhere near the infirmary, since most people who went in didn't come out again.

"Your cough is getting worse," Linda protested.

"It's just a cold." Despite the stinging pain that radiated from her lungs into her entire body with every violent coughing fit, Rachel denied the possibility that this could be something more serious.

After another hour of painful attacks that made it increasingly difficult to keep her fingers still or to concentrate on filling the bullet shells with explosives, she was at the point where she pondered whether to ask the foreman if she might be allowed to go to the latrine, just to inhale some fresh air. Inside the factory the air seemed to become thicker and dustier by the minute, until she could barely breathe.

"Hang on a few more minutes and we have lunch break," Linda whispered, as if she'd read Rachel's thoughts. Lunch break was twenty minutes exactly, and the meal consisted of a cup of *Ersatzkaffee*. On lucky days the women additionally received a slice of bread. It was nothing to look forward to, but today the thought of flopping onto the ground and doing nothing seemed like paradise.

Determined to make it through to the break Rachel tried to suppress another coughing fit, but it surfaced with a vengeance shaking her entire body. Just as she recovered and began once more to stuff the explosives into a shell, a brilliant light flashed several yards away, followed by a sound like rushing wind through a narrow space as the brightness intensified and seemed to move on her like a huge open-mouthed fire-spitting dragon. Before Rachel could process what was happening, she was engulfed in a torrent of pain and heat. Ugly flames danced in front of her, licking at her body with frenzied haste. But the worst sensation emanated from her hands and arms burning in a fierceness she'd never experienced before. The pain became more intense with every passing second along with the increase in heat.

Despite not wanting to inhale the hot burning air, she took a deep breath to scream at the top of her lungs. Her own high-pitched shriek coalesced with many others, echoing off the factory walls and, in a ridiculous train of thought, Rachel feared it would shatter the windows near the ceiling.

If she'd had the oxygen she would have laughed at her own stupidity. She definitely had worse problems than broken windowpanes. In addition to searing her skin and flesh, the fire guzzled up the oxygen in the air and her lungs fought for breath. She fell backward, breathing in the hot air and gasping as her throat was singed.

From somewhere loud voices screamed and she felt people grabbing her and beating her as she fought them. *Stop beating me*, she wanted to cry, but no words came from her mouth. The pain was so excruciating, so all-encompassing, she thought this must be how it felt to be a witch burning on a stake.

She opened her eyes, but they were blinded by the flash of light, and all she could see were bright stars on a white background. At the same time, she gagged from the intense smell of acrid smoke and burnt flesh. It was akin to the bone-chilling stench that came from the crematorium at Bergen-Belsen settling like an impenetrable blanket over the camp, just more intense.

Wondering what was burning, she blinked a few more times until her vision slowly returned and she realized it was the women from the work group next to hers, where the explosion had probably originated. More pitiful howling screams tore through the air, grating on her ears. Enveloped in a shroud of yellow-orange smoke, she fought for breath, but gagged again at the stench of sulfur, mixed with a coppery, metallic component.

Two women were frantically beating at her with rags. Rachel's brain was oxygen-deprived but she still realized they were trying to beat the fire out from her burning clothing and she stopped fighting them.

"Roll over!" someone yelled at her. Rachel obeyed and rolled onto her stomach with some difficulty, hearing a distinct crack in her ribs, while the two women she hadn't recognized kept lashing out at her. After what felt like an eternity, they finally stopped.

Someone lifted Rachel to her feet, half carrying and half dragging her to another part of the factory. She let her eyes roam back to the workstation next to hers, where mere minutes ago eight women had worked. The gunpowder explosion had wreaked havoc: the workstation was in shambles, dark grey-orange smoke hung in the air and several charred corpses were lying on the ground, still smoldering.

The guards yelled and shouted, but Rachel's brain was too confused to make out the meaning of their words. Her left hand screamed with excruciating pain, an agony that was a hundred times worse than anything she'd ever experienced before, including when she'd burned her hand with hot water as a child.

Left lying in a heap against the wall of the factory next to the exit doors, she welcomed the cold gusts of wind coming inside every now and then, bringing a short reprieve from the hot burning sensation invading her skin. She whimpered and moaned, drifting in and out of consciousness. Every time she woke, the pain was so intense that she would immediately slide back into the calming darkness, letting it engulf her.

When she reached consciousness once more, she saw Linda crouching over her with a bowl. Linda seemed to be unscathed, except for an angry red burn on her forehead and smears of soot all over her face. She carefully dipped Rachel's hand into the cool water and said, "Keep your hand in the water. It'll take the worst of the pain away."

Relief washed over Rachel as the water cooled the burns, and she mumbled some incoherent words.

"Did you understand? Keep your hand in the water!" Linda insisted.

"I'm so sorry…" Rachel closed her eyes again, fighting against the darkness overcoming her.

"There's nothing to be sorry about." Linda caressed her hair.

"… All my fault… Didn't pay attention…"

"It wasn't your fault. The explosion happened at the neighboring station to ours. But you didn't jump away fast enough."

"The women there?"

Linda made a sad face. "All dead. And many more injured, like you."

"… Want to die." Rachel was so tired of living and enduring all these horrors, she simply wanted to close her eyes and never open them up again.

"Don't you dare give up!" Linda said it with such outrage Rachel opened her eyes again to see her friend glaring at her. "You have to stay alive for your sister, remember?"

The mention of Mindel awoke that last hidden reserve of her spirits and she gave a slight nod. "Not dying. Not today." While Rachel couldn't care less what happened to her anymore, she also knew she couldn't leave Mindel all alone on earth, if there was even a chance she was alive. Her little sister was her only connection with the world of the living, and for her Rachel would make an effort to get through this.

"Leave the injured and get back to work. We have a war to win, lousy dimwits!" the guards shouted at the women.

"Can't slow down the war machine for anything, now can we?" Linda whispered, before she caressed Rachel's cheek and stood up to return to work.

A sardonic satisfaction filled Rachel's mind as she thought, *That explosion will make quite the dent in our daily production.*

She was slumped against the wall, softly whimpering, when the factory medic came around to take a look at the casualties. He grabbed her hand from the water to inspect it and she screamed out in pain.

"Shut up, filthy Jew!" he said, dropping her hand back into the bowl, splashing precious cool water. "It's just a burn. Clench your teeth and don't be a crybaby."

She would happily have stabbed a knife into his heart if she had one, but settled for glaring at him. Next, he ripped the shreds of her singed dress from her body, leaving her breasts exposed for everyone to stare at. He poked and pressed on her ribcage and once again she heard the ugly crunch.

"This one can't continue to work," the doctor said to the SS guard standing behind him.

"All right, we'll request a replacement and send her back."

Rachel was hurting too much to grasp the meaning of his words, except for the relief washing over her that she didn't have to finish her shift, for which she was very grateful.

When the doctor was gone, she finally dared to have a look at her hand and wished she hadn't. It consisted of ugly burned black skin and raw flesh. On the less damaged parts blisters were forming.

It looked truly horrific, but thanks to Linda bringing her the bowl of water, it barely hurt as long as she kept the hand immersed. But the moment she attempted to take her hand out of the bowl, the searing pain returned with force, making her dizzy, before she quickly immersed her hand again.

Despite the pain, exhaustion took over and she slept through the rest of the shift, until a guard kicked her with his boots.

"Get up, lazy-bones, it's time to walk home!"

Home? For a split second, Rachel believed he wanted to send her to the farm, but soon realized that *home* meant the Tannenberg camp.

She howled with pain when he took away the bowl of water, which earned her another kick in the midriff. In order not to infuriate him further, she did her best not to whimper as she used all her strength to get up. Without the cooling water, ripples of pain from her injured hand coursed through her entire body, making her sway. It felt like she was trapped by the raging flames all over again.

The image of medieval witches burning at the stake came to her mind once more, and she all but vomited on the guard's boots. Forcing the bile down, she staggered and stumbled to catch up with the rest of the women waiting for the injured to start the trek *home*, with aching ribs and singed clothes.

As she left the factory building, she caught a glimpse of several charred corpses and felt a twinge of jealousy. Those women had made it, they would suffer no more. Outside, the cold November air hit her half-naked body, causing her jaw to chatter, but at least it had the beneficial side effect of cooling her burned skin and easing the pain.

"Here, I grabbed your coat for you." Suddenly Linda was beside her, handing her the slight overcoat the women wore during the march but handed in before manning their workstations. There was no way she would be allowed to stop and put it on, but Linda hung the coat over her shoulders, closing the buttons while walking backwards in front of Rachel.

"Thanks."

At the Tannenberg camp Rachel was immediately taken to the infirmary, where the Jewish nurse could do nothing for her but bandage her cracked ribs and put the hand in water again, until the SS came to put her on the next transport back to Bergen-Belsen. In her current condition she didn't care either way.

She lived. She ached. And she was hungry.

Her hand was throbbing in rhythm with her heartbeat and the bumpy ride in the truck only added to the agony. When the truck stopped at the gates of Bergen-Belsen, she at once welcomed and feared getting off.

Upon arrival they were inspected and most of the women were assigned to the barracks, but Rachel and two others were hauled to the infirmary in the star camp. It was ironic, because she'd been wanting to come here all this time to look for Mindel, and when she finally reached her goal, she was in no condition to walk around and ask about her sister.

"Here you go," a kind Jewish doctor, who'd removed the dead skin and bandaged Rachel's hand, said. "I'll let you stay for three days, but I'm afraid then you'll have to return to the women's camp. Make the most of your stay here and try to recoup some strength."

Then he was gone and Rachel drifted back into her state of half-consciousness, not knowing whether the whimpering and moaning came from her own mouth or someone else's.

During normal times, she would have considered this infirmary atrocious: unhygienic, dirty and crowded. But compared to the conditions in the main camp, or even Tannenberg, it was paradise. Probably the best thing was that not even the SS guards peeked inside to harass the inmates. It was a well-known fact that the bullying, cruel members of the so-called Master race were also deathly afraid they might catch a contagious disease from the ill prisoners, so they gave a wide berth to anyone sick.

The next day Rachel felt slightly better. She was still weak, hungry and exhausted, but at least the incessant throbbing in her hand had stopped and she could finally form a coherent thought once again. Barely able to move due to her cracked ribs, she resorted to questioning anyone who entered the hospital about Mindel, but nobody had seen or heard of her little sister.

"How old is the girl?" the women in the bunk next to her asked.

"She's four… No, five now—" Rachel stopped mid-sentence, remembering her sister just recently had her fifth birthday. Once again her heart broke for the poor mite, who'd been all alone on such an important day, with nobody to celebrate with her.

Memories of Mindel's last birthday flooded her brain and Rachel was transported back to their farm. In place of the stench of disease and death, the smell of freshly baked apple cake wafted into her nose and she smiled happily. In a moment's time Mindel would come downstairs to find the entire family waiting for her.

Due to the circumstances, the table bore only modest presents. The apple cake, for which Mother had saved up weeks of sugar rations, a hand-me-down dress her mother had tailored to fit Mindel's tiny frame, the rag doll Rachel had been sewing every night for several days, and nine wooden marbles, with a scribbled note from Aron and Israel promising to teach her how to play "Lucky stone in the middle," where the child who got his or her marble nearest to the stone in the middle was the winner.

Minutes later, Mindel stormed down the stairs into the kitchen, her happy face a sight Rachel would never forget. She stopped in her tracks, grabbed the rag doll, pressed her against her chest and squeaked, "A doll! I have a doll!"

"Now you have a special friend who'll always be there for you," Rachel had said and Mindel had hugged her and told her she was the best sister in the world.

"What shall we call your friend?" Rachel asked.

"Paula," Mindel said, as if she'd known the doll all her life and then proceeded to present the doll to the family members, one by one. "Paula, this is my father. Here beside him are my two brothers, Aron and Israel. Over there is Rachel, and my dear mother."

Father cast an indulgent smile at his youngest child before he said, "I have to begin work on the fields. Can we cut the cake, please?"

Mother nodded and said, "Let's light the candles and sing 'Happy Birthday' for Mindel." Once they finished and Mindel had blown out the four candles, Mother cut half of the cake into six pieces, one for each person, leaving the rest for the next day.

Rachel savored the sweetness of the cake on her tongue, determined to keep the taste lingering in her mouth for as long as possible, since it had been the only dessert or cake they'd eaten for months—to be exact since Aron's birthday in May. These days sugar rations were scarce and precious, so the only sweets mother made were birthday cakes.

The rag doll soon became Mindel's most prized possession. In the beginning Rachel had scolded her little sister for dragging the doll anywhere and everywhere, but later on she had become grateful that her sister had at least one friend so she would never be alone.

A deep sigh erupted from Rachel's throat and brought her back to the unsavory hospital. Mindel's birthday had been their last happy occasion together as a family, before the fallout from Old Hans' death had sent their lives into a terrifying downward spiral.

In the afternoon, she was on the lookout for the nurse she'd talked to months before, but she never saw her and she didn't dare to ask anyone else out of fear she'd raise suspicions. Instead, it was a very young nurse called Christa who made the rounds in the infirmary, offering little more than kind words and a smile. Medicine wasn't wasted on inmates and the basic function of the hospital barracks was to separate the sick from the rest of the prisoners. The only means of healing was rest.

Rachel asked Christa, "Please, I'm looking for my sister, Mindel Epstein. I believe she's here in the star camp."

The nurse wrinkled her forehead and slowly said, "I believe... There was a cute little girl called Mindel. Brown hair, always carrying a raggedy doll and with a slightly older boy in tow, probably her brother."

Rachel's heart beat fast with excitement. "That could be her. Where can I find her?"

Christa's expression became sad. "I haven't seen her around in quite a while. You see, so many people die here, and the children especially don't last for long."

"I must find her." Rachel jumped up from the bed, only to groan at the intense pain in her cracked ribs.

The nurse pressed her back onto the bunk. "You will go nowhere in your condition." But as she noticed Rachel's desperately pleading eyes, she relented with a sigh. "I will put out the word to ask around, but you must stay in bed. You won't be of any use to your sister when you're dead."

Rachel relaxed and nodded. It was a sliver of hope—but no more.

She took Christa's advice and slept as much as possible, giving her battered and exhausted body time to recover. Sleep was also a respite from the pain in her hand, since painkillers were a luxury not wasted on the inmates.

On the third day, Christa brought encouraging news. "It seems there's someone who knows of a girl called Mindel, who's going around and asking everyone about her sister Rachel."

"That must be her!" Rachel shouted excitedly.

"Shush." Christa put a finger to her lips and then bent down as if she were having a look at Rachel's burns. "If you want to see your sister, it can be arranged. At a cost."

"I can pay," Rachel whispered, since she had held onto the cigarettes, despite the temptation to spend them during her dark moments in Tannenberg.

"Well, then, I'll make the inquiries and let you know." Christa left the hospital barracks.

Rachel felt for the cigarettes in her dress pocket when she remembered and howled in desperation. Her dress, along with the cigarettes, had been singed from the explosion and the vile doctor in Tannenberg had ripped the shreds away.

Later in the day, the SS doctor paraded through the infirmary and declared Rachel well enough to return to work.

Less than five minutes later, she was escorted to the women's camp past the barbed wire fence separating the two compounds. Rachel felt bereft. She didn't even have time to let the friendly nurse know, and could only hope that someone would give Mindel the message that Rachel was still alive and looking for her.

CHAPTER 21

One of the perks that came with living in the orphans' barracks was the absence of roll calls. Since the SS hated the disturbance the ever-fidgeting children brought to the roll calls, they had exempted Mother Brinkmann and her group from the daily counting. In fact, it didn't matter to them whether the children were alive or not. They couldn't be used for work and the probability of one of them trying to escape was tiny.

Every morning when Mindel watched the other inmates lining up in the courtyard, while her little group was allowed to stay by their hut, she felt a rush of relief surging through her veins. If for nothing else, not having to stand still for hours each day had been worth being taken under Mother Brinkmann's wing. Much to her relief, even Laszlo had come around and had reluctantly admitted it hadn't been such a bad move to come here.

The children were sitting outside to soak up the rare sunshine during this otherwise dark and cold month of November, when hundreds of people marched toward the camp, passing their barracks outside the barbed wire fence.

Mindel distantly remembered that was how she'd come here such a long time ago, walking—or mostly being carried by Rachel—from the train station to the main gate. Curious, the children approached the fence to get a closer look at the newcomers. But the moment Mindel caught a glimpse into the face of the most miserable human being she'd ever seen she shrieked and jumped backward, straight into another child who began cursing at her. "Hey, watch where you're going, idiot!"

Mindel did not answer, so severe was the shock of what she'd seen. Nobody in the camp had fat on their bones or looked remotely healthy, but these… creatures couldn't be humans. She dared a second glimpse at the ever-growing mass of bodies marching past.

"Are these men or women?" she asked Laszlo, who usually had an answer for everything.

"Dunno. Look like aliens to me."

"What is an alien?"

"A creature that lives on another planet. They're not people like us."

"What is a planet?"

"Stop asking stupid questions," Laszlo scolded her and she decided it was better not to pester him anymore. She still loved him, but his mood was becoming ever more volatile and he'd yell, shove, or hit her whenever he got angry. Not when Mother Brinkmann was around, because she didn't tolerate such behavior among her children, but as soon as she was out of sight, the older children began fighting with each other and bossing around the smaller ones.

Mindel turned her attention to the mass of bodies passing by the fence. They had seen newcomers every once in a while, but recently it was happening almost every day—although never such frightful creatures as these.

"Children, come inside, it's getting cold," Mother Brinkmann called and herded them back into the barracks. Her husband was waiting inside the hut for the daily class.

In the beginning Mindel had enjoyed the classes, because she'd learned to write her name with her finger in the dust. But lessons were so awfully boring and she was always so tired, her head wouldn't follow Herr Brinkmann's lessons, and then she got scolded for disrupting the class.

Today, though, she took the opportunity and asked him the question Laszlo hadn't wanted to answer. "What is a planet?"

Herr Brinkmann smiled and began to explain about the Earth circling the sun together with other orbs like Mars or Venus. It didn't make sense.

"Why do people from other planets come to our camp? Don't they know how awful it is?" she asked.

"Who told you this?" Herr Brinkmann asked.

"Nobody." Mindel bit her lower lip and stared at the ground, afraid to make herself look foolish if she said more. But the issue gnawed at her and the next morning she snuck off to visit Heidi. The older girl was clever and knew even more than Laszlo did.

"Mindel, what a surprise! How are you? We wanted to come and see you," Heidi greeted her.

Mindel shrugged, she had to ask her question before she lost the courage to do so. "Can I ask you a question?"

"Sure."

While she recounted the happenings from the day before, Laura settled beside them. As Mindel ended her story, both of the older girls laughed.

"They are not aliens. Those people come from a camp much worse than this one," Heidi said.

"Worse than this?" Mindel didn't think that was possible, but why would Heidi lie to her?

"Yes, it's called Auschwitz, and there they send people up through the chimney," Laura said, earning her a stern glare from Heidi.

Mindel drew her brows together, asking, "What does that mean?"

"Nothing. Laura is just being stupid," Heidi said in a tone that brooked no argument. A tone Mindel knew all too well. Grown-ups always used it when they had decided she was too young for something. From experience she knew there was no way of coaxing the older girls into telling her, so she shrugged again and decided to ask around later.

"By the way, yesterday a woman came asking for you," Heidi said.

"For me?" Mindel had no idea who'd want something from her.

"Yes, apparently there was a patient in the infirmary who might be your sister."

"Rachel? Why didn't you tell me right away? Can we go see her?" Mindel hopped up and down with excitement.

"It was too late to walk all the way to your barracks and return before curfew," Heidi said.

"I don't want you to get your hopes up too much. We don't know if the person asking for you really was your sister. Since we couldn't get you, we went to see her to find out. But she'd already been transferred back to the women's camp," Laura added and Mindel broke down in tears, unable to contain her disappointment. She'd been so close to maybe finding Rachel, and now she was gone—again.

"Hey, don't cry." Heidi wrapped an arm around her. "This is good news. Now we know your sister is alive."

"But… Laura… said… it's not sure." Mindel sniffed.

Heidi glared angrily at Laura and rocked Mindel on her lap. "We are sure. How many Rachels could there be looking for little girls with your name? She's alive, and she's looking for you. That's a good sign. As soon as she can, she'll come looking for you again."

"Can we send her a message?" Mindel asked on a hopeful note.

"That's a good idea. The nice nurse can maybe give your note to a patient from the women's camp."

Even though Heidi made it sound like an easy task, Mindel sensed the hesitation in her voice. But she wouldn't let this deter her from her plan. "We need pen and paper. And then will you write a note for me?"

Heidi nodded and together they entered the barracks to scrounge for a piece of paper. The camp children collected anything and everything they could get hold of, and they soon found someone willing to exchange a scrap of paper for two rusty nails Mindel carried in her pocket.

"I almost forgot," Heidi said. "This Rachel said your last name is Epstein. Is that right?"

Mindel furrowed her brows in deep thinking, but as hard as she tried, she didn't recognize the name, so she shrugged. "I really don't know."

Heidi nodded. "It doesn't matter." Then she wrote on the scrap of paper:

Rachel Epstein. Your sister Mindel is at the orphans' barracks with Mother Brinkmann. Heidi Wenzel.

On her way back Mindel peered through the barbed wire fence into the women's camp, hoping to see Rachel somewhere, but the only things she saw were hastily erected tents for the thousands upon thousands of women coming from this other camp called Auschwitz.

From then on, she walked to the fence every day, hoping to catch a glimpse of her sister. She would stay until some SS guard shooed her away, or until the bell for dinner time rang and she had to return to her barracks.

Never once did she see Rachel, but every day there were more tents and more people in the formerly empty courtyard. It would be impossible to find her sister there. With sagging shoulders she decided not to return, at least not until she heard back from Heidi that someone had delivered her note.

That evening dark gray thunderclouds rolled in, covering the entire sky. One of the dimming memories of her days on the farm was how she and Aron had jumped from puddle to puddle, happy at the sensation of rain pelting down on them.

Here, though, she hated the rain. It wetted her dress, and for lack of a change in clothing, she'd spend the rest of the day moist and freezing. No, in the camp bad weather was no fun. Not even jumping puddles was a game the children would play, because with the holes in their shoes, the awful chill would soon numb their feet and then creep up their legs.

She increased her pace, wanting to be in the hut before the skies opened up. Later at night, lightning and thunder shook the barracks as a deluge came down with strong gusts of wind. Mindel huddled closer to Laszlo, shivering each time a squall blew through the cracks in the thin wooden wall. To make matters worse, the wind howled as if ghosts and other creatures were coming to destroy them.

"It's just the wind, Mindel," Laszlo consoled her.

"But it's so loud and scary."

They kept silent for a while, until he whispered, "Can you keep a secret?"

"Yes."

"There's another transport going to Switzerland and I'm going to sneak onto it."

She gasped. "You can't. The SS will kill you if they find out."

"They won't catch me. I have talked to a man from the repair crew. He knows the people in the special camp, and he says there's a foolproof way to get onto the transport."

"Please don't go," Mindel begged him. She was afraid for him, but also for herself. Despite being under Mother Brinkmann's care, how would she cope without Laszlo? "I will miss you, and Paula will, too."

"Then come with me."

"I can't. Heidi said my sister is alive and looking for me."

"You can't be sure about that! What does Heidi know?"

Mindel hated how he always needed to appear smarter than her and she pouted. "We sent her a note. I just have to wait for the answer."

"And then what? Do you think the SS will allow her to come here?"

"Then I go to where she is."

"Ah, Mindel." He wrapped his arm around her. "You'll be better off coming with me. Please. I promise everything will turn out just fine. You can leave your sister a note and after the war she can come to live with us in Switzerland."

The entire idea seemed much too daunting to even entertain it. As bad as being in the camp was, who could assure her that this Switzerland wouldn't be worse? Maybe it was as bad as this Auschwitz camp where all those horrible creatures came from? She involuntarily shuddered and decided she'd rather stay with Mother Brinkmann and the other children. "I really can't."

"Think about it, we'd have so much fun in Switzerland. I heard they have loads of chocolate there."

Chocolate? Mindel's mouth watered as she thought back to Christmas on the farm, when she'd received two pieces of the rare treat, together with a raspberry jam cake. It seemed like an awfully long time ago.

CHAPTER 22

In the early hours of the morning, the raging storm abated, and the prisoners were called outside for roll call. On the way to the assigned assembly space for her hut, Rachel passed the temporary tent area.

She blinked several times to make sure what she saw wasn't a hallucination. Where the night before there had been hundreds of tents, now nothing remained but muddy earth, shredded tarpaulin and desperate women. She hadn't personally spoken to any of the newcomers, but camp gossip had it they came from Auschwitz, a camp ten times worse than Bergen-Belsen. According to the accounts of the new arrivals, people there, in Auschwitz, were selected straight from the train ramp—one line for those who could work and another line for those who had to die. Even after experiencing unthinkable cruelties at the hands of the Nazis, and the SS especially, she had difficulties wrapping her head around the news.

It seemed too outrageous to be true, but then, what was normal or even decent where the Nazis and their treatment of the Jews was concerned? Rachel shook her head, as if she could shake the horrendous images from her mind.

After being kicked out of the camp hospital, she wasn't returned to Tannenberg, and had been lucky enough to be selected for a work detail inside the women's camp, which served her just fine in her quest to find Mindel.

That evening after work she returned to her barracks, only to find out that the women from the destroyed tents had been assigned to the already overcrowded barracks. Last night she'd shared her bunk with one other woman, but now she found two more people in there.

"The *kapo* assigned these two to our bunk." With a sour face her bunkmate introduced the newcomers who looked to be about Rachel's own age.

There was nothing they could do about it. Rachel didn't welcome the idea of having to share the small bunk with three women instead of just one, but she put a brave face on the matter and said, "Hello. I'm Rachel."

"I'm Margot," the older girl said with a peculiar accent. "And this is my sister Anne."

Rachel made an effort to be kind, because she remembered how lonely she'd felt when she first arrived here and how Linda's friendship had helped her to settle into the awful conditions. "Where are you from?"

"The Netherlands."

"That's a long way from here." Before being deported, Rachel had never ventured farther from her home than into the next town, about one hour's walk away.

Anne sniffed. "We've been to a hundred places by now."

Margot, who seemed not only to be the older, but also the calmer sister, explained, "We were actually born in Germany, but emigrated to the Netherlands because our father thought we'd be safe there from the Nazis. Until Hitler's Wehrmacht marched into the country and we had to go into hiding."

"Into hiding?" Rachel thought about the time on the farm, where the entire family had hidden in plain sight, more or less unbothered.

"Yes. We lived for two years in an *achterhuis*, a secret annex to a house in Amsterdam."

"All the time? Did you go outside?"

"We didn't," Margot said.

"What? That must have been so hard." Having grown up on a farm, Rachel had basically lived outside and couldn't imagine being confined in a hideout day and night for a week, let alone for two years.

"It was. And you wouldn't believe the constant quarrels we had with eight people all crammed together in such a small space. It was hell," Anne said.

"Not as hellish as what came after the Gestapo found us out."

Rachel nodded. Everybody in the camp had their own horrific experiences and could relate. Exchanging stories, it became clear that the odyssey Anne and Margot had endured had been exceptionally awful, especially in that camp of horrors called Auschwitz, for compared to the physical appearance of the two sisters, Rachel and her bunkmate looked positively rosy.

Apart from piling more people into the already overcrowded huts, nothing else changed. There wasn't more food nor other provisions like blankets. The same barrel of soup per hut that had not sufficed to satiate the hunger of a hundred women was now used to feed three hundred. A gnawing and growling stomach was Rachel's perpetual companion, and together with the itching and biting of the lice, fleas and bedbugs, it kept her from sleeping despite her complete exhaustion.

Apart from her constant frantic worries about Mindel, days in the camp were filled with hunger, pain, and boredom. She wasn't sure whether she preferred the horrible work in Tannenberg or the equally horrible tedium here. At least in the factory she hadn't had time to think and worry.

Good news was rare, but the Auschwitz women claimed that the war was as good as lost, and that the Red Army had already conquered half of Poland.

Anne and Margot confirmed the rumors about what was happening in Auschwitz, though, and what they recounted seemed to come straight from Dante's twisted mind in his description of the ninth circle of hell. In all of her eighteen years Rachel had never believed that she would witness such evil.

A lifetime ago, Rachel had sneaked Dante's book from her father's bookshelf and read it hidden beneath her blanket... Memories of better times returned and she allowed her mind the luxury of drifting away and forgetting everything around her. It was her only respite from the horrible present and she seemed to retreat more and more into a peaceful and happy world—even if only in her imagination. For a short while she wasn't in Bergen-Belsen, where the stink of human excrement and burned corpses lingered everywhere, but on the farm, inhaling the scent of freshly cut grass, feeling the warm sun on her skin while she milked the cows, tasting ripe, sweet strawberries on her tongue.

"Hey, get out of my way," someone grunted and elbowed her.

Rachel blinked a few times, but reality had snatched her away from the dream and as much as she tried, she couldn't get back to that wonderful place she missed so much.

Life at the farm hadn't been a bed of roses, because even with Old Hans' protection and their remote location they'd felt the increasing hardships placed on the Jews. Sadness filled her heart as she remembered her last day of school.

Juden verboten! No Jews allowed, was the new rule in the nearby town of Mindelheim. It did not only apply to school, but also to public parks, benches, the library, the ice cream parlor, restaurants... everything. The town hall had special hours—or should she say minutes—when Jews were allowed to pursue their official business, and in the shops Jews were served only at the end of the day, when everyone else had shopped already. Many times, even with ration cards, there was nothing left to be bought.

Thankfully the farm was mostly self-sufficient and while the family hadn't lived in luxury, they'd always had enough to eat and clothes to dress properly.

She looked down at the sturdy shoes she'd been wearing day in day out since her capture more than a year ago. The soles had worn thin and on rainy days the moisture from the ground found its way inside.

Lost in memories she then found herself thinking back to the time when her mother had unexpectedly fallen pregnant with Mindel. In stark contrast to her parents' joy over the births of Israel and Aron, this time they seemed hopeless.

"What will we do with another child?" her mother had said.

"I agree, now is not an ideal time," her father had responded.

"Every day we struggle more and have less food to put on the table. How will we feed another mouth?" Mother seemed clearly upset.

"Don't worry so much. Things will get better. The Germans are a civilized nation full of culture. They'll soon come to their senses and give Hitler a good running."

"From your lips to God's ears."

"We're safe here under the protection of Old Hans."

"But what if something, God forbid, happens to us?"

"You worry too much. Rachel is thirteen already, she will take care of her brothers and the little one. But it won't come to that, you'll see."

Mother sighed. "I guess you're right. In any case another child is a blessing, even in such a cursed time."

CHAPTER 23

Laszlo grabbed Mindel's hand and pulled her behind the kitchen barracks. They hadn't come here since living with Mother Brinkmann because she kept a close eye on her children, always cautioning them to stay away from the guards and outbuildings, lest they get caught in some sort of trouble. But, as always, Laszlo only paid attention to her when it suited his plans.

"We need more food," Laszlo whispered to her.

Mindel agreed, because the rations had gotten smaller with every arriving trainload of prisoners. But she was also scared. There were too many people around, both prisoners and guards. "Let's not do it today, please. You will get caught."

"I'm quick. Nobody will even know I was there." Laszlo puffed out his chest. "You and Tina can keep watch." He nodded to one of the girls from the orphans' barracks who had taken to following them both around like a puppy.

"What's he gonna do?" Tina asked.

"Scrounge food," Mindel whispered back, watching as Laszlo stood up and walked toward the back of the building. From their position, they couldn't see the back door, just the corner of the building. Laszlo turned and waved at her before he disappeared around the side.

The girls waited in the shadows, pretending to be sitting on the ground playing with Mindel's doll when several SS guards passed them by. Mindel had learned never to look them in the face because that only seemed to invite their interest and that was the last thing she or Laszlo needed right now.

But she let out a loud whistle the way Laszlo had taught her, as soon as the SS walked down the path toward the kitchen barracks, hoping her friend would be quick enough to disappear before they entered the hut, if they even did. Most of the times they just marched by, looking grim.

Long minutes passed and Laszlo didn't return. Mindel grew ever more anxious, wanting to go and see what had happened. Only Tina's small hand on her arm kept her from storming into the kitchen. All of a sudden she heard shouts and a kerfuffle and moments later saw the SS guards coming out of the back of the kitchen.

She gasped with horror when she saw Laszlo dragged behind, covered in blood. They gave him several more knocks with their batons for good measure, before they left him bleeding on the ground.

"Oh no," Tina cried out.

"We have to take him to Mother Brinkmann," Mindel whimpered. She tucked Paula away in her too-small dress and scampered across the open space, stopping just before rounding the corner of the building that housed the kitchens. She swallowed several times and then peeked around, making sure the SS were gone.

"Laszlo!" she screamed and rushed to his side. He was so battered that she stopped her hand midair before touching him, not wanting to hurt him.

"They got me…" he whispered, barely able to keep his eyes open.

"Shush. We'll get you back to Mother Brinkmann. She'll know what to do," Mindel said. Mother Brinkmann always knew what to do; she would be able to fix Laszlo.

"I can't walk."

Well, that was a problem Mindel hadn't considered.

"We'll help you," said Tina, who'd caught up with them. Both of them were much smaller than he was, but somehow they managed to drag him up and with his arms slung over their shoulders he hobbled along. Despite their best efforts, holding Laszlo up became harder with every step and Mindel had to bite on her lips in order not to cry out from the pain. She almost collapsed in relief when two of the older boys saw them and took over.

Mother Brinkmann came out of the barracks and assessed the situation with a single glance, ordering, "Karl and Thaddeus, you get him inside on my bunk. Sandy, you bring me the first aid box, and Tina and Mindel, I'll have a word with you both later."

Mindel quietly observed how the bigger boys settled Laszlo on the bunk.

Sandy came running with a cardboard box used as the first aid kit. It contained a few strips of cloth, ointment and small white pills that were cut into quarters and given to seriously ill children. Sometimes they helped and the child got better.

Mother Brinkmann returned with a small bowl of clean water from a secret stash that the children weren't allowed to ever touch and began to clean Laszlo's wounds.

Mindel wrung her hands as she watched her friend wince and cry out, but was too fascinated by the efficiency of Mother Brinkmann's actions to look away. When Mother Brinkmann finished cleaning the wounds, she gave Laszlo a quarter of the white pill, and then turned around to glare at Mindel and Tina.

"Now, would you care to tell me what happened?"

"The SS…" Tina whispered.

"Yes? And why did they beat him?"

Tina stuttered and Mindel felt her ears burn under the scrutinizing gaze. "He was in the kitchen…"

"What on earth was he doing there?" Mother Brinkmann's voice became raised.

"Organizing food."

"He got caught *stealing*?" Mother Brinkmann looked so angry that Mindel almost wished to face an SS guard instead of her. Lost for words, she merely nodded.

What followed was a long sermon about proper behavior that ended with, "There will be no more stealing while you live in my barracks. Let Laszlo's injuries be a lesson to you all. Anyone caught stealing from here on out will have to find another place to live."

All the children looked shamefaced, except for Laszlo, who'd dozed off, groaning. Mindel had no idea how he could sleep in such a grave situation. Now Mother Brinkmann would get even angrier with him.

Surprisingly, she didn't. Instead she covered him with a blanket, shooed the other children out of the barracks and said, "He needs rest. You go and play outside."

Three days later Laszlo was able to get up from the bunk and came limping toward Mindel, with a victorious look on his face. But before he reached her, Mother Brinkmann said with a voice cold as steel, "Laszlo, I have to talk to you."

Mindel was pondering whether she should stay to listen or not, but in the end, curiosity won out.

"You put every one of us in danger with your behavior," Mother Brinkmann scolded Laszlo. "We live in slightly better conditions than in the other barracks, because the SS mostly ignore us. But if they find out that my children are stealing food from the kitchen, they might well close these barracks. Do you really want to return to having roll calls, and fending for yourself?"

Her piercing stare made Mindel shiver. "What you did, Laszlo, was stupid and dangerous."

"No, what these monsters are doing is stupid. They have no right to starve us to death and I won't let that happen to me! Or Mindel!"

"Laszlo!"

"No!" He was shouting angrily. "You can't tell me what to do. You're just another helpless Jew. The only ones who can make me do anything are the bloody SS and I defy even them! Because I'm not a coward like the rest of you."

"I understand you're upset but you need to listen to my words. No more stealing." Mother Brinkmann was keeping surprisingly calm in the face of Laszlo's anger.

"I'm good at it."

"And it's going to get you killed," Mother Brinkmann warned him.

Laszlo defiantly stared at her. "That's going to happen anyway. What do I care if I die today or a month from now? Nobody will cry for me and the other children can eat my share of the food."

Mindel's ears were ringing with shock. He couldn't be serious about not caring about dying. Secretly wiping the tears from her eyes, she snuck out of the barracks, kicking a few pebbles around.

"What are we going to do without Laszlo?" she asked her doll, but not even Paula had words of solace for her.

That night, when she crawled into the bunk beside Laszlo, she plucked up the courage to ask him, "Do you really want to die?"

"Why not? Let's face it, none of us will survive this camp."

"I don't want you to die. I love you and I would cry awfully when you're gone."

He rolled around with a pained groan and hugged her with one arm. "I'm going to find a way for the two of us to get out of here. I promise."

"I don't want to leave the orphans' barracks. No one tries to steal my food or our blankets, and it smells a lot better."

"When we're in Switzerland we'll have more food than we can eat. And fluffy eiderdowns!"

She sighed, remembering the heavy but soft blanket her mother had always tucked her into during winter. So, he'd not given up on his plan to go to Switzerland. To her it seemed daunting—too daunting. It was certainly better to stay here than to escape to someplace unknown that neither of them even knew where it was. She liked Mother Brinkmann and being around the other children. Most of all, she liked the nighttime stories about Fluff.

Fluff had become a dear friend, like Paula, and every day she looked forward to another of his daring adventures. This night's story had been about him learning to swim with a duck. She still smiled at how he'd been afraid of the water at first but with the duck's encouragement frolicked in the lake for hours. Something she wished she could do as well.

CHAPTER 24

"Anne? Rachel, where are you?" Margot called out as she entered the barracks.

The two girls were sitting on the bunk, the threadbare blanket slung around their shoulders, knitting gloves with threads taken from said blanket.

"What's up?" Rachel asked.

Margot handed her a dirty slip of paper. "Look!"

Rachel Epstein. Your sister Mindel is at the orphans' barracks with Mother Brinkmann. Heidi Wenzel.

Rachel read the curly handwriting and gasped. "Oh my God! Mindel is alive!"

"Who's this Mother Brinkmann?" Margot asked.

Karin, a woman who worked in the kitchen and was an ample source of gossip and true information alike, looked up. "You don't know about Mother Brinkmann? She's like the Pied Piper, scooping up orphaned children. She's been in the star camp for years. Came here with her husband and a daughter. When the girl died, she took in a little one who'd lost her parents. And then another one."

Rachel was in awe at the efforts this stranger was making to save orphaned children, perhaps including her own sister.

Karin continued talking. "I heard when she had five or six little ones under her care, the other women in her hut complained to the SS about the constant noise. Nobody could sleep at night because of the whining and moaning. The younger ones often wet the bed and people would wake up with pee dripping into their faces." She made a disgusted face. "The SS took her and the children away. But much to the surprise of everyone, she was given her own hut at the very end of the camp that had formerly been used as quarantine barracks. So she and her husband are living together in what is now called the orphans' barracks and are left in peace by the SS and the Lagerkommandant, just as long as they keep the children in check and don't bother anyone."

"She sounds like a wonderful woman," Rachel said.

"If you ask me, she's nuts. Left a good job in the kitchen to care for these children who'll die soon anyway. Nobody will thank her for it and she might even die herself because of it." With all her information given out, Karin lost interest in the conversation and turned around.

"You must go and see her," Anne said. Since she hadn't been here long enough, she didn't know it was impossible to cross into the other compounds.

"I've tried already. There's no way to cross over. It's on the other side of the barbed wire fence in the south corner of our compound."

Anne shook her head, a stubborn light entering her eyes. "The note got here, right? The least we can do is get a note back. Let me see the paper."

Reluctantly Rachel handed the paper to Anne. It was her only connection to Mindel and she wanted to hold onto it, press it against her heart, feel Mindel's presence linger and imagine she was here by her side.

Anne read the note and turned even paler than usual. "This… this can't be true."

"What's wrong?" Margot asked.

Anne shook her head. "It's signed Heidi Wenzel. Heidi! Don't you remember my friend Heidi?"

Margot reached for the note in her sister's hand. "I'm sure there are a thousand girls with that same name."

Rachel looked from one girl to the other, not knowing how to feel. Joy over the possible reunion with their long-lost friend, or sadness that their friend was in this hellish place, too.

"Look at the handwriting. I'm sure it's her," Anne insisted. "I have to see her!"

"You can't. Haven't you heard what Rachel just said? There's no way to cross."

Anne stubbornly shook her head. "I'm going to see Heidi no matter what. But first we need to get a note to her. How do we do it?"

"There's a nurse working in the infirmary over there, but living here. Her name is Christa and she might be able to help. Although…" Rachel shrugged.

"What?" Margot and Anne said in unison.

"She requires payment."

Anne frowned, but then held up the glove she was knitting. "A half-finished glove maybe?"

Rachel remembered the ten cigarettes she'd gathered so many months before to try to bribe the other nurse to let her through. If only the cigarettes hadn't been burned. Smuggling a note into the other compound must be a lot cheaper, though. "That feels like too much, but maybe we could bribe her with a bunch of threads."

Anne immediately made to unravel threads from the blanket until she held about a dozen in her hand. "Let's go!"

"No, we have to wait until after dinner. She'll be working right now," Rachel said.

Anne pouted, before she agreed. "You're probably right. And we need a plan."

For the next hours they tossed ideas at each other on how to best contact Heidi. Rachel felt her hopes rising with every passing minute. If this Heidi girl was as astute and quick-witted as the Frank sisters, she might be the perfect person to reunite Rachel with her sister.

They finally settled for a note indicating they'd wait for her each night from after dinner until curfew at the far end of the fence separating the two compounds. There was exactly one spot where waiting people could linger without being seen from the watchtowers.

"I'll stay here and cover for you, if you ask your friend about Mindel," Rachel said as the time came for them to leave.

"Thank you, and we will certainly ask about your sister," Anne said, giving her a hug.

Rachel waited for their return to the barracks with high spirits, while she took over the sisters' chores of sweeping and scrubbing. She was barely able to concentrate and more than once received a warning slap on her arm from the *kapo*.

Seconds before curfew, Anne and Margot finally slipped into the barracks, with slumping shoulders. Once they'd climbed into the shared bunk, Margot said, "Heidi wasn't there."

"We'll try again tomorrow evening. I'm sure she'll show up. I know she will." Anne wouldn't let a single failed attempt defeat her.

Rachel had come to admire the younger girl for her spunk and determination. While Margot was soft-spoken, kind and obedient, Anne was the complete opposite. Extrovert, outspoken and determined.

The following days passed excruciatingly slowly. Rachel didn't even mind standing for hours during roll call, as long as the seconds ticked by, bringing her closer to finding her little sister. She already imagined seeing her sweet little face, and kissing her soft cheek.

Every evening Margot and Anne left for the agreed-upon place, walking purposefully in the shadows until they reached the fence, where they lurked waiting for Heidi to show up. On the fourth night, Anne returned beaming with joy. "It was my Heidi! Can you imagine that? I'm so happy she's alive."

Rachel bit on her lip, anxious to hear more.

"She promised to return tomorrow night with your sister," Margot said.

"Do you think it's really her?" Rachel asked.

"Probably, yes. The little girl doesn't know her last name, but she knows that she is four years old and used to live on a farm."

"That does sound like it could be my sister." Rachel didn't want to get her hopes up, but couldn't help but pray it really was her Mindel. Then it occurred to her that Mindel was already five and her heart sunk.

"I'm sure it's her. It has to be her," Anne said.

Moved to tears, Rachel couldn't utter a word. Both of the Frank girls hugged her and Margot said, "Tomorrow I'll cover and you go with Anne. I hope you can talk to your sister."

"Talk?" Rachel perked up her ears. "Won't I be able to see her?"

"They put straw inside the barbed wire just a day ago, because there were too many people standing by the fence hoping to catch a glimpse of relatives in the other compound."

"Damn!" Rachel felt cheated, but quickly consoled herself with the fact that talking to her sister was better than nothing. *At least Mindel is alive*, she thought, and despite her intentions not to, a fresh surge of hope blossomed in her chest.

CHAPTER 25

Winter had come with snow and bitter cold. Mindel had always loved the snow. Back home, she and her brothers had used to play outside for hours, building snowmen and igloos, and take the sled for a ride, wrapped in warm clothes from head to toe. When they had returned inside hours later, exhausted and cold, her mother would make them hot milk with honey and settle them in front of the oven, in their terrycloth pajamas. How she missed that time.

Here, she was always cold. She couldn't remember the last time she'd felt warm, not even at night wrapped in the thin blanket and cuddled up against Laszlo and Tina. Since more and more children had arrived, Mother Brinkmann had assigned three or four of them to each bunk, which was actually good, because the other bodies gave off heat, but it also meant they had to sleep pressed together without moving.

Mindel was waiting her turn in the food line, blowing on her hands to get some warmth into her fingertips, which had lost most of their feeling.

She remembered her first winter away from home in another camp with Rachel by her side. In her memory it had been much warmer. She certainly couldn't remember her hands being this cold. She tried to pull the sleeves of her dress over her hands to keep them warm, but found out it wasn't possible.

Without her noticing it, the sleeves were suddenly ending mid-forearm, just like the rest of her dress seemed to have shrunk, barely covering her knees, and she was having a hard time getting the buttons done up.

Since the incident with the SS beating up Laszlo, she'd been scared of the kitchen hut and had refused to set foot anywhere near it. However, that day Mother Brinkmann sent her to fetch their daily ration of bread from there, a chore that normally fell to an older girl, but she had died the day before and most of the other children were too sick to go outside, so Mindel had reluctantly obeyed. With winter Mindel had noticed so many more children dying than usual, it was quite the horrible situation and one could never be too sure not to wake up beside a corpse.

As she now stood waiting for her turn, the horrible images came rushing back and she fidgeted her feet, wanting to run away. But then they'd have no bread. And Mother Brinkmann would be angry with her. Very angry.

The line moved slowly and with each step, her scrunched-up toes painfully bumped against the confinement of her shoes. She curled her toes as much as she could, but that didn't make it any more comfortable either. Walking in these shoes had become excruciatingly painful over the last weeks, but it was still better than going barefoot.

When it was her turn, she reached out her hand to receive the two loaves of bread, recognizing the Russian woman who'd once been so kind when she'd caught her stealing potato peels a long time ago.

"Poor mite," the woman said with a sad smile. "Wait over there until I'm finished, will you?"

Mindel was scared out of her wits, but didn't dare to run away in case the woman called the SS on her. Once the bread was distributed and everyone had gone, the kitchen worker approached her with some ugly gray things in her hand and said, "Here. Take these."

Mindel looked at the woman and back to the things she offered. When recognition hit her and she identified the ugly things as knitted gloves, she almost screamed out with joy. "Thank you so much!"

"You are welcome. Now your fingers will not be so blue," the woman replied in broken German.

Mindel pulled the gloves on, feeling as if she'd been given the most beautiful present in the history of mankind. She thanked the woman again and walked out with her new gloves and two loaves of bread. The bread was the shape of a brick and didn't taste much better than one, but she was still tempted to eat just a tiny bit on her way back. The only thing keeping her from doing so was the fear of punishment by Mother Brinkmann.

Stealing was one of the worst offences a child could commit and the punishment was severe. Since the incident with Laszlo, even more so. First time offenders weren't allowed to listen to the bedtime story about Fluff. Mindel shivered, she wouldn't miss story time for anything in the world, but it could even be worse. Karl, one of the older boys, had eaten half a loaf of bread on his way home from the kitchen, and since it hadn't been the first time either, Herr Brinkmann had expelled him from the barracks.

"Hey, Mindel." Heidi stepped into her path.

"Oh, Heidi, hello! Have you heard from my sister?"

"Can you keep a secret?"

"Of course I can." Mindel stood as tall as possible, trying to show the other girl just how big she was.

"You can't tell anyone and you can't scream."

"I won't." This was getting strange.

"I think I have found her. In the women's camp."

Mindel's heart felt like it stopped for a moment, while tears filled her eyes and her lower lip began to tremble. Suddenly her voice was gone and all she could do was nod.

"Can you sneak out tonight? We can talk to her through the fence. But since any conversation with people from the other compounds is strictly forbidden, we have to be careful. Nobody must see us. Can you meet me at the fence to the women's camp after dinner?"

Mindel nodded, overwhelmed by the emotions storming in on her. She would be there, come hell or high water. For Rachel she would even miss bedtime story with Fluff. "I won't tell anyone."

"Good." Heidi seemed content with Mindel's answer and waved at her as she walked away. Returning to the orphans' barracks Mindel started to worry. What if Mother Brinkmann found out? That woman had the uncanny ability to notice everything. Just like her own mother, Mother Brinkmann seemed to be able to look through walls, blankets and straight into the minds of her charges. Someone had to explain her absence during story time, just in case.

Laszlo. He would help her. A tiny twinge of guilt stabbed at her, because she'd promised Heidi not to tell anyone. But Laszlo didn't count. He would never betray her, and she would need him to cover for her anyway. Heidi would understand. Although to be on the safe side, it was best not to let her know.

Armed with this great news she returned to the orphans' barracks, so elated she barely noticed the pain in her toes.

"Look what I got!" she yelled as soon as she entered the hut, holding up her gloved hands with the bread in them.

"Where did you get those gloves?" Mother Brinkmann cast her a suspicious glance.

"I didn't steal them. Honest! The Russian woman from the kitchen gave them to me. Isn't she nice?"

"Indeed, some people still have kindness in their hearts. You may not believe me now, but in the end, good will prevail over evil." Mother Brinkmann smiled and took the bread from her hands, cutting it up into small slices and giving Mindel half of a slice. Mother Brinkmann never distributed all of the bread, but kept the second loaf of it for dinner, claiming it was best not to eat it all at once, which the children naturally bemoaned. With Mindel's tummy hurting so much, why wouldn't Mother Brinkmann allow them to eat their entire ration? But Mindel had learned not to argue and walked away.

"What's wrong with your leg?" Herr Brinkmann asked as she limped past him. As always, he was rolling cigarettes from the butts the children had picked up from the ground.

She'd never seen him smoke, but since cigarettes in the camp were still considered as good as gold, he used them to buy some of the things they needed.

"Nothing. It's just my shoes that are hurting my feet."

"Let me have a look," he said and she slipped out of her shoe. When he put her bare foot beside the shoe, her toes surpassed the tip by almost an inch.

"Aw, well, you children grow too fast. Let me see what I can do."

Mindel nodded and climbed into her bunk to eat her break-fast—soup and the half slice of bread—and to get some warmth under the thin blanket. Now she just had to wait until evening to go and finally see her sister again.

CHAPTER 26

When the horn sounded for roll call, it felt as if Rachel had only fallen asleep minutes earlier. But despite her tiredness, she jumped off her bunk like the healthy, energetic girl she'd been a year ago.

Anne gave her an encouraging smile. "You look so happy today."

"I am. I can't wait to talk to my sister again. Maybe there's a way to see her. Maybe if I talk to the camp commandant, he'll reunite us?"

Margot shook her head, but Anne touched Rachel's arm and said, "I'm sure something can be done."

Rachel was grateful for the kind words. Anne wasn't like most of the other girls or even women who came here. She was determined and ever mindful of the feelings and needs of others, even though she was only fifteen. For her age, Anne Frank was very mature, but then again, who hadn't grown up way too fast in the midst of this war?

On her way to the assembly place, Rachel examined her orange fingernails, which were slowly growing back in pale pink. It looked quite artistic, as if she'd used orange nail polish and had forgotten to paint a tiny strip. The angry red scar on her hand reminded her of the awful burn that had cut short her ordeal in the Tannenberg camp. Taking up her assigned spot in the courtyard, she let her mind wander back to the ammunition factory.

Since she'd returned to the main camp, despite the smaller rations, she felt better and the constant coughing had subsided. But the best thing was that after several days she'd lost the acid taste in her mouth. She thought about Linda, her companion and friend, who'd always brought positive energy with her. What might have happened to her? Was she still alive? How about her other former workmates? How many of them were still alive? She shrugged, and determined she shouldn't be thinking about those types of things. It was too depressing.

Living in the here and now was awful enough, there was no need to burden herself with worries she could do nothing about. In that moment, she wanted to concentrate her entire energy on finding Mindel, who there was a real chance had survived—against the odds. She squared her shoulders, standing straight with the newfound hope, and couldn't help the tiniest trace of a smile appearing on her face as memories of her tough little wildcat of a sister flooded her. That day before her birthday, hanging precariously from the apple tree—

"You, over there," the guard barked at her.

Rachel blinked several times as she realized she'd allowed her mind to drift and didn't have a clue as to what was happening. When the guard raised his baton, she hurried to the area he indicated, fear gripping her as she didn't have the slightest idea why or for what she had been selected.

"What's going on?" she asked one of the other women, dismayed that while she'd been daydreaming, she'd forgotten to actively try looking sickly enough to avoid being selected.

"Work detail. Salt mines."

"The salt mines?" Rachel's knees wobbled and were about to give out. Only the thought of a truncheon slamming down on her kept her from falling, while her mind screamed: *No! Not now! Not when I'm so close to seeing my sister again!*

She wanted to hurl herself at the guard, scratch out his eyes, strangle him… or beg for mercy… but she did none of those things. Instead she stayed frozen in place, knowing that nothing she did would change the guard's mind, but the wrong thing could mean her death. And then she would never see Mindel again.

There was still hope: this might be one of the work details where people returned each night to the camp to sleep in the barracks and with some luck she might return in time for dinner and be able to meet Mindel at the fence.

"Move! Fast!" the SS guard barked.

Rachel forced her feet to walk in line with the other women, resisting the urge to look back. But with every step away from the camp her hopes vanished some more, until one hour later they approached the same train ramp where she and Mindel had arrived so many months ago.

No! Please not in the railcars! But there was no doubt about the Nazis' intentions and soon enough all the women had been herded into the waiting cattle wagons. Once the doors were locked and bolted, the only shred of hope left was that the journey would actually take her to the salt mines and not to the unimaginable horrors of the extermination camps that the women coming from Auschwitz had told them about.

CHAPTER 27

Finally, the day drew to an end and it was time to line up for dinner. Mindel was the first in the queue and wolfed down her tepid soup even more quickly than usual. She impressed once again on Laszlo the need to cover for her absence and darted off to meet Heidi next to the fence.

It was such an exciting turn of events, her cheeks were burning hot and, for the first time in weeks, she didn't feel cold. Once she'd found Rachel everything would turn out just fine. Maybe her sister could even come to live with her in the orphans' barracks. Mother Brinkmann for sure wouldn't mind having another big girl to help her with the smaller children.

"Heidi!" she gasped, out of breath, as soon as she saw the girl.

"Shush!" Heidi scolded her. "We mustn't draw any attention to ourselves. We'll stay in the shadows waiting. No words until we hear steps approach, understood?"

Mindel nodded, ashamed of her exuberance. Like everyone else she knew it was never a good idea to alert the SS. As long as the children kept quiet, the SS usually left them alone, since they had more important things to do.

Heidi held her hand as they stood near the fence and waited. Once they heard steps approach and Mindel's heart beat so fast she couldn't hear anything but the rushing of blood in her ears.

Heidi held a finger in front of her lips and Mindel understood. She wouldn't make a single sound.

The steps were loud and heavy—SS. Once they were gone, Mindel whispered, "Why have they put this straw in the fence? How are we supposed to see my sister?"

"The straw was put there because too many people were looking for friends and relatives in the other part. That's why you can only talk to your sister, not see her."

The explanation felt like a punch to her gut and Mindel had to hold back her tears. Why wouldn't the SS guards want them to see their family? There were so many things she didn't grasp. Nothing in this camp made sense to her, but since grown-ups tended to behave in a peculiar way, she'd always shrugged it away. But this time? Someone had to stand up to these men in black uniforms and tell them how ridiculous their behavior was. She promised herself that when she grew up she wouldn't let anyone push her around.

Mindel's feet were getting numb standing motionless in the too-small shoes and icy cold crept up her bare legs. Mother Brinkmann had shown her how to wrap them in sheets of old newspaper, held together by threads from a blanket. It had taken Mindel hours of practice until she finally managed to properly loop a bow that was neither too loose nor too tight. The newspaper helped somewhat, mostly against gusts of wind, but couldn't stop the chill spreading from her feet deep into her bones.

She gave a cursory glance at Heidi, hoping the older girl would allow her to jump from one leg to the other, to get the blood circulating again. But Heidi shook her head and put her finger over her lips again. Soft footsteps approached and then stopped.

"Heidi, are you there?" a female voice whispered from the other side of the fence.

Mindel couldn't contain her excitement any longer and yelled, "Yes. Yes. Is Rachel with you?"

A silence ensued on the other side, until Heidi scolded her in a low voice, "Not so loud, Mindel."

She pressed her hand over her mouth, anxious to do as she was told. But the words spoken next shattered all her resolve.

"It's me. Anne. But Rachel couldn't come. She's been selected for a work detail."

Mindel had no idea what that meant and wanted to ask a thousand questions, but Heidi warned her, "Keep silent. We'll talk later."

Then Heidi and this other girl called Anne chatted for a while. The disappointment was so huge that Mindel was completely focused on keeping the tears at bay and thus didn't pay attention to anything the two girls talked about.

"We have to go," Heidi said and nudged Mindel's elbow.

Almost automatically, she put her feet into motion, when Anne called over the fence. "Hey, Mindel. Rachel always talked about your special friend, Paula. Do you have her with you?"

With a sad smile Mindel withdrew her doll from inside her dress and held her up high, even though Anne wouldn't be able to see her. "Paula, my doll. Rachel made her for me and she always called her my special friend."

Heidi wrapped an arm around her shoulder. "Now we know that she really is your sister."

"But…" Mindel courageously held back her tears and wanted to send Anne greetings for Rachel, but at that moment a vicious voice barked on the other side of the fence.

"You! Get away from the fence. *Schnell!*"

They heard shuffling feet, stomping footfalls and then nothing. Anne was gone.

"Don't be sad," Heidi tried to console her. "We know your sister is alive, and that's more than some others can say about their family."

"But… why did they take her away?" Mindel lost her battle not to cry and heavy tears rolled down her cheeks.

"I don't know why any of this is happening, but hopefully she'll be back soon. I'll go and talk to Anne whenever I can, and as soon as your sister returns to the camp, she'll find a way to let us know."

Mindel was so sad. Devastated.

Despite Heidi's reassuring words she couldn't see anything positive in what had just happened. She'd been so excited to talk to Rachel and now this!

Scuffing her feet and wiping the tears off her face she returned to the orphans' barracks, sneaking inside just when Mother Brinkmann closed the book about Cin-cin, and asked what Fluff's newest adventure should be about. But not even Fluff could brighten her mood this night.

Much later, when she heard the heavy breathing of the sleeping children, she finally let her tears fall and cried herself to sleep.

The next day, Mother Brinkmann returned from running an errand in the middle of the day with a pair of shoes in her hands.

"Mindel, these are for you."

Mindel looked at the brown, battered shoes that seemed to be at least double the size of her own.

"Try them on," Mother Brinkmann urged her.

The shoes were way too big, and her heels slipped out with every step. Mindel giggled. "It feels like walking in Father's rain boots."

"They were the only ones we could get. Wait a moment." Mother Brinkmann went to her secret stash of useful things and returned with two newspaper sheets. She crumpled them and stuffed each one deep into the shoes. "Try again."

"Much better." Mindel beamed at the prospect that her toes wouldn't hurt so much anymore. She walked around, still unsteady in her oversized shoes. When she walked back, Mother Brinkmann was holding her old shoes in her hand, a furrow across her forehead.

"Timmy, come here," she called and a small, skinny boy of four years obeyed. Mindel looked at him. Timmy was so much smaller than she was. How come he was the same age?

Mother Brinkmann gave Timmy Mindel's shoes, and then she gave Timmy's shoes to a girl of two who'd just learned to walk in her stockinged feet and for lack of shoes hadn't been allowed to leave the hut when winter had set in.

"Can I have new shoes, too? My toes always feel bruised," Laszlo said.

Mother Brinkmann asked him to remove his shoes and socks and then frowned when she saw his toes. "Laszlo, why didn't you say something sooner? These are going to get infected if you're not careful. You can't continue to walk around in these shoes, and I don't know when Herr Brinkmann will be able to trade for a pair of shoes big enough for you. The bigger, the more in-demand they are." She shook her head. "I'll have to cut a hole in the toe of each shoe. That would give your toes some room to move about."

Laszlo grinned. "Let's do that."

"But you'll have to make sure and wiggle your toes when standing in the food queue. If you don't they'll freeze up and fall off."

"No, they won't," he said with a cheeky grin.

"Yes, they will. Now, promise me you'll keep moving your toes and I'll make a hole in your shoes."

"I promise."

Mother Brinkmann went to work and when she was finished, he walked around the barracks, modeling his open-toed shoes for everyone. The other children giggled with delight.

One of the girls who always pretended to be grown up looked at Laszlo and rolled her eyes. "He's going to be freezing all of the time now and his shoes will be full of snow and mud."

"Well, at least he won't have to worry about getting an infection that requires him to lose his entire foot," Mother Brinkmann said, effectively ending that discussion.

Several children begged Mother Brinkmann to cut the caps off of their shoes as well. She refused, explaining she wasn't going to disfigure perfectly good shoes. The children accepted her ruling and immediately set their minds to making up a rhyme about Laszlo's toes falling off. A few of them, including Mindel, started to walk around on their heels, pretending they had no toes at all. Giggling hilariously, they bumped into each other, and played at being angry about the clumsy toe-less people milling about.

CHAPTER 28

Utter desperation had conquered Rachel. Two interminable weeks earlier, she'd found her sister and missed meeting her by a whisker when the evil Nazis had selected her to work in the salt mines.

With exhaustion tugging at every fiber in her body, every day she trudged the short march from her new camp to the mine. Everything here was deplorable: the living conditions, the food, the work… and above all the salt.

It was everywhere, settling like dust on the skin of the women—converting them into whitish ghost-like creatures, entering every crevice of their bodies, rubbing them raw, destroying skin, and preventing wounds from healing. The salty smell pursued her every minute of every day and its taste kept her in perpetual thirst. Soon her lips became chapped and her throat ached. She swore that she'd never again eat a single morsel of salt should she make it out of there alive.

From morning to night, the women had to toil in the underground mines, never once seeing the light of day. The rations were so meager she never noticed the difference between before a meal and after, and regularly forgot whether she'd already eaten or not. After a while she decided to stop bothering. It didn't matter. Nothing mattered anymore. Not the hunger, not the pain, and certainly not the world outside this damned mine.

Armed with a pickaxe she hacked at the rock, breaking out the salt. Where the work at the ammunition factory had been tedious and perilous, here it was back-breaking physical labor, the kind that could wear down even a strong and healthy man.

But since there were no strong men around, the emaciated women made of skin and bone were the ones destined to break out the salty rock and then grind it to tiny pieces that were later used to refine the pure salt. Every day Rachel and her work detail climbed into the shaft, where the salt was deposited between layers of rock deep inside the earth.

There was no respite from the salt and it took only a few days until Rachel's skin was raw from exposure. The slightest sweating or rubbing irritated her skin to the point that she believed it was catching fire. The worst, though, were her hands. Covered with blisters from the pickaxe there seemed to be no patch of intact skin left on the raw flesh and every time she came into contact with the vicious salt—which was constantly—it was literally salt rubbing into her wounds.

Rachel was in so much agony at all times that she had forgotten how it felt to be pain-free. The only good thing about working in the shaft was that the SS rarely bothered them down there. Even the comparatively mild temperatures in the mine turned out more of a curse than a blessing, because every time she returned back to the face of the earth the harsh cold bit into her bones and numbed her limbs. Though at least then, she didn't feel the pain anymore.

Every day Rachel collapsed deeper into a state of depression, until she no longer found a reason to stay alive. *Let the Nazis win*, she found herself thinking. She was ready to give them the satisfaction of dying right then and there. Rachel wasn't the only one pushed to the edge of sanity, since most of the women had lost the will to survive, simply existing in a state of complete apathy.

In her few lucid moments she remembered her shock at the first sight of those beings who were called *Muselmänner* in camp jargon, during her first days in Bergen-Belsen. Back then she'd sworn never to become one of them, however much she suffered from the deadly hunger disease—a combination of starvation and exhaustion.

But now she realized, with even greater shock, that she was on her way to becoming one of them, maybe she had already turned into one—a former human being who'd become apathetic to anything including her own fate and was unresponsive to even the most barbaric treatment by the Nazis. And she found she didn't care anymore. She'd reached the point where she truly and honestly couldn't gather up enough strength to even feel concerned about what was happening to her. It was as if she had already ceased to exist and by some divine mistake, her dried-up shell continued to walk the earth without an actual being inside.

Those women who still had a clear thought in their minds often actively sought to end their misery. Just this morning one of the women had broken away from the line during their march to the salt mine. The SS guards hadn't wavered for a second and shot her in the back, leaving a darkened spot on the pristine white snow.

Rachel lifted her shovel once more, her muscles screaming in protest and her heart filling with envy at the stranger's escape from this living hell. She ignored the pain, emptied the shovel into the mine car and picked up another load.

Her agony didn't matter. Nothing mattered. Her mind seemed to be filled with cotton balls and the viscosity of her thoughts wouldn't allow her to imagine anything beyond her current surroundings. Shovel up. Unload. Down. Fill. Up. Unload. Down. Fill. Up…

Working back to back with another woman, she never once paused. Her throat was rougher than a grater, and what wouldn't she have given for a glass of water? Alas, there'd be no water until dinner time, and even the alluring snow tantalizing her to bend down and grab a handful on her march to the camp was off limits. *Verboten.* Bend down and die. Stop working and die. Continue working and die another day.

At night, Rachel lay down on the bunk and closed her eyes, wishing death might claim her in her sleep and save her from another miserable day in the mines. The agony from both her sore muscles and bones clashed with a different type of pain coming from inside her body. It was more than just the ubiquitous hunger, and felt as if her very organs were not cooperating anymore. Together they created an explosion reaching every single cell in her body, causing her heart to stutter, red stars to appear in front of her fluttering eyes and her mind to go numb.

A few days later, she snapped. As the mine car rolled along the tracks, Rachel suddenly stretched her back, threw down her shovel and launched herself in front of the railcar.

"What are you doing?" the woman working next to her asked, jerking Rachel back.

"I'm done."

"So, what? You're going to let the railcar run over you? That's completely idiotic."

"Why, because I want to take control back of when I die and how?"

"No, I understand that, but there are changes happening. The war is in its last throes. I can feel it."

"I can't," Rachel said, trying to shake off the other woman's arm as she took a step forward. But the opportunity had passed; the car was already in front of her.

Rachel felt like crying but no tears would come. The SS wouldn't let her live, and this woman wouldn't let her die. She didn't want to be here any longer in this twilight zone between life and death. But with the railcar passed by and an SS guard approaching, what choice did she have but to pick up her shovel and go back to work?

"Hold on, dear, because it won't take much longer," the other woman said. "And because we have to survive. We just have to."

CHAPTER 29

Mindel and Laszlo were standing in line for the orphans' barracks bread ration when Heidi's friend Laura came along.

"Hey, Mindel, hey, Laszlo. Have you heard there's another transport going to Switzerland real soon?" she said, coming over. When her gaze fell on Mindel's oversized shoes, she glared at her. "Where did you get those from?"

"Why? Herr Brinkmann gave them to me, because my own were getting too small."

"You... little thief... you... vulture... body-stripper... you...!" Laura's voice heaved with emotions and Mindel couldn't make any sense of her words. "Give me the shoes, right now! They belong to Augusta!" Laura screamed, attracting the attention of the adults, and unfortunately of the SS guards, who strode toward them, menacing with their truncheons.

It took Laszlo only a second to take a decision and he whisper-yelled, "Run. Fast."

Losing their place in the line was an awful thing, because it meant risking that all the rations were distributed before they reached the end, and then they'd get scolded by Mother Brinkmann. But on the other hand, being beaten by the guards was an even worse prospect.

The three children took off and arrived breathless behind the latrines, where they sought cover. Because of the horrible stink, the SS wouldn't follow them there.

When Laura recovered her breath, she raved at Mindel, "Take those shoes off."

"Now, wait a minute. I'm sure Mother Brinkmann paid for them. Maybe we should ask Augusta?" Laszlo defended her.

"You can't! She's dead!"

"Dead?" Mindel yelled, looking in horror at the shoes that suddenly felt like millstones around her feet, dragging her into the mass grave where Augusta waited for them. Desperate to get rid of these cursed things, she bent down to undo the laces.

"What are you doing?" Laszlo asked.

"I don't want them. Not if Laura's friend died…"

"Don't be stupid," he said harshly. "That's how it works in the camp. Augusta can't use them any longer and if you take them off, you'll be walking around barefoot in the snow."

Mindel stopped what she was doing and considered the impact of returning the shoes. Mother Brinkmann's warning echoed in her head and she whispered, "I don't want my feet to freeze and fall off."

The prospect of Mindel freezing to death brushed away Laura's outrage and she conceded generously, "You can have them. Augusta would want to help another child with her shoes."

Mindel had noticed for a while now that even her best friends had become increasingly irritable and lashed out at anyone with no reason at all. She shrugged it off as a thing that happened when children grew up. Graciously, she extended her hand to Laura. "Friends again?"

"Friends again." Laura shook her hand and trotted off.

Mindel and Laszlo returned to the food line where they were lucky enough to receive the last two loaves of bread. On the walk back to their barracks, Laszlo tried to persuade Mindel to sneak with him onto the transport to Switzerland, but she wouldn't be swayed. Instead she begged him to stay, but to no avail.

That night he snuck out, promising Mindel they'd see each other again after the war, when he'd be waiting for her in Switzerland. When he left, she returned despondently to sleep.

In the morning she refused to get up and even to have breakfast. With that many children in the barracks she didn't expect anyone to notice, but sometime in the morning, Mother Brinkmann sent Sandy to come looking for them.

"Mindel, are you sick?"

"No. Just tired." She pressed her face into Paula's dirty dress.

"Where's Laszlo?"

Mindel looked up at the older girl, and although Laszlo had impressed on her not to tell anyone, she couldn't resist the piercing gaze. "I'm not supposed to say."

Sandy's stare intensified. "What exactly aren't you supposed to say?"

Mindel studied her bitten fingernails and whispered, "He snuck out last night to go to Switzerland."

"He did what?"

"To sneak on that transport to Switzerland." Mindel felt the shame burn her ears.

"Oh my God, why are you little ones always so stupid?"

Mindel didn't even protest being called little and stupid in the same sentence, so desolate was she.

"We have to go and get him back," Sandy said.

Relief flooded her and she nodded. Everything would be just fine and Laszlo would come back to her. Then a frightening thought occurred to her. "We can't tell Mother Brinkmann, she'll be furious."

"Furious might be an understatement." Sandy sighed. "We won't tell her. If she asks we can say Laszlo went to the latrines real early in the morning because he was so sick with the runs."

Mindel nodded, grateful that Sandy was taking charge of the situation. As soon as they had left the barracks, Sandy asked her, "Where is this transport to Switzerland gathering?"

"In the special camp."

Sandy's eyes became big as saucers. "We can't just go there. How did Laszlo plan to pass the fence?"

"I'm not sure…" Mindel noticed the urgency in Sandy's voice and squeezed her eyes shut in an effort to think very hard. "He said something about a repair crew. And a surefire way to get on the truck." She almost broke down in tears, because she couldn't remember any more details.

Sandy took her hand. "We'll go over to the fence and see if we find him there."

They trudged across the length of the star camp to the fence that separated it from the other compounds. Usually Mindel never got outside this early in the morning and seeing all the inmates standing for roll call on the *Appellplatz* caused goosebumps to erupt all over her body.

"We have to hide behind the barracks," Sandy said, since nobody was supposed to walk around during roll call. They continued their journey creeping under the cover of the flat barracks and had just reached the one closest to the fence, when turmoil broke out at the gate to the special camp.

Mindel's heart missed a few beats when she recognized Laszlo dangling like a kitten from the arm of an SS man who had him by the scruff of the neck. Without thinking, she rushed forward to help her friend, but a few steps later Sandy had caught up with her and yanked her back into the shadow of the barracks.

"What the hell are you doing?"

"I have to help Laszlo," Mindel whined.

"There's nothing we can do, and you know it!" Sandy scolded her.

"But… but… they will hurt him!" Now that she was crouched against the wall, catching her breath, she realized how stupid her action had been.

Sandy gave her a sad look, but whatever she was about to say was interrupted by Laszlo's pitiful howling when the guard set him down just long enough to crack his whip and unleash his wrath on the boy.

"Sandy! We need to do something!" Mindel screamed, until she felt a hand wrapped tightly across her mouth.

"Shush. Or do you want them to beat us, too?"

Her entire body trembling, Mindel couldn't even nod her agreement and barely registered when Sandy said, "We'll have to go get Mother Brinkmann." The next thing she knew Sandy had dragged her around the corner and, taking the path at the far end of the camp next to the latrines, she stumbled behind the older girl until they reached the orphans' barracks.

"What on earth has happened to you?" Mother Brinkman apprised with a single glance at the two girls that something truly awful had transpired.

Mindel herself was too shaken to speak, so she let Sandy do the explaining. "Laszlo got caught sneaking into the special camp."

"Whatever does the stupid boy want over there?"

"He wanted to get on the transport to Switzerland," Sandy said.

"Oh dear." Mother Brinkmann paled. "How bad is it?"

"Very."

Mother Brinkmann gave a gasp of dismay, turned and headed for the door to the barracks. "You children are to stay inside until I return. I mean it. Not one of you is to leave this building. Do you understand? Sandy and Michael, you are in charge." Then she hurried out of the barracks, concern etched on her emaciated face.

"What's wrong?"

"Where's she going?"

"What did you do?"

The questions kept coming until Mindel decided she might as well answer. "Laszlo was trying to get onto the transport to Switzerland… A guard caught him."

Her statement was met with shocked silence. Several long seconds later the children began talking all at once; they were still sitting in the hut, speculating about Laszlo's fortunes, when Mother Brinkmann called to them from outside the barracks.

"Open the door and be quick about it."

One of the older boys opened the door and everyone stood up and watched curiously as Mother Brinkmann walked in, carrying Laszlo in her arms. Though Mindel could scarcely believe it was the same boy she'd seen half an hour ago dangling from the SS man's arm, because his face and body were completely covered in blood, his eyes swollen shut and an open cut crossing his face. His arm hung at a strange angle from his shoulder and Mindel involuntarily groaned. The whip lashing she witnessed had looked horrible from far away, but seeing Laszlo's battered body from close up was almost too much to bear. Cold fear gripped at her heart.

"Hurry, children, we must see if we can help him. If I'd arrived a moment later they would have beaten him to death."

Mindel stared at her friend in horror as Mother Brinkmann began to assess his injuries. Laszlo's mangled face was barely recognizable and the new adult teeth he'd been so proud of were missing, making him look worse than a scarecrow. He only had one of his shoes on, his toe poking comically out of the hole that Herr Brinkmann had cut into them. She looked away, because it made her stomach hurt. After the first shock she became angry. Why did the SS have to do this? Why did he go there in the first place? Hadn't she warned him this was too dangerous?

But then she looked at Mother Brinkmann, confident the woman could make everything better. Under her care, Laszlo would soon be as good as new again, playing with Mindel and the other children.

"We have to take him to the infirmary," Herr Brinkmann said, assisting his wife in undressing the boy and cleaning his wounds. Laszlo didn't even stir when the wet cloth touched his bruised skin.

Mindel crept forward. "Please don't. People don't come back from there."

Mother Brinkmann glanced at her for a short moment, before she returned to her work. "Mindel, Laszlo is hurt very badly. He might not survive this."

"Please, don't let him die."

"I'll do my best, child. Now, everyone go, I need to concentrate."

Mindel moved to her bunk and watched as Mother Brinkmann tended to Laszlo's injuries. She kept waiting for him to wake up, but his eyelids were barely even fluttering. Since there was no way he could climb up to his bunk in his weakened condition, Mother Brinkmann put him in the lowest tier of the bunk next to hers.

Mindel pressed Paula against her heart and walked over to get the treasures she and Laszlo possessed: a few round pebbles, a glass shard and a long string that must have been a shoelace once. Here in the orphans' barracks they didn't have to fear for their mugs at all times, because Mother Brinkmann stored them all next to the entrance and no child would have dared to steal one of them.

Carrying their possessions she walked the way back to where Laszlo was lying and said, "I'll stay with him."

"He'll be asleep most of the time," Mother Brinkmann said, stroking Mindel's head. "You go and play with the other children."

"No. I will take care of him."

Mother Brinkmann must have noticed her determination, because she simply said, "Make sure he's always covered with the blanket and doesn't get cold."

Mindel nodded seriously. She would make sure Laszlo was comfortable and got well.

***

For the next few days, she watched over him, day and night, refusing to leave his side unless she absolutely had to. She talked to him in the same way she talked to her doll, not minding that he didn't answer. In the depths of her soul she knew he heard and understood her and that was all she needed. But when he still didn't open his eyes, she became scared. What if… No, she wouldn't let herself finish that thought. It was too awful. She settled beside him, simply staring at the wall and reliving all the funny, scary, and wonderful things they had done together. Without his support, she felt so lonely, and it was her own fault.

"I should never have allowed you to leave. I should have made sure you stayed in our bunk that night," she whispered.

"You knew he was planning to do this?" Mother Brinkmann had appeared by the bunk with the hot stinking soup they were given for dinner.

Tears spilled as Mindel couldn't keep them inside any longer. Mother Brinkmann gave the mug to some other child and then pulled Mindel onto her lap, rocking her back and forth the way Rachel had always done after Mother… Her sadness overwhelmed her and a flood of tears rushed down her cheeks.

Sometime later, when she'd finally stopped sobbing, she told Mother Brinkmann what weighed so heavily on her conscience. "He wanted me to go with him, but I said it was too dangerous. It's all my fault."

Renewed sobbing, albeit without the tears, shook her body in Mother Brinkmann's arms as she tried to come to grips with her guilt for not taking care of her best friend. Laszlo had been watching out for her for such a long time and the one time he'd needed her, she'd abandoned him.

"It wasn't your fault. Laszlo is such a determined boy. When he set his mind to doing something, there was nothing you could have done to keep him from doing it."

Mindel snuggled against the woman who'd become her surrogate mother, wanting to believe her, but she knew better. She could have prevented all of this, if only she had... "I should have told you about his plans."

Mother Brinkmann didn't protest. She simply held Mindel closer in her arms and gently kissed the top of her head.

CHAPTER 30

A new trainload of women arrived at the salt mine, bringing with them news of what was happening in the outside world. According to these women, who'd been transferred from other camps in occupied Poland, the Red Army was storming across Poland, and the Nazis were struggling to keep the prisoners from being liberated at their hands.

Rumors also suggested that the Western Allies had already crossed into German territory over the Rhine river. Not that anyone could confirm the rumors, but if the nervous behavior of the guards was anything to go by, then Germany really was about to lose the war. And soon.

Rachel found a tiny shard of hope again. She'd withstood the harsh treatment for such a long time, she was determined to hang on to her life just a little while longer by sheer willpower, counting the days until the Allies—Eastern or Western, she didn't care—liberated them.

One of the encouraging signs was what seemed to be constant Allied bombings, presumably of German cities. Underground in the salt mine, the women weren't privy to anything going on outside, but during the march to and from the camp, and at night in their freezing barracks, they heard the aircraft flying over their heads.

They were invariably American or British planes. The last Luftwaffe fighter Rachel had seen must have been weeks ago. She didn't especially like the bombing raids, but so far, all the planes had passed their tiny village and flown on, she guessed to more populated places. Sometimes at night, she saw the flicker of what had to be a burning city on the horizon.

Trudging to the mine for another grueling shift, Rachel heard the air raid siren scream across the landscape and like rabbits in flight the SS guards took cover, leaving the women in the middle of the road.

For a moment, Rachel considered running away, but discarded the thought as they too attempted to take cover by the side of the road. It was impossible to escape. In her current condition she couldn't run, only move very slowly, and even if she found cover in the flat surroundings, she'd be discovered in no time at all. The villagers were hostile to the Jewish prisoners and one glimpse at her skeletal appearance would alert them to the truth and they'd be able to bask in the glory of returning an escaped prisoner to the camp.

She had often wondered how and when people had turned into anti-Semites. The area around the salt mines reminded her of her home in Upper Bavaria, except for the missing hills. But the fields, currently covered with snow, the cattle fences, the forlorn farmhouses huddled against the shelter of a copse of trees and the small village nearby, it was all eerily similar to the place where she'd grown up and spent many happy days before the Nazis had come to power.

Born in 1926, even with her limited experience, she had witnessed how the Jewish people were steadily treated worse, ostracized, having things they'd taken for granted taken away, until they ultimately ended up being taken away themselves. Even though she had been too young to understand the reasons, she had certainly felt the results. Having to leave school, not being allowed to go to the dances with her former classmates, and having to give their own farm to Old Hans, just so they could stay. It was a scandalous wrongdoing, but nobody had stood up and raised his or her voice.

Nobody had spoken up for the Jews. Not even the Jews themselves. Her parents had always hoped it wouldn't get worse, that somehow people would come to their senses one day and see that the Jews weren't the reason for their ailments. That they were Germans like everyone else.

Crouching in a ditch together with several women she mused once more about the injustice in this world, when she heard a rattling noise and looked up to see in the distance a train making its way through the landscape.

Within moments two bombers that had been flying high in the sky, swooped down, strafing a train with their deadly load. A bomb burst and the train abruptly halted, spewing its fleeing passengers outside. Rachel shut her eyes against the blinding light from the darting flames, hearing deafening explosion after explosion. Covering her ears, she crouched deeper into the ditch until the noises stopped.

She opened her eyes again and saw multitudes of people, small as ants, fleeing from the train and desperately seeking cover, but the flat land provided none. Squinting, her gaze followed several of the fleeing passengers and sighed with relief when she saw none of them wore the telltale striped uniform of prisoners—that in fact they were Nazi troops. A swooshing sound indicated the return of the planes and she screamed at the sight of them nosediving to the ground and then turning horizontal in an impossibly low altitude, flying at the same height as the tops of the trees and hunting the running passengers.

The strafing was vicious and desperate screams of people who were mowed down by the Allied aircraft drowned out the roaring motors. She couldn't help but cheer for the pilots, spurring them on to kill as many of the hated Nazis as possible.

After two more rounds of circling back and forth, no running people were left. The bombers had accomplished their goal and gracefully wiggled their wings as they returned high into the sky, flying back in the direction from which they had come.

It didn't take long after the planes were out of sight until the SS guards emerged from wherever they'd been hiding and unleashed their wrath on the women over the destruction of the train. Everyone suspected of dallying or enjoying the Allies' success received a share of whiplashes or baton blows.

While the air raid had given Rachel and the other exhausted women a small respite, now the marching speed was doubled, meaning more than one woman fell behind. Those who didn't die instantly were poked and punched with batons until they got up again, or were shot in the head.

The incident had given yet more hope to Rachel, though. That woman who'd thwarted Rachel's attempt at suicide must have told the truth, and the end was near. The end of the Nazis' "Thousand Year Reign" after less than a decade. And with it, surely there would be liberation of all their prisoners by the Allies? With that thought in mind, Rachel gathered the strength to keep up with the column, keeping hold of the hope that the sight of enemy planes on the horizon had planted in her heart.

She just prayed the rumors they were hearing were true and the end of the war was really coming, that it wasn't just the fevered imagination of prisoners like her, holding on to whatever they could. Albeit she couldn't muster much sympathy or compassion for the German civilians who had died today, because they were the same people who hadn't lifted a single finger to help the plea of the persecuted Jews, even if they hadn't actively participated in the atrocities.

I wish the Allies would kill all of them! Every last one! The violence of her thoughts shocked her to the core. Before her deportation, she'd never wished evil on another person, well, maybe with the exception of Herr Keller, but it seemed the last shred of her humanity had been rubbed away by the penetrating salt and she'd become an evil soul, just like the Nazis themselves.

Too exhausted to come up with any further coherent thoughts, her mind shut down and once again she was reduced to a barely functioning shell. Down in the salt mine, her hands seemed to take up the pickaxe all by themselves and she listened only with half an ear to the whispers of the other women.

"The Allies must be close."

"God, I can't wait for the time they liberate us."

"And kill all the Nazis."

"If the Allies don't kill them, I swear to God, I'll strangle the Mouse with my own hands."

Rachel found herself nodding. The women used nicknames for most of the guards, and the Mouse had received his for his mouse-like face. His behavior, though, was that of a cat, playing cruel games with the prisoners, before killing them for the joy of it.

CHAPTER 31

Mindel returned to Laszlo's side, watching over him, wiping his forehead when he was sweating and snuggling against him when he froze. She fed him his soup with a sippy cup that was usually reserved for the babies. And finally, one day, he opened his eyes once more, looked at her and whispered, "Mindel? What are you doing here?"

But before she could answer, his lids fluttered and shut again.

"Please, Laszlo," she begged him. "If you wake up again I promise I'll do whatever you want. I'll play Jews and SS with you all day long and I'll even be the Jew."

His eyes fluttered open and he croaked, "Mindel."

"Mother Brinkmann, he's awake!" Mindel cried.

Mother Brinkmann and her husband both rushed to Laszlo's bedside at the encouraging sign of consciousness, but judging by their grave faces when looking at him, they didn't seem very happy.

Mindel didn't understand why. Laszlo had finally spoken to her and his pale face had taken on a reddish hue.

"Laszlo, do you know where you are?" Herr Brinkmann asked.

The boy glanced around, wordlessly staring at the two adults, before he slipped back to sleep again.

"He was awake. He spoke to me. Really."

"I'm sure he did." Mother Brinkmann patted Mindel's shoulder. "It must have exhausted him. But it's a good sign."

The next day Laszlo developed a fever, though, and Mother Brinkmann made leg compresses for him out of two rags soaked with snow. Mindel's heart constricted every time she looked at her friend who seemed so small and weak in his bunk.

By dinner time, Mother Brinkmann shooed Mindel out of the bunk to eat her soup and when she returned, Laszlo was sitting upright in his bed for the first time since the horrible incident. He seemed to be fever-free and broke out into a huge grin at the sight of her.

"You're up," she said and rushed toward him to give him a hug, but he winced under her embrace. "Ouch."

"Oh, I'm sorry. Are you still hurting?"

He put on a brave face. "Only a little bit."

"Now he's going to be fine, right?" She turned around to look at Mother Brinkmann who was bringing Laszlo a few biscuits from her secret stash.

"We can only hope. He's not yet over the hump."

Mindel didn't believe a single word. Laszlo was fine. The children gathered for their bedtime story with Fluff, and he received the honor of choosing the night's topic.

"Fluff wants to play in the snow."

Mother Brinkmann smiled and started telling the story, while Mindel sidled closer up to Laszlo holding his hand. Despite Fluff's thrilling adventure, Laszlo fell asleep halfway through story time. When all the children were in their bunks, and a silence fell over the barracks, Mindel felt a lightness she hadn't felt since Laszlo's beating. Everything would turn out fine.

During the night she woke, because someone had hit her square in the face. She blinked a few times, until she realized it was Laszlo thrashing like a madman beside her, whispering incomprehensible words. Once again, cold fear took hold of her, even as she tried to comfort him.

"Shush. Laszlo, be quiet. Are you hurt? Or cold? Anything?" With every unanswered question her panic grew until she couldn't take it any longer and jumped out of the bunk to wake Mother Brinkmann. But the woman was already up and on her way, bending over Laszlo with a worried expression on her face.

"His fever is back," she said, after pressing her hand to his forehead.

"Can you wrap his legs with the cold rags again?" asked Mindel, but Mother Brinkmann only shook her head.

"I'm afraid not. The barracks are locked at night. We can only hope he makes it until morning."

Despite Mother Brinkmann's attempts to convince her otherwise, Mindel refused to leave Laszlo's side. "He needs me now. I will take care of him." She placed his head on her lap, stroking his hair the way Rachel had done to her so often. "You'll be just fine. Paula and I are watching over you, don't you worry," she whispered, and then remembered what he'd said to her in the early days. She repeated his own words while stroking his hair. "You just have to stay alive a little while longer. It won't be long before the Allies will come and rescue us."

Throughout the night, his breathing came in rags and spurts, and several times he thrashed about, mumbling unintelligible words, but every time she stroked his head, he relaxed and fell asleep again.

When the wake-up alarm sounded and the barracks' doors were unlocked from outside, Mindel wanted to weep with relief. Now Mother Brinkmann could gather some snow to make those leg wraps for him and then he'd be fine again.

But in that moment, a full ten days after he'd been beaten, probably at the same time as he should have arrived in Switzerland, he simply stopped breathing. Mindel looked at him aghast and shook his shoulders. "Stop playing, Laszlo! That's not funny! I order you to breathe! Don't you know that you'll die if you don't breathe? Wake up now, Laszlo. You need to wake up!"

Alerted by Mindel's yelling Mother Brinkmann rushed to the bunk, but there was nothing she could do for him. Mindel felt a hand on her shoulder, trying to gently pull her away from her best friend. Desperate, she wrapped her arms around Laszlo's thin, bruised body, willing him to wake up again. He was only joking, teasing her like he always did. He wasn't really dead. He couldn't be. He was her best friend.

"You can't be dead! I won't allow it!" She stomped with her foot and balled her hands into fists. "You have to come back. I need you!"

But Laszlo had left the world behind. As his body turned cold, she knew then that, despite his promise never to abandon her, he had done just that and she would never see him again. That she was all alone. Not even Paula was a solace, because she was only a stupid doll… Tears streamed down Mindel's cheeks and she found herself in Mother Brinkmann's warm embrace, while Herr Brinkmann carried Laszlo's body outside.

She couldn't stop crying, didn't even eat or drink for two days, so deep ran her grief. She missed him so much, missed his arm around her shoulders when they were sleeping, his mischievous glance when coming up with new games—heck, she even missed the way he used to pester her. And, with no word from Rachel, the truth was that Mindel missed the only person left on earth who had loved her with his entire heart.

CHAPTER 32

The New Year had come and gone without the children noticing it. Every day in the camp was like the last one: a constant struggle to stay alive. It had been weeks since Laszlo's death, but Mindel still missed him ever so much.

One morning, Mother Brinkmann told the children, "Today is a very special day. Today is Tu BiShvat, also called Rosh HaShanah La'Ilanot, the New Year of the Trees and Plants."

"There are no trees in the camp," one of the older boys murmured, seemingly fearing a lesson about Jewish holidays.

"I know," Mother Brinkmann answered with serenity. "One more reason to celebrate this holiday. Because without plants, we humans cannot exist. Traditionally on Tu BiShvat the table is set with the best fruits nature provides us with."

"What is a fruit?" asked Rita, a girl of two and a half, who'd been born in the camp.

"Fruits are foods that grow on trees or other plants," an older girl explained, but Rita only shook her head, since she'd never seen a tree or other plant in her life.

Mother Brinkmann produced two crumpled apples and showed them to the children. "To celebrate Tu BiShvat, everyone will get a piece of apple, and then you'll know what a fruit is. After, we will take the seeds and plant them near the fence."

"That'll never work," Michael, one of the older boys, whispered.

"Even if it does, people will rip out the sprig and eat it," Sandy whispered back.

"Wherever did she get the apples from? I haven't seen one since I arrived here," Katrin asked.

Mindel turned her head to look at Katrin, before her eyes returned to the apples in Mother Brinkmann's hand. They were yellow and crumpled with a few brown spots, nothing like the plump and shiny red apples she'd eaten on the farm.

Her memory about the time before the camp had faded, but she'd kept a few special moments in her heart, conjuring them up whenever she felt sad and lonely. The time when she and her brothers had climbed the apple trees in the orchard to pick the best ones. Of course, her brothers had always climbed higher than she dared and had teased her that the apples up there tasted a lot better than those she could reach.

Thinking about apples invariably made her mouth water, as that other memory rushed into her brain. The yummy apple cake her mother had made for her birthday. Everyone in the family had been standing around the table, patiently—or in the case of her brothers, not so patiently—waiting for Mindel to blow out the candles and make her birthday wish. She didn't remember what wish she'd made, but she vividly remembered how her mother had cut half the cake into pieces, giving one to each family member, while putting the other half away for the next day.

It felt as if it was yesterday that she'd tasted the sweet-and-sour delight, and she involuntarily closed her eyes to conjure up the smell of freshly baked goods wafting through her mother's kitchen. Her birthday had been in autumn, shortly after the harvest, when the entire family including her had been out in the fields from dusk to dawn bringing in the crops.

"What season is it?" she asked out loud.

"Winter," Mother Brinkmann answered.

"Does autumn come before or after winter?"

"It comes before. The year starts with spring, summer, autumn and then winter."

Mindel cocked her head, thinking hard. "When did I arrive here?"

"You and Laszlo came to us in the autumn, but your arrival in the camp was probably around April, which is springtime."

The mention of Laszlo's name stabbed at Mindel's heart, but she ignored the pain, using her fingers to count the seasons. She was pretty sure she'd turned four when Mother had made her the cake, since that was the last birthday celebration she remembered. So, if four seasons had passed, and it was already winter again, she must be a year older by now.

Aware of the enormity of her discovery, she straightened her shoulders and said as loud as she could, holding up all five fingers of one hand, "Then I'm five now."

Mother Brinkmann smiled and asked, "Do you remember when your birthday is?"

A shadow of doubt crossed Mindel's face. "Not exactly, but it was in autumn, I'm sure of that. My mother baked me an apple cake with fresh apples from the tree when I turned four."

"Well then, how about we make Tu BiShvat your new birthday?"

"I would like that." Mindel was moved to tears to finally have a birthday again and—even more importantly—knowing that she had grown older and now belonged to the five year olds.

"I guess that's a reason to celebrate." Usually, Mother Brinkmann saved up part of their rations for special occasions like this and made a kind of cake with breadcrumbs glued together with jam or margarine. Today, though, she was unprepared.

The children sang "Happy Birthday" for Mindel and once they finished, Mother Brinkmann declared that to mark the occasion

Mindel would receive two pieces of apple instead of just one like everyone else. Mindel beamed from ear to ear as she savored the special treat.

The next day even more surprises showed up. Mother Brinkmann was called into the camp administration because the Red Cross had been allowed to deliver parcels for the prisoners, and these were being distributed between the barracks.

She returned with a happy face, holding up a large box. "We received this from the Red Cross."

"What's the Red Cross?" Mindel asked.

"An organization that helps the injured and the poor," Sandy explained.

Mindel cocked her head. Nobody in their barracks was injured and she wasn't sure whether they were poor. "Why don't they come and take us out of here? Wouldn't that be better?"

Sandy gave an exaggerated sigh. "Don't ask stupid questions. Because the SS doesn't allow it."

Mindel knew that too many questions weren't appreciated, but she needed to clarify one more thing. "Why do they even keep us in here?"

"Now, that is an even more stupid question," Sandy said and walked away, while some of the other children poked their tongues out at Mindel. But before she could retaliate, Mother Brinkmann called them to order.

Everyone settled in a circle around her. It was completely silent in the hut, except for the rustle of cardboard, as she opened the large box. From what Mindel understood, the box was going to be stuffed with goods.

Mother Brinkmann removed one thing after another and put them onto the bunk where she was sitting. Pairs of socks, gloves, caps, two shirts, one dress, one pair of trousers and several packages that looked like food came to lie on the bunk.

Mindel's eyes, along with those of the other children, became wider with every precious thing exhibited. She had not seen such an abundance of treasures ever in her life, not that she remembered. And judging by the beaming faces of her friends, they felt the same. It really was like a birthday, just with all the children being the birthday girls and boys on the same day.

Her eyes were mostly glued to the goods, but Mindel also observed how Mother Brinkmann handed the foodstuffs to her husband to put into the secret stash and then carefully scrutinized each of the children. Being familiar with numbers by now, Mindel quickly counted the children, since the number varied from day to day. Some died, but other new children arrived at the orphans' barracks to live with them. It was just the way things were.

She counted forty-five in total. There wouldn't be a gift for each one of them. Mindel waited with bated breath to find out whether she'd be one of the lucky ones.

"Come here, Sandy," Mother Brinkmann said, and every child in the hut hissed in a breath, waiting to see what Sandy would receive. She was one of the older girls and the tallest one. Mother Brinkmann took up the pretty dress, holding it up against Sandy, who made short work of shedding her old dress and pulling the new one over her head.

It fit to perfection, made of dark blue wool that looked soft and warm, even from a distance. Mindel so wished she'd been given this dress, though she had to admit it was much too big for her. Sandy gave a twirl in her new dress and all the children clapped their hands.

Mother Brinkmann held Sandy's old dress up, measuring the size with her scrutinizing glance, before she let her gaze wander across the children once more. "Franzi, this should fit you."

Franzi was eight and just like Mother Brinkmann had suggested, Sandy's dress was the perfect size for her. Franzi's face though showed clearly that she'd much rather have received the brand new, soft, woolen dress from the Red Cross box and Mindel thought she should really be a bit happier, because her own clothing had become way too small for her lanky bones.

Mindel was so preoccupied in thought that she didn't hear Mother Brinkmann call her name and only looked up when the child next to her elbowed her in the ribs. "You've been called up."

Walking toward the bunk with the presents she tried not to get her hopes up too high, although she eyed a pair of dark green woolen socks that certainly would keep her ever-freezing feet warm. But instead of the coveted socks, Mother Brinkmann handed her Franzi's dress.

It wasn't what she'd wanted, but she smiled nevertheless. Franzi's dress fit her like a glove: the sleeves covered her wrists and the waist didn't pinch at every movement. It had buttons down the front and the skirt was long enough to cover her legs down to mid-calf.

Mindel's own dress was handed down to the next smaller girl, and the same happened to the shirts and trousers in the box. The old socks of the children who received new ones unfortunately were much too holey to be handed down, so Mother Brinkmann tasked the boys with unraveling them and the older girls with knitting new socks or gloves from them.

Not a single thread was wasted, which was a shame, because Mindel had hoped that she'd be able to keep some material to make something new for Paula, who was completely naked since her dress had literally fallen off a few weeks ago. But naturally Paula was the very last in line and nothing remained for her to wear. At least Paula stayed warm under Mindel's dress and never suffered from cold feet or hands.

"Don't you worry," Mindel comforted her doll. "Once we get out of here I'll buy you as many beautiful dresses as you want. In all the colors of the rainbow."

Paula smiled at her and Mindel made her nod.

In the afternoon, Mindel walked all the way to the other side of the camp to show Heidi and Laura her new dress.

"Hey, Heidi," Mindel said and did a full turn, coming to stand in front of the older girl with a curtsy. "How do you like my new dress?"

"It's very beautiful, Mindel. You look like a princess," Heidi complimented her. The dress wasn't new or beautiful by any standards, even camp standards, but it fit her and all the holes had been patched up.

"Have you heard from your friend Anne?"

Heidi's face fell. "She's so ill. The last time we spoke she could barely talk loud enough for me to hear her and was coughing all the time."

"Oh." Mindel furrowed her brows. "Does that mean she will die soon?"

"I hope not. They distributed packages from the Red Cross and I grabbed an empty box and am now asking everyone to contribute something to toss it over the fence for her."

"You can do that?"

"Yes, the fence is not that high and the box is not heavy, despite most everyone giving a little something."

Mindel was excited and wanted to do her part. But she didn't have anything to give. No extra clothes or special trinkets... Nothing except... Paula. She fought a heavy fight with herself and then reached under her dress to fetch her doll.

"Here." She held out the doll, her heart breaking a little inside.

But Heidi shook her head. "No, you can't give away Paula, she's your special friend."

"But I don't have anything else to give."

"Don't worry. Anne will be happy with whatever is inside the box already. And I think she's too old for a doll anyway."

Mindel was secretly relieved and put Paula back inside her dress. It would have been so hard to give her away, especially now that Laszlo was dead. She couldn't help but think of him often, and having Paula nearby always helped to dispel the fear and sadness.

Suddenly, Mindel had an idea and she darted out of the barracks, calling out, "I'll be right back. Wait for me."

Mindel hurried to the back door of the kitchens, hoping the Russian woman would be working today. She made sure there were no SS guards around before she crept inside, searching for the kind woman. As soon as she saw her she walked over, and said, "Please, could I have just a small piece of bread? Please?"

The woman scowled down at her. "What are you doing here? We'll both get in trouble if the guards see you."

"I was very careful not to be seen. It's not for me, but for a very sick friend. Please."

The woman sighed, turned around and cut a small slice from a half-loaf of bread. "Here, take this. Be gone with you now. Don't tell anyone where you got that."

Mindel nodded earnestly and rushed out, remembering her manners at the last moment and turning around even as she was half through the door. "Thank you!" She scanned the surroundings the way Laszlo had taught her and then ran back to Heidi's barracks as fast as her weak little legs would carry her.

Completely out of breath, she had to stop a few times on the way to recoup her strength. The smell of the bread in her hand reached her nose, making her aware of the gnawing hunger in her intestines. *Just a little bit, nobody will know.* But she shook her head, closing her hand tighter around the bread and moving on. This bread was for Heidi's friend.

She held out the crust of bread and proudly showed it to Heidi. "Here, for Anne."

"Where did you get that? Please tell me you didn't steal it."

"No. The Russian woman gave it to me... But I wasn't supposed to tell you that."

Heidi hugged her. "Thank you so much. Such a wonderful contribution to the box."

"Can I come with you when you toss it?"

"No, you shouldn't. The guards have become more alert and I will only go minutes before curfew. You'll have to be in your barracks by then."

Mindel pouted, but after Heidi promised to recount every detail of the toss-over, she marched off. Once she arrived at the orphans' barracks her legs were so wobbly she could barely stand on them.

Mother Brinkmann shook her head. "Oh, Mindel, child, you shouldn't walk that far, not with the little food we have."

Mindel wondered what exactly the amount of food had to do with walking, but she was too tired to ask.

A week later Heidi came to the orphans' barracks with a sad look on her face.

"What's wrong?" Mindel asked her.

"Nothing."

"Did Anne get your box?"

Heidi shrugged and Mindel had the suspicion there was something the older girl didn't want her to know. She hated how the adults, and even the older children, always assumed she was too young for one thing or the other. She had just turned five, for crying out loud! Five! She wasn't little anymore.

"I want to know," Mindel insisted.

Heidi gave a deep sigh. "Another woman stole it."

"What? How dare she? What happened? How?" A million questions stormed out of Mindel.

"She must have overheard us talking about the box and waited in the shadows until I threw it. Then she pushed Anne over, scooped it up and ran away, even before Anne knew what happened."

"How mean! Didn't she know the box was for Anne and not for her?"

"For sure, she knew, but she didn't care. I have been at the fence every evening since, but have never met Anne again. I'm afraid something has happened to her."

Mindel felt so sad for her friend, she put her tiny hand on Heidi's arm and said with the same soothing voice Mother Brinkmann used to console a child, "Don't worry. She's probably dead by now, but you shouldn't be sad, because these things happen."

"How dare you say this!" Heidi yanked her arm away from Mindel and rushed off, leaving a very confused little girl behind.

Mindel had only wanted to be helpful. Everyone knew that death was part of the daily life at the camp, thus she didn't have the slightest idea why her friend had reacted in such a strange way. It wasn't like Heidi and Anne had been best friends like she and Laszlo had been. Thinking of him, her heart squeezed and grief overtook her once again.

CHAPTER 33

The only indication of time passing was the weather. With spring arriving, the harsh cold had abated, but now Rachel and the other women had to combat alternating humidity, pelting rain and muddy roads. Keeping clean in these conditions was all but impossible and Rachel had given up any pretense of being a normal person long ago.

One day they were woken as usual before daybreak. After a meager breakfast the women assembled in columns to march to the salt mine. But instead of walking down south, they were steered up north. Rachel groaned. As always, the guards didn't give any explanation or even the slightest hint of what was about to happen and speculation among the prisoners was rife.

Some whispered about death marches, sure they'd be sent on one of them, as the SS wanted to avert prisoners' being liberated by the Allies. *Leave no evidence behind* was the order of the day, at least according to the *kapos* who often were privy to conversations between guards. Flesh-and-blood people like Rachel were considered nothing more than evidence of the Nazis' crimes that had to disappear before the Allies swooped in.

Not sure whether she'd withstand walking for days or weeks on end, Rachel all but wept with relief when the group arrived at the train station. Not even the cattle cars waiting for them could put a damper on her mood. As long as she didn't have to walk, things weren't half bad.

Somehow, she climbed into the wagon and huddled together with the lot of tired, hungry, and dirty women. The stench of unwashed bodies, human excrement, urine, and death was all around her and she feared she would never get the smell off her skin again.

She must have collapsed from sheer exhaustion, because the train suddenly stopped, the doors were opened and SS guards forced them to disembark with their incessant "*Schnell! Schnell!*"

But *fast* wasn't in Rachel's vocabulary anymore. Everything she did was slow, since this was the only way her emaciated body managed to do anything at all. As she reached the doors of the cattle wagon, the woman in front of her wouldn't move, despite the generous whiplashes from the guards. Frantic lest she become a victim of their wrath herself, Rachel shoved the surprisingly lightweight body aside. The dead woman fell onto the ramp with a dull thud and looked up at her with lifeless eyes.

There was no time to mourn or even acknowledge that a human being had died. In her hurry to get down from the cattle car, Rachel trampled across the dead woman, who was nothing but another number, a scratch mark on a list of corpses to be removed. One less person to toil in slavery for the Aryan master race.

The platform seemed strangely familiar, but her barely functioning brain needed a full minute to recognize it was the train ramp of Bergen-Belsen. A glimmer of hope that Mindel might still be somewhere nearby in the camp warmed her heart, although that warmth dwindled to almost nothing as she thought of the one-hour march to the camp she would no doubt have to endure before arrival. Only then might she get a chance to even look for Mindel.

The guard in front of her swung his whip over his head, seemingly boasting to his comrades about his versatility painting figures in the air with it. He stumbled and all but fell, catching himself at the last moment.

Rachel flinched back and was about to move on when she saw something glittering in the mud, where he'd been seconds ago. She dropped to her knees, risking being lashed, while her hand grabbed whatever glittery thing he'd lost. Within a split second she recognized it as a gold ring, undoubtedly stolen from one of the prisoners, since it seemed much too small for his pudgy fingers.

She shoved guilty thoughts aside, reassuring herself that the rightful owner was probably dead and the possession of a gold ring might mean the difference between life and death. No, the time for scruples was long gone, as they headed toward the end of the war and hopefully their liberation by whatever Allied army might reach them first. So the thing foremost on Rachel's mind was to hang on for just another day.

She hurriedly slipped it inside her shoe and managed to get up before one of the guards could hit her with his truncheon. For the next minute she held her breath, hoping nobody had noticed what she'd done. The ring in her shoe added to her discomfort, seemingly getting bigger and more lumpy with every step she took toward the camp.

The march was an endless ordeal, forcing bodies that had been depleted to the minimum to keep on walking. Many women straggled and whenever one unfortunate soul couldn't catch up to the group anymore, inevitably a shot rang out as that one was put to her final rest. The first few times, Rachel flinched, but when the shots became more frequent, she stopped batting so much as an eyelid since every movement drained valuable energy from her body. It was as it was, nothing she could do about it.

She gasped in horror the very moment she marched through the gate with the odious words *"Arbeit macht Frei."*

Free of what?

The camp was even more horrific than she remembered it, the most awful stink of sickness wafting into her nose. Bergen-Belsen was bursting at the seams. Everywhere she looked there were women standing, sitting, lying, squatting. Since her departure a few months ago, the camp population must have tripled at the least.

The stench of death was ubiquitous and, for a brief moment, Rachel considered begging to be returned to the salt mines. As opposed to her previous arrivals at Bergen-Belsen, this time she wasn't processed or registered. This time the newcomers were simply dumped inside, and left to fend for themselves.

With chaos raging and apparently no SS guards even bothering to maintain a semblance of order, Rachel took the initiative and made her way to the barracks where she had been living last, hoping to find Anne or Margot. The hut was incredibly overcrowded with five to six women sharing a bunk and despite having been exposed previously to the most awful stenches human misery could produce, she gagged as she ventured deeper inside the darkness of the barracks.

Neither of the Frank girls were there and none of the women she asked knew anything about them. Back at the door she glanced one last time into the hut, deciding it was preferable to sleep rough than to try and find a space inside this hell on earth.

Outside, dozens of women had secured themselves protected spots under the small awning of the hut. They were leaning against the wall, soaking up the warming sunshine of early spring, looking more dead than alive.

Rachel recognized a former barracks mate and approached her. "Hey, aren't you Wanda?"

"Hm." Wanda gave a barely perceptible nod. In her early thirties, she looked like an octogenarian.

"I'm looking for Anne and Margot Frank."

"Both got sick."

"Where are they?"

"No idea. Caught typhus and one day disappeared. I reckon they died and their corpses were put out front to be taken away."

Rachel flopped down at the empty spot beside the woman, the lost hope draining all her energy to stay upright, since the Frank sisters had been her only link to Mindel.

Wanda moved aside to make room for Rachel to lean against the wall and murmured, "It'll all be over soon. If I were you I wouldn't set foot into the barracks. There's nothing but typhus and dysentery in there."

Rachel nodded. Sitting out here was as good as anywhere else, and since the SS apparently had abandoned the camp—except for the men guarding the fence—she decided to stay in this very spot until she either died or the Allies came to liberate her. Whatever happened first—she'd long since stopped caring.

In the morning, Rachel woke with a start when a ray of sunshine danced across her face. Her entire body was frozen stiff, but out of habit she scrambled to stand upright. Judging by the sun high on the horizon it must be mid-morning already. How could she have missed roll call?

Anxiety settled in her bones, since she was certain she'd have to pay for such a transgression of the rules. Not showing up for roll call was something nobody, except for those already in the clutches of death, would dare to do.

Frantically looking around she didn't see SS guards, or any semblance of order in the camp. Just women sitting, crouching, lying. Even outside the smell was debilitating, as women were urinating and defecating wherever they found themselves, too weak or too far gone to bother getting up.

Rachel entertained the idea of doing the same, but somehow found the strength to put her feet into motion and go to the latrines, where she finally dared to remove the ring from her shoe to inspect it. It was a fine gold ring with a tiny diamond, probably an engagement ring stolen by the SS guard from some unfortunate soul—and now it was hers. She thought about the best place to hide it on her body, and finally decided to wear it—on her toe. Tucked beneath her socks and shoes it was the safest hiding place.

On her way back, she passed the kitchen barracks, where a single woman sat inside, her forehead on the counter.

"Hey, where's the line for breakfast?" Rachel asked her.

The woman raised her head and stared at her with empty eyes. "No line. No food. No nothing." Then her head dropped back on the counter.

Rachel looked around in the kitchen. Normally in every camp, the kitchen barracks were spit-spat clean, and not a single tool was out of place, since working in the kitchen was one of the most coveted work details only given to favored prisoners. None of them wanted to risk losing the job and being sent somewhere else and did their best to please the *kapos* and SS by showing impeccable work ethics and cleanliness.

But this kitchen looked as if had been ransacked. Nothing was in place, and every last morsel of food or portable utensil had been stolen. Rachel shook her head. If one couldn't even count on the SS to keep order in the camp anymore, the end must truly be near.

She turned around, just as two young soldiers came inside, hauling a sack of wheat behind them. She stared at them as if she'd seen a mirage, but when she blinked, they were still there, dumping their burden. They stared at her, apparently unsure what to do, then shrugged and left again in a hurry to leave this godawful place.

Rachel opened the sack, dug her hands into the wheat, shoving it into her mouth, choking on the dry mass. She swallowed and swallowed, her mouth dry as sand. Nearly suffocating, she frantically glanced around the room, located the faucet and stuck her head beneath. When she opened it, water burst into her mouth, almost drowning her, and then died down to a trickle.

With her face wet and smeared, she returned to the sack of wheat and stuffed as much as she could into her pockets, before shoving more of the mass into her mouth. After two days without any food at all, it was a feast. Other camp inhabitants must have seen the soldiers, too, and approached the kitchen in an angry mass of starving people poised to fight for survival. Rachel quickly assessed the situation and slid out the back door just as the crowd entered the kitchen and an awful fight over the raw wheat broke out.

As the days passed more and more inmates from other camps arrived in the most precarious conditions and were dumped inside the barbed wire fence, while the camp organization had basically ceased to exist. There was no order, no food being distributed, no nothing.

Suddenly she missed the horrible brown liquid they'd called coffee and the equally horrible muddy liquid they'd called soup. At least it had given a semblance of normal life. But this here, this was pure anarchy.

In a last, superhuman effort she walked to the connection between the women's camp and the star camp, still hoping she'd somehow find a way to cross into the other compound and get to Mindel there. But all the guards who'd abandoned the women's camp seemed to be concentrated by the fence, sitting with nervous expressions outside their watch posts, making sure nobody crossed from one compound into the other.

She bided her time, observing the guards for several hours before identifying one that didn't yell and threaten like the others. Ignoring the gnawing hunger and the pain, she sat on her haunches, immobile, waiting for an opportunity to contact him. It came long after dark, when his companion said, "I'll grab a bite, want me to bring you some?"

"Nah, I'll take my break once you return."

Then the other guard disappeared into the guardhouse.

Despite the cold sweat running down her back, she got up and approached him. It was now or never.

"Excuse me, sir—"

"What do you want?" he asked with a surprised, but not necessarily angry face.

"My baby sister is in the star camp. She's only five years old. Please, is there a way I could go search for her?"

"Five? Why wasn't she allowed to stay with you?"

"I don't know. We got separated when we arrived," Rachel said softly. "Please, can you help me?"

His face showed that he was struggling, but after several moments of thought, he shook his head. "No. I can't help you. It's *verboten*."

"It wouldn't be for nothing," she whispered.

He gave her a suspicious glance, but she noticed the flicker of greed in his eyes. "What do you have?"

"A gold ring."

"Pah… it's probably brass."

"It's real gold with a small diamond. It was my engagement ring and my fiancé paid three months' salary for it." Rachel was trembling inside as she made the story up. "It's all yours if you let me pass into the star camp." She prayed he'd bite. If she had misjudged him, he might force her to give the ring to him and shoot her to show his gratitude.

"Where is it?"

"Not here. Safely buried."

The guard eyed her and seemed to consider what to do. "Come back at midnight. Don't approach me if I'm not alone. Now go," he hissed as his colleague stepped out of the watch post.

"What's that bitch want?"

"Begging for food," he said, swinging his truncheon at Rachel, who quickly moved back into the shadows.

She stayed hidden nearby, until complete darkness had settled over the camp. Then she removed the ring from her toe and pressed it deep into her pocket and waited until she could approach the guard again.

CHAPTER 34

Two months had passed since TuBishvat and typhus was wreaking havoc in the orphans' barracks. Several of the children had died the previous night and more were seriously ill. In an effort to break the chain of contagion, Mother Brinkmann changed the sleeping arrangements, cordoning off part of the barracks and telling the uninfected children that they were no longer allowed to talk with the others.

Mindel had a slight cough and a runny nose like most everyone in the camp, but apart from that—and the itching, biting lice—she didn't feel any worse than normal. Nevertheless she hated the fact that she wasn't allowed to play with her friends.

"What is 'contagious'?" she asked.

"It's when someone is sick with something and everyone else catches the disease if they get close to them," Sandy explained. After a glance at Mindel's confused face, she added, "For example a cold. When one person gets a cold, suddenly everyone has it. That's contagious."

"Only typhus is much more serious than a cold and many people won't recover," Mother Brinkmann added before heading back to check on the sick children.

Mindel thought about the explanations for a minute, trying to process the information, before she asked, "Is hunger a contagious disease, too?"

"Why would you think that?" Sandy said in the way that clearly indicated she thought the younger girl stupid. But Mindel wouldn't be deterred. She'd grown used to being considered daft and annoying for asking so many questions. What the older children didn't know was that in fact they were the daft ones, because their explanations never made much sense.

"Because everyone living here is hungry."

Some children laughed. "Hunger and typhus aren't the same thing."

"Why not? Being scared and hating people are contagious, aren't they?"

The laughing stopped and Michael asked, "Where do you get these strange ideas from?"

Mindel paused for a moment, frowning. "It's just if one child is afraid, soon after we all are."

"Fear and hate *are* contagious, Mindel. I wish it wasn't that way, but it is." Mother Brinkmann had returned. "Hate is a disease worse than typhus and the very reason why so many of our people have been killed. First the Nazis feared us, then they blamed us for whatever problems there were in Germany and once they started hating us, it was the beginning of what we're experiencing now."

Mindel nodded, although she didn't completely grasp the meaning of Mother Brinkmann's explanation. But she didn't ponder for long about that issue, since she yearned for clarification of so many other things she didn't understand.

The infirmary, above all. Over the last few weeks she'd watched person after person removed from their barracks and hauled off to the infirmary. It was a known fact that people who went there rarely returned. She just didn't know why.

Knowing very well that the other children would only laugh at her once again, she waited until Mother Brinkmann was busy patching up torn clothes, then sidled up to her and asked, "Are you keeping our sick kids here so that they won't disappear?"

"Disappear? What do you mean?"

"Well, sick people go to the infirmary, but no one ever comes back from there. Is that why you are keeping our children here?"

"Oh, Mindel," Mother Brinkmann said and patted Mindel's head without giving an answer. Another annoying adult habit. They always resorted to vague comments like this one when they didn't want to answer a question.

Mindel still hadn't quite figured out whether they tried to hide the fact that they had no idea, or because they thought she was too young to know the truth. Probably a mixture of both. If only she had someone who was honest with her… Laszlo… he'd always told her the truth, unpleasant as it was.

Memories of Laszlo made her sad and she took out Paula from under her dress, whispering in her ear, "You and I, we won't get typhus, don't you worry. I'll take good care of you and everything will be fine."

Sometime later Mother Brinkmann turned around and said, "Time to go to bed. Everyone get into your bunks and I'll tell you another story about Fluff."

Even the children who hadn't caught typhus were too starved and tired to protest and climbed into their bunks. Lately, Mindel felt like all she did was sleep or lie around dreaming. Even after the harsh winter had passed and the weather had become warmer, the children rarely ventured outside and never played tag or hide-and-seek like they used to last summer.

She huddled in her bunk that she now shared with five other girls, eager to hear another story about Fluff. It was a comforting, predictable part of their existence and Mindel hugged Paula close as she listened. Why couldn't the rest of their days be as nice and peaceful as those minutes when Fluff helped them escape into a better world?

CHAPTER 35

"Do you have the ring?" the guard asked when Rachel approached him several minutes after midnight, as he had told her to do.

"Yes and it's yours once you let me pass into the star camp."

"I want to see it first."

This was a crucial moment and Rachel went stiff with fear. If she'd misjudged him, he could simply steal the ring from her hands and send her back to the women's camp.

But now it was too late, there was nothing she could do, so she stretched out her hand, opening her fingers to reveal the shiny ring on her palm. The diamond caught the rays of one of the floodlights illuminating the camp perimeter with the electric fence and glimmered in all colors of the rainbow. It truly was a beautiful ring.

The guard grabbed it and buried it deep in his pocket before he motioned for Rachel to follow him. Her heart thumping high in her throat she pretended to be absolutely calm, well versed in these kinds of bribery as she kept close to him, but not too close, impatiently waiting until he unlocked the gate in the fence and beckoned for her to pass.

Despite the growing fear in her stomach she held her head high and slipped through the gate the very moment it opened up, afraid the guard might change his mind before she was safely on the other side.

It felt like stepping into a completely different world. Where the women's camp had been filled to the brim, here she didn't see a single person, and assumed they must all be sleeping in their barracks. The few people lying around turned out to be dead, and afraid of the guards enforcing the curfew, she decided to find a sheltered spot and wait until morning before she began her search for Mindel.

In the morning she woke to an unusual bustle in the compound. Even back in the days when the SS had still kept a tight regimen, there had never been such a nervous tension in the air. Something was definitely brewing, but she wouldn't let herself speculate or be frightened. Whatever it was, she could do nothing to prepare, let alone to prevent it. That much she'd learned in the past year and a half.

Therefore, she focused on finding Mindel. Much to her surprise, this part of the camp was still somehow organized and at dawn the kitchen workers came carrying soup pots to the barracks. Her stomach grumbled loudly at the sight of food and she decided to keep Mindel waiting for a little longer and instead queued up at one of the pots with her mug in hand.

When it was her turn, the soup handler looked at her warily for a moment, but then shrugged and poured one ladle of soup into her mug. Rachel hurriedly moved away, lest someone ask questions and take the murky, stinking liquid from her. She grabbed some of the wheat from her pockets and threw it into the soup, hoping that both the soup and the wheat would improve by mixing them together, although food was food and she would have eaten almost anything by now.

She might not go as far as some other women she'd seen in the women's camp cutting off pieces of flesh from the fresh corpses lying around, but certainly wouldn't be above eating tree bark, leaves or rain worms. Not even a slimy brown Iberian slug would have been too yucky to forego.

What had the Nazis done to them? Reduced them not only to beast-like sub-humans, but to actual cannibals. People with no qualms at all. Where survival was at stake, nothing else mattered: not decency, pride nor basic humanity. Sometimes she wondered whether it was actually worth it to survive this ghastly hell and if she would ever lead a normal life again.

Once she'd gobbled down her breakfast and the gnawing in her intestines had eased up a bit, she began asking people for the orphans' barracks, until a kind woman pointed to the far end of the compound.

The feeling of trepidation about the long trek grew into full panic when, mere minutes later, SS guards swarmed the camp. For a change they looked like frightened mice instead of showing their usual smug arrogance, but even this difference in attitude couldn't ease her worries.

A sense of urgency gripped Rachel and she hurried through the camp, determined to reach the orphans' barracks at the far end. She berated herself for wasting precious time to stop for food. With only three more huts to go, two SS men caught up with her and one yelled, "Hey, you! Assemble in the courtyard."

Sheer panic coursed through her veins and she wavered—one moment too long. His truncheon hit her on the shoulder and the awful thud reverberated through her entire body. There was no room for decision-making; she had to obey.

So, she turned around and shuffled in the opposite direction, putting more distance between herself and the orphans' barracks with every pained step. A tormenting thought crossed her brain. She wasn't supposed to be in this part of the camp. If they were going to do a roll call she'd be found out and the SS would surely kill her.

Disappointment over having come so close to finding her sister and once again failing at the last moment rushed over her, draining her will to live. When she arrived at the assembly yard, she barely believed her own eyes: instead of lining up the inmates into orderly rows, the guards herded everyone toward the gates.

As opposed to earlier times when she'd been transferred, this time there were no lists, no names, and no order. It was all a complete shambles, one last-ditch effort of the Nazis to cover up their crimes.

She didn't know what exactly was going on, but the tension grappling the entire camp tied her stomach into knots, and from the guards' unabated anxiety she gleaned that the Allies were close. Unfortunately for her, they weren't close enough yet and together with thousands of star camp inmates she was marched toward the train ramp—again.

The walk was strenuous and more than once she gazed with longing at the ditch beside the road. To sit down and relax for just a minute seemed like the most wonderful thing on earth, but everyone who succumbed to the yearning was promptly shot. She did not want to be shot. Not now that she could smell the coming freedom in the air. After hanging on for such a long time, she determined to cling to life just another day more.

There was no train waiting when the bedraggled group finally reached the train ramp. Rachel flopped down on the gravelly ground, sharp stones pricking into her buttocks. Thirst was gluing her tongue to her gums. She cast a look into the sky, wishing for clouds to roll in and the detested rain to pelt down on her. But all she saw was a blue sky and a cruelly bright and happy April sun shining down on the miserable crowd.

Anger at the sun erupted in her like a volcano spewing lava, and she literally shook her fist at the celestial body that looked down onto the earth day after day, illuminating nature with bright yellow rays, bringing the seedlings to sprout and the flowers to blossom, unaffected by the horrid human misery.

All around her she stared into gaunt and gray faces atop emaciated bodies, each one of them emanating hopelessness and an ocean of despair. One person looked exactly like the next one, indistinguishable skeletons covered by parched skin, except for... *Mindel!*

The girl looked as horrid as everyone else, but it was unmistakably her little sister. She was only twenty feet away from her, sitting on the lap of an older girl. Rachel would have cried, but her tears had dried up many months ago.

"Mindel!" she yelled, even as she struggled to her feet and weaved her way through the crowd.

CHAPTER 36

Mindel was burning up from the inside. Ever since the SS had entered their barracks in the morning and herded everyone out, she'd been feeling awful. In addition, her legs were too short to keep up with the tempo of the group and if it hadn't been for Sandy, who'd dragged her behind, Mindel would have given up and thrown herself into a ditch.

She knew quite well what happened to those wanting to rest, but right now she was too weak to care. The moment they'd reached the train ramp, she flopped onto Sandy's lap, instantly falling asleep. After the long and agonizing march, where dirt and pebbles had gotten into her shoes, she was so tired she simply couldn't keep her eyes open. Her feet were freezing, but the rest of her body was hot.

"I'm tired," Mindel whimpered.

"I know you are."

"And thirsty."

"Me, too. I'm sure they'll give us some water soon."

Mindel didn't even bat an eyelid at the blatant lie. When had the SS ever cared about the inmates' needs? "How much longer?"

"I don't know. I'm sure it won't take long."

Her head fell forward and right before she fell asleep again, she wondered why everyone thought death was such a bad thing. If it meant she wouldn't be thirsty, hot and aching anymore, she'd rather be dead than sitting in misery on the ramp. At least the dead could roam freely and fly with the angels, playing in the clouds.

"Mindel!" someone yelled. "Mindel!"

She didn't want to wake up, but her brain recognized the voice and she forced her eyes open, scrambling to turn around to see where it was coming from.

"Rachel?" She saw her sister pushing through the crowd, struggling to get to her.

"That's my sister," she told Sandy. "That's Rachel!"

"Mindel! Stay where you are, I'm coming to you," Rachel hollered. She pushed and shoved but it seemed to take an eternity for her to make her way through. "Almost there!" Rachel shouted, her voice being drowned out by the screeching sound of the train's brakes as it drove into the station.

Mindel saw Rachel and how she was swept away by the sea of bodies that somehow had gotten up. She struggled to get away from Sandy, who heaved them both to their feet. "Let me go!"

"No way. You'll get hurt."

"I need Rachel."

"Your sister is almost here."

The crowd around them began moving forward and Mindel panicked. She couldn't lose Rachel again when she'd just found her.

"Pick me up!" she demanded. From up there she had a much better view and when her sister was only a few steps away, Mindel jumped and launched herself at her. Somehow, she managed to grab hold of Rachel's arm and held on tight, even as the crowd began to move faster, engulfing them.

"I found you, my sweet little darling." Rachel swooped her up in her arms, and kissed her cheek. "I thought I'd never see you again."

"I missed you so much," Mindel said, before exhaustion and the strain of living in the camps overwhelmed her little body and she closed her eyes.

CHAPTER 37

Rachel pressed her sister's limp body tight against her chest as the emotions welled up, shaking her. The poor mite in her arms looked so ghastly, crouched over her shoulder light as a feather. Her heartbeat was weak and irregular and she was burning up with a fever, but there was nothing Rachel could do for her, except to hold her.

When the train came to a full stop, she noticed some passenger carriages among the usual cattle cars. A novelty for her. She'd been forced to travel like an animal ever since the Nazis had captured her. As expected, the mass rushed toward the passenger carriages and scuffles broke out as everyone tried to get into the more comfortable compartments.

Rachel was too weak and handicapped by having Mindel on her shoulder to participate in the rush and resigned herself to travelling once more in the dreaded wagons. Much to her surprise, though, the SS forced the mass back and called for the infirm and women with small children to come forward.

It took her a moment to realize that she belonged to that group. With Mindel sleeping in her arms, she approached the train and was indeed fortunate enough to get into one of the compartments. As overcrowded and decrepit as they were, it was a far cry from having to travel in the cattle cars.

Before the train departed, the SS distributed bread, jam and cheese along with some water. Rachel settled in her seat, holding

Mindel in her arms, feeding her sips of water and morsels of bread. At intervals, she wiped the sweat from her sister's forehead, fanning air over her burning body, and holding her close when the fever turned into violent shivers, wracking her little frame.

For hours Mindel would fall in and out of consciousness, talking to Rachel each time as if it were the first time she'd seen her. That worried Rachel, but not as much as the way the fever kept spiking. Mindel was so thin and her haunted eyes seemed to belong to an ancient woman instead of a girl of five.

Rachel was no doctor, but anyone could see that Mindel was suffering from the feared typhus, a disease that had wiped out a vast percentage of the inmates in the Bergen-Belsen camp. Not that it had made a difference in the overcrowding, because the Nazis had apparently kept dumping trainload after trainload of transferees from other camps into Bergen-Belsen, until this morning, when they'd started herding them back out.

Whoever was the genius behind that erratic plan, Rachel hoped he'd rot in eternal purgatory for what he was doing to them.

The train moved in spurts and breaks, often standing for hours during an air attack, before it moved again. Mindel hadn't woken since the night had settled, and the only indication she was still alive was her erratic heartbeat. Rachel grew more desperate with every passing minute, fearing her little sister would die right there in her arms.

"You can't die on me, sweetie," she murmured. "Not when I just found you." She knew Mindel couldn't hear her, but nonetheless she murmured words of comfort into her sister's ear, telling her sweet little lies, ones she didn't believe herself. "Everything will be fine, you'll see. The Allies are almost here, coming to liberate us. You just keep going, right?"

With every passing hour Rachel's murmurs became more desperate. As the hope of keeping her sister alive faded ever more, guilt raised its ugly head again, arguing with her. "You promised to take care of her, and see what you did?"

"I couldn't… The SS tore her from my hands…"

"Why didn't you hold her tighter? Why didn't you go after her?"

"There was nothing I could have done."

"You could have fought, you weak wretch!"

Rachel knew she was being too hard on herself, but she also knew that inner voice would never be silenced if Mindel died. Lost in desperation, she suddenly noticed the train had stopped again. Droning noises indicated the approach of low-flying Allied aircraft. Moments later she saw an entire squadron through the train window, but even before she had processed the vision, gunfire erupted all around her.

She sat there, holding her breath, praying that the pilots would realize the train was full of prisoners and spare their lives. Her prayers seemed to have helped, because the planes flew past the long train full of miserable Jews. The locomotive puffed and the journey continued.

In the morning she woke with a start when the train stopped once again. For hours nothing happened. The train stood in the middle of nowhere, but neither SS guards nor Allied aircraft appeared. After some time, the first courageous women left their compartments to venture out and soon returned with the news that the SS and the driver had abandoned the train, leaving it and all of its passengers standing on the open track. Rachel argued with herself whether it was better to stay inside and wait for things to come or to venture out, carrying her sick sister in her arms.

Her decision process was cut short by shouting and machine-gun fire. Staying inside definitely had become the preferred option. Peeking out of the window, she spotted tanks approaching—tanks without the Iron Cross.

Even before Rachel had finished the thought, another woman screamed, "The Americans! The Americans! We're free!"

Not much later, Rachel stared into the shocked eyes of a fresh-faced soldier in an American uniform.

"*Ihr seid frei.*" His German was heavily accented when he told them they were free. Rachel couldn't believe her ears at first, but evidence suggested that he was telling the truth and she gave him her brightest smile.

"Hello. I'm Rachel Epstein, a Jew from Kleindorf in Bavaria."

The women stumbled from the train and when it was Rachel's turn, one of the soldiers tried to peel Mindel off her shoulder.

"No, she's my sister!" Rachel screamed, grabbing Mindel tight.

The man looked slightly confused and explained something she didn't understand until finally someone translated for her. "He says he just wants to help. You'll get her right back."

Rachel nodded, not having expected so much kindness.

The young soldier looked with unabated horror at the hollow-cheeked child in his arms and when Rachel had joined him on the grass next to the track, he said, "*Krank. Arzt.*"

Rachel nodded. "Yes, please, she needs a doctor." He probably hadn't understood, but since he looked so friendly, she let him carry Mindel and when he beckoned her to do so, she followed him.

With the help of prisoners who spoke English, the officer in charge explained to the liberated masses that they were going to bring food from the nearby town as soon as possible and would also organize proper accommodation, but this could take some time.

Nobody moaned or complained, because the elation over being liberated ran high in everyone. Rachel stood next to the young American who was holding little Mindel. It broke her heart to see the specter-thin body fighting against the deadly disease. As much as she understood that the Americans couldn't do magic, she feared that waiting by the train with the others until proper accommodations were organized would cost Mindel's life.

Together with a woman who spoke English, she approached the officer in charge.

"Please, my sister needs a doctor."

The officer cast a single glance at Mindel and then yelled to one of his men, "Get this girl to the nearest hospital right away."

"Yes, sir. I'll take care of it." A younger soldier turned to her. "Miss, if you could come with me, we'll take you and your sister to the hospital."

Rachel nodded and followed him to one of the Jeeps that had come after the tanks. "Where are we?"

"Hillersleben."

She'd never heard that name and must have looked confused, because he added, "Our nearest field hospital is in Magdeburg, about fifteen miles from here."

***

In the field hospital the doctors and medics did everything they could for Mindel, but she wouldn't wake. Since their liberation four days before she'd been in a deep slumber that the doctors called a coma and for two more days the fever remained dangerously high. Rachel grew increasingly desperate when her little sister kept sleeping even after the fever finally broke on day three.

She rarely left Mindel's bedside, even though the doctors insisted she must rest. One of the medics only got her to go to the delousing procedure by promising to watch over Mindel himself.

By day four nobody would have bet a single cent on Mindel's life, but Rachel stubbornly refused to believe her little darling wouldn't wake up again. She faked a certitude she didn't possess, and only when everyone was asleep at night, did she allow her tears to flow, for the first time since she'd arrived in Bergen-Belsen, what felt a lifetime ago.

She cried for the beautiful little girl lying in the bed who had watched her entire life explode into a thousand disjointed pieces. It wasn't fair that things would end this way. Mindel would have had her entire life ahead of her and now…

Rachel dropped her head to the bedside, soaking the sheets with her tears. Mindel had been her sole reason to keep going this last year. If she died, Rachel didn't want to be alive either.

CHAPTER 38

Everything was soft and plush. Mindel gingerly moved her fingers across what felt like linen sheets, not a scratchy mattress. She held still for a moment, afraid to open her eyes and destroy the beautiful dream.

It was surprisingly quiet and she missed the constant coughing, burping, moaning, whimpering that had been with her every minute of every night since she'd first arrived at the camp. Something was entirely wrong.

Was this how it felt to be in heaven? Curious, she tried to open her eyes, which wasn't an easy task. She blinked several times, but it still took a while until the whitish fog cleared from her vision and she finally saw her surroundings.

Now she was sure she'd died, because all the men wore white coats, the beds were covered with white sheets and when she moved her head she felt the plush pillow beneath. It even smelt fresh and clean, just as she imagined heaven to be.

Somehow she must have missed her own death and had woken up as an angel. More curious than scared, she lifted the blanket to look beneath and, yes, she wore a white nightdress just like the angels did. But much to her disappointment she couldn't find her wings peeking out from under her shoulders, not even when she rolled onto her side.

They must not have given me wings, because I was asleep. A surge of panic bolted through her body, as she considered the idea that she'd overslept the distribution of wings and would now forever be an angel without the ability to fly.

A white-coated man approached her with a big smile. "Welcome back. You had us all very worried, young lady."

"Where am I?" Mindel asked with a cracked voice.

"In a field hospital."

Mindel took a moment to consider his answer and then asked for clarification, "Where are my wings?"

"I wouldn't know about that." The man looked somehow confused.

She scrunched up her nose; how come he couldn't answer such a simple question? Wasn't he the one in charge of this thing? She tried again: "Am I dead?"

Now he smiled kindly. "No, you're very much alive, although we were very worried about you."

"Oh." Mindel wasn't sure how she liked being back on earth, but since the man seemed willing to satisfy her curiosity, she pressed for more answers. "Are you going to send me back to the camp?"

He shook his head. "No, sweetie. The war is all but over. There are no more camps. You'll never have to return."

"Really?" She couldn't believe her ears. "You promise?"

"Pinkie promise," he said holding up his little finger and wrapping it around hers, which she found slightly strange. "And now I want to examine you. Can you sit up?"

She nodded and with his help she sat upright in her soft and white bed while he took the stethoscope from around his neck, placing it in his ears. He listened to her heart and her lungs and then removed the earpieces. "Everything's fine."

Mindel decided she was done with examinations and it was time to address the really important issues. "I'm hungry and thirsty."

The doctor chuckled and summoned a nurse. "This young lady needs some food and a glass of milk. Could you get this for her, please?"

"I'll see what I can rustle up."

Just then Mindel remembered the march from the camp to the train ramp and how she'd found her sister there. She grabbed the doctor's coat and asked with anguish, "Where's Rachel? Where's my sister?"

"She's over there, sleeping." He pointed at the cot next to her. "She's been watching over you the whole week."

Mindel followed the direction of his thumb and when she recognized her sister's face, tears welled up and she thought that maybe it wasn't all that bad that she hadn't died. "I want her."

"I'll wake her up and tell her that you're back with us. She'll be very happy."

Mindel watched as the doctor walked over and gently woke her sister. Rachel bolted to a sitting position, panic evident in her face until she looked in Mindel's direction and their eyes finally met. Moments later, they lay in each other's arms.

"My little darling, I was so worried you'd never wake up again."

"I missed you so much." Mindel dug her face into Rachel's chest, happy beyond words that she'd finally found her again.

A young soldier arrived with a glass of milk and some oatmeal. "This will get her feeling better in no time."

"Hungry?" Rachel asked as she spread a cloth over Mindel's lap.

Mindel eyed the food, but when Rachel went to offer her a spoonful of the cereal, Mindel refused to take it.

"What's wrong?"

"You eat first and then I'll…"

"I've already eaten."

"You have?"

"Yes, they eat well here and they don't mind sharing."

Mindel was confused, but she quit fighting Rachel as she fed her the cereal.

"The doctor said I was sick."

"Yes, you had a fever on the train and went to sleep, what they call a coma, for just over a week."

"I was asleep for a week?" Mindel asked with big eyes.

"Yes, silly. You scared me, too. I thought you were going to die."

Mindel smiled at her then and shook her head. "They can't kill us. We're stronger than they are."

"How do you figure that?"

"Because we have each other." It was all very simple. As long as she was with Rachel, everything was going to be all right.

"What happens now?" Mindel asked after finishing her breakfast.

"The war is still going on and we have to stay here until you're fully recovered. Then we'll be moved to a refugee camp."

Mindel flinched. "Another camp? But the doctor promised…"

Rachel stroked her hair. "It's a much better place with enough food, real beds, doctors and no roll calls. We're in good hands with the Americans. And as soon as we can, we'll find a way to travel home and look for Aron and Israel." Rachel removed the empty cereal bowl and hugged Mindel close. "I'm so glad you're feeling better."

Mindel snuggled into her sister's arms for a long while until a frightening thought occurred to her. She sat up and hurriedly scanned the surrounding area.

"What are you looking for?" Rachel asked.

"Paula. Where is she?" Mindel began to get agitated.

Rachel laughed. "Paula took a much-needed bath and got a delousing. I'll get her for you."

"That's good. She was a bit stinky."

The doctor and nurse overheard their conversation. "Things that stink seem commonplace around here. The good news is, your doll is no longer one of them."

The nurse retrieved a much cleaner Paula. Mindel insisted on checking up on her to make sure she was feeling well, and the kind doctor even let her use his stethoscope to examine Paula.

"She's much better, but needs to take a nap," Mindel concluded with a bright smile, although her eyes were drooping.

"Why don't you lie down with her?" Rachel suggested.

Mindel hid a yawn and slid under the clean blankets. "You won't go away?" she murmured sleepily.

"I won't leave you alone ever again," Rachel promised her.

EPILOGUE

Tel Aviv, January 1965

Mindel stood at the window in the small apartment where she lived with her new husband. She still had quite a lot to do before Rachel arrived. Like every year on Tu'Bishvat she became sentimental and looked back into her early childhood, although she didn't remember much.

A few images of her on the farm where she'd grown up. Running in the fields with her brothers. Climbing the apple trees. Her mother's soothing hands as she'd scratched her knee. She swallowed down the clump forming in her throat. Neither of her parents had survived the war, both gassed in Auschwitz. And no pictures of them had survived either, because that despicable mayor, Herr Keller, had destroyed every personal belonging of the Epstein family once he'd taken possession of the farm.

Having to steady herself against the windowsill, she thought back to the moment when she and Rachel had finally been rescued by the Americans, literally at the last minute.

After spending some time in the American field hospital in Magdeburg they had been transferred back to Bergen-Belsen, much to Mindel's horror. Although she'd soon found out that the new owners, the British, were running the displaced persons camp very differently from the former Nazi owners.

For six months she and Rachel had lived there, regaining their strength and putting some meat on their bones. Thankfully no pictures of her from that time existed, but she still remembered the awful shock when she'd first seen herself in a mirror. Despite having seen the other children turning into hollowed out skeletons, she'd never once entertained the idea that she looked equally horrific.

Several months into their stay, word had come to them through the Red Cross that both their parents had perished in Auschwitz, but there was no news of their brothers. It was as if they'd disappeared from the face of the earth, since no records of any kind existed.

Rachel though, had stayed hopeful, impressing on Mindel that their brothers might have reached the convent in Kaufbeuren and been able to live there under a false name. As soon as both of them were strong enough, they had gone to the British Administration and asked for permission to relocate to the small town in Bavaria where they'd grown up and that now lay in the American zone.

Irmhild, Rachel's former classmate who had provided them with fake papers, had perished in the Ravensbrück concentration camp—punished for the crime of wanting to help Jewish children. But there had been no news of her brothers whatsoever. She shivered involuntarily and wrapped her shawl closer around her shoulders. Even today, twenty years later, there was no confirmation of their deaths, nor their survival. She'd read in the newspaper of children without papers showing up in so many places that she clung to the idea her brothers had somehow made it and lived happily under a different name with a kind family that had taken them in.

Over the years they'd reunited with some friends, like Heidi and Clara who both lived nearby, and heard about the demise of others. Linda, a woman who'd become a friend to Rachel in the camp, had succumbed to typhus during those last days of April 1945 when the disease rampaged through Bergen-Belsen and ultimately killed about one third of the prisoners.

"Are you all right?" Dov, her husband, wrapped his arms around her from behind. As someone who'd grown up in Palestine, or Israel as it was now called, he didn't fully comprehend what she'd gone through, but he always picked up on her nostalgic moods and tried to dispel them.

"I'm fine. It's just that the past always catches up with me on this day. It's my birthday, after all." After her liberation from the camp, she'd kept thinking of Tu'Bishvat as her birthday, and every year she lit a candle for Mother Brinkmann on that special day. That courageous woman had not only saved Mindel, but so many children who would have otherwise died without an adult to take care of them.

Tragically Mother Brinkmann had perished a week after the liberation, succumbing to the typhus contracted from tending to the sick children in the camp during those last awful days. Mindel of course had been sick herself and had only found out about Mother Brinkmann's death months later.

"Typical for you to claim two birthdays, just so you can receive presents twice a year." Dov rested his chin on her shoulder and she turned around to face him.

"That piece of apple Mother Brinkmann gave me in the camp was the best present I ever got. I can still remember its taste."

Her gaze fell on the big table, set for eight. Dov's parents, his sister and her husband would join them, and of course Rachel and her husband Simon. A wave of guilt swept over her, because after returning to the farm the relationship between Rachel and her had taken a turn for the worse. Back then, she'd been too young to understand that Rachel had never been able to come to terms with what had happened, and had sunk deeper into depression month after month, despite the fact that the war was over and—at least for Mindel—life was wonderful again.

In 1948 Rachel had decided the two of them would emigrate to Palestine, starting a new life far away from the ghosts of the past. Things had improved, but somehow the old wounds still stood between them. While Mindel herself adapted quickly to the new environment and took to the Hebrew language like a duck to water, Rachel had struggled for many, many, years. Oftentimes Mindel felt like the adult who had to watch out for her older sister, instead of vice versa. It had been difficult for both of them, because the experiences in the camps had turned Rachel into a bitter woman, unable to trust anyone. That was, until she had met a man who'd lived through a similar experience, but had never lost his positive outlook on life. Rachel's wedding to Simon three years ago had changed everything.

The sisters had had a long talk and Rachel had admitted that she'd never been able to shed the feeling of guilt for not protecting her little sister during the horrible time in Bergen-Belsen. Mindel had been flabbergasted, because never in her wildest dreams had she thought Rachel would blame herself for their ordeal. After some ugly crying in each other's arms, they had felt the old closeness between them return.

Mindel sighed.

"Thinking of your sister?" Dov asked.

"Yes. She had it so much harder than I did. I mean, for me it was awful and everything, but somehow I believed that was how it was supposed to be. But Rachel, she had experienced better times and gradually everything was taken from her until she was reduced to an object. Less worth than even an animal, but a numbered slave, working for them."

"But she's better now, isn't she?"

"It's amazing, really. Since she met Simon she's become a completely different person."

Simon was an Auschwitz survivor whom Rachel had met three years before and instantly fallen in love with. "Despite his awful experiences, Simon has never once stopped believing in the goodness of humanity. Just like that friend of hers in the camp, Linda. I don't remember her, but she must have been the most wonderful person on earth."

"Simon has definitely been a good influence on your sister. So good, he made her a mother at the ripe old age of thirty-seven." Dov grinned, ready to accept the scolding he knew was coming.

"Don't you dare say anything bad about Rachel, she's not old!"

"I would never go up against fierce women like you or her." He caught her hands with his and pressed a kiss on her mouth. When he released her, he turned both of them around and glanced at the table. "Is everything ready for our guests?"

Traditionally for Tu'Bishvat three plates should be on the table: one with fruits that had a non-edible peel like oranges or hazelnuts. The second one should offer fruits with stone, like avocado, olives or dates. And the third one with fruits that could be eaten in their entirety, like grapes, strawberries or apples.

According to the tradition, they should be the most beautiful fruit, but Mindel always honored the occasion of her other birthday, by offering two crumpled yellow apples with brown spots.

They sat in the middle of the table, commemorating the most awful time during her life in the Bergen-Belsen camp but also representing the kindness she'd experienced there despite everything—from Mother Brinkmann, Laszlo, Heidi and the other children. And, of course, two sisters reunited after incredible hardship.

Tonight was extra special because she and Dov had an announcement to make. Just six months after their wedding day, she was carrying a child under her heart. A child that was part of a new generation, unburdened by the horrors of war.

Secretly she wished for a little boy whom she would name Laszlo, after her first true love, the seven-year-old boy who'd offered her comfort, kindness and protection when she had no one else. And if it was a girl she'd name her Rachel after her wonderful, brave and determined sister, who'd faced impossible odds to be reunited with her.

A LETTER FROM MARION

I want to say a huge thank you for choosing to read *Not Without My Sister*. If you did enjoy it, and want to keep up to date with all my latest releases, just sign up at the following link. Your email address will never be shared and you can unsubscribe at any time.

www.bookouture.com/marion-kummerow

This was a tough book to write, almost on par with *Unwavering*, the third book in my Love and Resistance Trilogy, where I was bawling for days on end.

I had the idea for *Not Without My Sister* a few years ago when I visited the concentration camp in Bergen-Belsen and their temporary exhibition "Children in Concentration Camps."

The interviews with child survivors were powerful, harrowing and thought provoking. There was one photograph that captured my attention. Her cute face with the intense brown eyes haunted me and inspired me to write a tale about the suffering of so many nameless children: a small girl of four or five years, cuddling a stuffed animal. She became my inspiration for Mindel. You can see the picture on my website together with an article about my visit to the camp: https://kummerow.info/bergen-belsen-concentration-camp

Due to the harrowing nature of the topic, I procrastinated on the project as much as I could, but the nameless little girl and her story kept nagging in the back of my head. To understand my reluctance to write this book, you must know that I have a daughter who was Mindel's age when I first had the idea, and every time I sat down to work on the plot, my heart squeezed into a tight knot, thinking this might have happened to her. But the characters in my head have the annoying habit of pestering me, until I give in and tell their stories.

Doing my research into child survivors of Bergen-Belsen I glimpsed into the minds of children, which are so different from ours. I certainly don't want to trivialize the Holocaust and the experience of imprisoned people, but to paraphrase Ladislaus Löb, a Hungarian Jew who was ten years old during his time in Bergen-Belsen: The children bore the hardships better than the adults, mainly because they were not aware of how desperate it really was. He admitted to being afraid, but at the same time feeling like being part of an exciting adventure. In his memoir, he also mentioned the awful games the children were playing like "Jews and SS" or "Who dies next." I have no reason to doubt the veracity of his memories, because another well-known but horrible children's game not much later was "*Frau, komm*," where children in Berlin played how Soviet soldiers were raping the women.

Ladislaus and the other children mentioned in his book, *Rezsö Kastner—The daring rescue of Hungarian Jews: A survivor's account*, became the inspiration for Laszlo and The Gang.

Rezsö Kastner was a Hungarian Jew working closely with the Nazis to save as many Jews as he could. Thanks to his negotiations 1,686 Hungarian Jews bought their "free passage" from the Nazis and were shipped from Hungary via Bergen-Belsen to Switzerland.

The scene with Obersturmbannführer Krumey in Chapter 17 actually happened, although not in the star camp, but in the adjacent Hungarian camp, where the first batch of 300 people were chosen to be sent to Switzerland. Obviously, everyone was desperate to get onto the first transport, since waiting for an elusive second transport might be in vain. 318 Jews travelled from Bergen-Belsen to Switzerland in August 1944, while the remaining 1,368 (including Ladislaus Löb and his father) arrived there in December 1944.

The International Red Cross had been allowed to deliver parcels to Bergen-Belsen on a few occasions. Apparently they weren't actually able to see the prisoners, but had to deliver the parcels to the camp administration, and the SS distributed the parcels to the barrack *kapos* (after pilfering I assume).

You have to remember that Bergen-Belsen was a special camp, where Jews were held to be exchanged for German nationals, although this apparently never happened. Conditions were slightly better than in other camps in the beginning, but deteriorated extremely toward the end when the SS simply stopped distributing food. Vile as they were, they even cut off the water supply to the camp during the last days before liberation.

The female guard Susanne Hille, called *Die Schwarze* because of her black hair, is a real person, too. She worked in the KZ-Außenlager (a sub-camp to the main camp of Bergen-Belsen) Tannenberg bei Unterlüß, which is why I sent Rachel to work there in the ammunition factory. In reality, this sub-camp only functioned between August 1944 and April 1945, so I bent the timeline a few months to keep the story moving.

Susanne Hille is remembered by many survivors for her exceptional brutality. Before the British arrived, she escaped, together with the other Tannenberg camp personnel, and for a long time it wasn't clear what had happened to her. Years later it was found out that she made it all the way across the Elbe river, where she died on May 7, 1945, one day before the capitulation of Germany. The exact circumstances of her death are unknown.

You may wonder why I didn't mention the most infamous guard of Bergen-Belsen, Irma Grese. One of her sobriquets was "The Beast of Auschwitz" and she certainly matched the much-less infamous Susanne Hille in sadistic cruelty. Grese was also one of the very few women executed for her crimes by the Allies. I didn't include her in the book because she only came to Bergen in March 1945, having been in Auschwitz and Ravensbrück before that.

Starting in 1957 several compensation lawsuits against the Rheinmetall Berlin AG (formerly Rheinmetall-Borsig) were instigated and according to court material, one of the main indicators whether a woman had indeed been forced into slave work at the Tannenberg camp was the mention of the orange hair and skin or the glass of milk. Women who remembered this, were immediately acknowledged as having worked for Rheinmetall and given compensation without further evidence.

The very last train Rachel and Mindel boarded is one of three trains that left Bergen-Belsen just before the British arrived to liberate it. The trains meandered for more than a week through Germany and one of them was finally stopped in Hillersleben near Magdeburg, where the Americans liberated the prisoners and distributed them into nearby towns.

You probably have recognized Bergen-Belsen's most famous inmate Anne Frank and her sister Margot. The two of them arrived at the end of 1944 on a transport from Auschwitz. The exact date when the two sisters died is unknown, it's only clear that they became sick with typhus and perished in February 1945. According to a former inmate, "one day they simply weren't there anymore."

Mindel's friend Heidi is inspired by the real person Hanneli Goslar, who had been a classmate of Anne's in Amsterdam. She managed to communicate several times with Anne across the fence, and she threw a package to her friend, which was stolen by another woman. Two days later she threw another one, which apparently was received, but that was the last time she and Anne had contact. Hanneli survived the war and later emigrated to Jerusalem, where she's still living in 2020.

If you have read my War Girl series, and especially *War Girl Lotte*, you may recognize Rachel and Mindel as the Jewish neighbors Lotte was hiding in her aunt's barn. For dramatic purposes not all details in *Not Without My Sister* align exactly with my other books.

I hope you loved *Not Without My Sister* and if you did I would be very grateful if you could write a review. I'd love to hear what you think, and it makes such a difference helping new readers to discover one of my books for the first time.

I love hearing from my readers—you can get in touch on my Facebook page, through Twitter, Facebook or my website.

Thanks,
Marion Kummerow

AutorinKummerow

@marionkummerow

kummerow.info

ABOUT THE AUTHOR

Marion Kummerow was born and raised in Germany, before she set out to "discover the world" and lived in various countries. In 1999 she returned to Germany and settled down in Munich where she's now living with her family.

Her books are filled with raw emotions, fierce loyalty and perpetual resilience.

She loves to put her characters through the mangle, making them reach deep within to find the strength to face moral dilemma, make difficult decisions, or fight for what is right. And she never forgets to include humor and undying love in her books, because ultimately love is what makes the world go round.

You can find all of her work here:
https://kummerow.info

Made in the USA
Columbia, SC
12 February 2022